I0557258

Slow Comes the Dark
Volume 3
Darkness Descends

Slow Comes the Dark Dark Volume 3 Darkness Descends

Vic Broquard

Slow Comes the Dark Volume 3 Darkness Descends

First Edition
ISBN: 978-1-941415-70-2
Copyright ©2013, 2014 by Vic Broquard

http://www.Broquard-ebooks.com
Broquard eBooks
103 Timberlane
East Peoria, IL 61611
author@Broquard-eBooks.com

Artwork by Crooked Willow Studios.

For Morgan and L. Ron Hubbard

Table of Contents

Chapter 1—And So It Begins
Chapter 2—Origins
Chapter 3—Back Story
Chapter 4—Civil War
Chapter 5—Recovery
Chapter 6—Disaster
Chapter 7—Brand New World
Chapter 8—Establishment
Chapter 9—First Contact
Chapter 10—Understandings
Chapter 11—Dealing with Natives
Chapter 12—Unexpected Development
Chapter 13—Salvage Operations
Chapter 14—The Battle of Johnsville

Chapter 1—And So It Begins

The place: Bleaker Rare Earth mines in the rugged foothills of the Dark Mountains on Ragnar-B, a remote world in the rim sector of Twillis. The 33rd Infantry Platoon of the 653rd Federation Military Forces, the FMF, was assigned to guard these valuable mines. Until now, noon, the war with the metal heads had bypassed them. Giant explosions of incoming artillery tossed small mountains of dirt, gravel, talus, and bodies high into the air, creating a brownish, noontime shower, but the rain was anything but friendly!

"We're out of position!" yelled Hammerhead, Sergeant Bill Sharke, to Hard Ass, Lieutenant Hard Ass Janine Alouse. Their captain had foolishly placed the three squads on the open plains near the center of the rugged valley. From here, four back roads led to the strip mines behind them. The captain's argument had been, "We'll be centrally located and protect all the mines from the tin cans." On paper, it sounded fine, but here on the battlefield, it left the platoon totally exposed. Now the silver robot fighters, the CAM or Cybernetic Android Mobile, had finally begun their move to take control of these mines. Rare earths were vital in the construction of many electronic devices, including these metal robot fighters.

Six artillery launchers rained death and destruction down upon the pinned-down platoon, softening them up for the coming onslaught from dozens of the CAMs, who stood motionless, shining brilliantly in the noontime sun high in the cloudless, blue sky overhead. The initial volley eliminated six men and the captain of the platoon.

"What the hell do we do, Hard Ass?" yelled Hammerhead. "We can't stay here."

Hard Ass raised her head and looked for her captain. "Shit! He's toast!"

"Yeh, an idiot. Okay, you're in charge, Hard Ass," Hammerhead yelled back. He too was prone, some five feet to her right.

"Hammerhead, Rocky, Sam," Hard Ass yelled above the

1

deafening noise of the artillery barrage that continued to crater their left flank, "fall back to that boulder field. We're out of position. Run, you goddamn rats! Run! Forget covering fire! Run!"

Hard Ass got her nickname for being just that. Janine was short, just barely tall enough to make it into the infantry, but her constitution more than made up for her lack of size. She was well muscled and tough, but more importantly, she never took anything from anybody, which is why she had not made captain. She'd been in more scrapes than anyone else in her platoon, dishing out bruises faster than anyone could give them to her. Everyone in her platoon respected her and desperately wanted her to be their captain, not the dead jackass who outranked her, and now he'd gotten himself and others killed because of his stupidity.

Without question, the surviving platoon members followed her orders. Ignoring the incoming barrage, men and women got up and raced backwards, diving for cover behind a small ridge line of boulders. "Okay. Who has our mortars? For god's sake, fire them now! Hammerhead, set up a defensive line there and there. Don't let the CAMs flank us or we're as good as dead. Where's our mortar fire? Damn it! You all got a death wish? Fire, goddamn it! Fire," Hard Ass yelled.

Thump. Thump. She heard the sound of mortar shells dropping into the tubes. She didn't need to see the shells lifting off, but grabbed her binoculars and began spotting the landing shells. "Hammerhead, tell Sam to aim for their artillery positions on the far ridge over there," she pointed out to Sergeant Bill Sharke.

Corporal Samantha Bearings was in charge of their mortar squad. Hammerhead moved off to their right, where Sam was assisting two of her men with the mortar. "Over there, ridge line. Take out their artillery."

Sam looked and yelled, "Can't out of range!"

"Shit!" Hammerhead yelled, and crawled across the uneven ground back to the large boulder where Hard Ass was yelling orders to their medic, Jascar "Bite Me" Long. Another barrage had taken out yet another squad member. "Out of range, Hard Ass. What now?"

"Where's our fucking engineer?" Hard Ass yelled.

"Over here!" yelled Sergeant Felicity Heavens, an attractive blonde engineer, a jack-of-all-trades. If it was broke, Fel could fix it.

"Call in for an air strike. We can't hold out like this! Tell them to hit their artillery battery on the far ridge line," Hard Ass pointed to the source of the rain of death.

"On it!" Fel yelled back, barking into her portable comm device.

"Shit! Here they come!" Hard Ass yelled. A line of shiny, metal robot fighters began marching towards them, each one more or less humanoid in shape. Their heads looked much like an oatmeal box, that is, a cylinder, with four eye sensors and microphones attached to it, along with a speaker where a mouth should have been. CAMs were not known to say much of anything though. Each weighted three hundred-fifty pounds. Their titanium steel shells stopped all normal gunfire. Even a blaster barely affected it. Their right hands held giant 50 caliber guns, much like ancient Gatling guns, that fired dozens of rounds in short order, brass shell casings falling like copper rain beside their feet. None knew just how much ammo one of these CAMs carried; it seemed unlimited. Their other hand held what looked like giant claws, but each was sharp as a razor, designed to rip a human body to shreds, should the human venture that close to them. Their feet looked more like giant chicken claws. However, they were not swift a foot, moving half as fast as a human, at best. Still, they were tireless and could move at their top speed all day, if necessary.

Hard Ass watched as her fighters fired their automatic weapons at the slowly advancing line, their bullets and shells bouncing harmlessly off the tin cans. "Shit! Aim for their heads, you fools. Where's our RPG?" Their RPG was the only weapon, short of a direct mortar hit, that could stop a CAM, though if enough of their head sensors could be knocked out, the CAM would simply cease operations, waiting to be repaired.

"On it," yelled Fel. Their engineer unpacked the rocket launcher and got it ready to fire. She took careful aim and fired off a round. Swoosh. The rocket shot off at blinding speed, streaking towards one of the advancing CAMs. Fel was a good shot. The round hit the tin can in its head and exploded. When the smoke cleared, a headless CAM stood motionless, while its companions continued spraying the bounders with their heavy caliber automatic fire and slowly moved forward.

"Good shooting, Fel! One down, lots to go. Where's our air strike?" Hard Ass yelled.

Fel yelled back, "Might not get it. None to spare." She proceeded to load another round into her RPG.

"Well shit! If we don't get it, we're pinned down here," Hard Ass yelled. She turned and looked behind her. The far ridge line would give them superior cover and where the damned captain should have positioned them in the first place. Trouble was, with all the incoming artillery fire, she knew they'd take heavy losses if they made the long dash to get to the ridge, if not mowed down by the automatic fire from the marching CAMs. An air strike was desperately needed. If it didn't come—what to do, she thought.

Another shell exploded close to her position, throwing up a pile of shattered rock. Fragments smashed her binoculars and pelted her body, which she ignored. Just then, Hammerhead yelled, "Hard Ass back there, behind the line. What are they doing?"

"Hell, can't see! Blast took out my goddamned binoculars. Someone hand me yours," she yelled. Hammerhead was closest to her and tossed his, while pointing in the direction for her to look.

Looking through his binoculars, she saw two more CAMs setting up something. What was it? A silver dish? Surely, this wasn't a comm center relay dish. That didn't make sense. "Oh double shit!" Hard Ass screamed. "It's a goddamn Shadow Maker! Shit! Shit! Shit!"

The Shadow Maker was the newest weapon in the enemy's arsenal and greatly feared. When it fired its cone of energy beams, any human body that it reached began slowly to disappear! By this time, everyone had seen videos of this diabolical weapon in use. Men and women just grew thinner and thinner until their bodies vanished into the shadows, hence its nickname. What happened to the person after they vanished wasn't known for certain. Some wild rumors claimed that the person was somehow then forced into one of these new CAM bodies and made to fight for the enemy, but no one truly believed that rumor. For sure, only a fine, powdery dust remained where their bodies had once stood. However, that rumor actually was true, but only the captains and lieutenants of the infantry division and higher ranks were told this was what did happen to those who were shot with this hideous new weapon, developed by their own local corporations! Hence, Hard Ass's reaction.

"Fel, for god's sake, take out that dish they're setting up behind the line of CAMs or we're all doomed!" Hard Ass yelled to her engineer.

"Out of range, Hard Ass. Hit it with mortars is our best bet," Fel yelled back.

After ducking from another spray of debris from an exploding artillery shell, Hard Ass relayed her order to Sam. Precious time was wasted as Sam and her crew shifted from dropping mortar shells at the line of the advancing tin cans and focused on the dish. As the shells began landing, Hard Ass yelled spotting orders to Sam, "Long. Short. Bit to the left."

A minute later, Hard Ass cursed again. "Shit. The tin cans are setting up another dish out of range of our mortar! Why do they have to get smart right now? Shit! Bingo! Good shooting Sam! That dish is history!" Sam nodded and redirected her mortar fire to the slowly advancing line of metal men, wishing that they could be hit as easily as the dish had been. So far, for all her mortar shots, she'd eliminated only one tin can, blowing its head off. She had knocked four others off their feet, when her shells landed at their feet, blowing a small crater in the rocky ground, causing the chicken feet to stumble, but the CAMs merely got back onto their feet and resumed their relentless, though slow, march towards their boulders.

Hard Ass knew they were in deep trouble. No air strike. Pinned down. Four minutes from now, the metal heads would be on top of them. Worse, by then the second dish would be up and running. The Shadow Maker would wipe them all out, but she didn't dare tell her troops that they'd then end up

5

somehow forced into one of these metal head bodies and forced to fight for the enemy!

Janine looked behind her. If they could make that ridge, there they would have far better cover and be out of range of the Shadow Maker, forcing them to have to reposition it closer. Stall. If they could make that ridge, they'd gain valuable time, but it would be a suicide run without that air strike! However, it would also be suicide to stay put. Another couple of minutes and they'd be wiped out by the damned Shadow Maker. Hard Ass made a tough decision.

"Everyone, listen up!" she yelled. Prone faces pivoted to look her way. She paused until the next artillery shell's explosion died down. "Pack up everything. One minute from now, we're going to make a mad dash to that rear ridge line. Don't look back. Run like hell! That Shadow Maker will take us all out, so run like hell! Sixty, fifty-nine," she began counting down, watching the mortar crew frantically packing up. "Now! Run like hell!" she yelled, and got to her feet and began running as fast as possible up the hill, dodging rough patches, small boulders, and shell craters. She didn't look back. If a bullet hit her, tough. She was more terrified of that Shadow Maker.

As she ran for her life, from the corner of her eyes off to her right, she saw several men from the third squad! Their run slowed down and halted. In horror, she saw their bodies slowly disappearing, vanishing from sight! *Oh God*, she thought, but continued her race for life. Reaching the rugged ridge line, she dove over it, hit the ground hard, and rolled. As she got back up, she saw trees, boulders, and a rugged valley system, incredibly good cover. "Form up a line here," she yelled as platoon remnants appeared, racing for cover themselves. "Count off," she added. As her members began counting, she hoped for the best. At least, soon she'd know how many of their original thirty-six member platoon was alive. She was pleased to see that Fel, Sam, and Hammerhead had made it safely.

Twenty were left. Hammerhead yelled, "Shadow Maker. Got six from third squad."

"I saw. Shit. Damned that captain to hell! If he would

have listened to me and positioned us all up here, we could have held them off without losing half the damned platoon!" Hard Ass barked.

Just then, they heard the noise of approaching delta wing fighters! Their air strike was coming, a bit too late for six, but welcome nevertheless. "Heads down!" Janine yelled, cradling her own head, trusting to the steel helmet to protect her head.

Fel yelled, "Shit! They have an anti-aircraft battery!" Hard Ass's heart skipped a beat. She'd missed spotting that battery and prayed the delta wing fighters weren't shot down. Two massive explosions shook the ground. The CAM artillery battery fell suddenly silent! Then, an aerial explosion caught their attention. Overhead, one of the two incoming delta wing fighters exploded in the air. Fortunately, the debris continued onward, smashing into the distant trees. As she looked up, she saw smoke coming from the second fighter and knew it was coming down as well.

She spotted a parachute. The pilot from the destroyed ship had managed to eject! She said a brief prayer. "Smoke and Lou—you two head out back. Find the downed pilot and see if the damaged one lands. Get the pilots back here safely."

"Aye, aye, lieutenant," Smoke replied, glad to get away from this mess, if only for a short while. Janine watched, as the two men rushed off into the trees. *Well, at least we can rescue the pilots.* She got out her binoculars and inched her way back up to the ridge line to survey the damage.

"Good. The artillery battery is history. So is that Shadow Maker." She saw the line of silver robots falling back, regrouping, she concluded. However, she saw two others carrying what looked like third Shadow Maker out of their own transport. Well, it would take them a half hour at best to get it up and running. She had bought her platoon time.

Jascar called out, "Sorry, I couldn't save Jackson. Damned Shadow Maker got our three injured mates. I'm running out of supplies, Hard Ass. So don't any more of you go getting yourselves shot up."

"K, Jascar. Not your fault," Janine replied. "We couldn't have evacuated them. If only the idiot captain had positioned

7

us up here in the first place." She yelled to the others around her, "So you heard him. Don't get yourselves shot." Several laughed. This was a war after all.

Since things were a bit quite, Janine made another decision. "Hammerhead, most of the MK40's were in the third squad who are history, but I can see a stash of them way down there. We need them if we are going to have any chance of holding these tin cans off. Take two men, sneak back down there, and recover them. The artillery is out, and the CAMs are focusing on removing their headless robots and getting a new Shadow Maker up and running, so you should be able to sneak back down there. Flank off to the far left. Your best cover is over there."

"Aye sir. Peters, Jones, you are with me," Hammerhead barked. Janine watched carefully as her risky move was executed. The foolish captain had put all the big MK40's in the hands of the third squad who were blasted by the first rounds of the artillery barrage. Unless they got some of them back, Janine knew they would be hard pressed to hold the ridge.

She called out, "Sam, how many mortar rounds are left? Fel, how many RPG shots you got left?" Her mind was racing ahead to the next battle, working out just what they could potentially do to hold onto the ridge and keep the tin cans from getting a hold of the rare earth mines.

Sam yelled, "Ten sir!"

"Five left," Fel added.

"Shit! Fel, you got any explosives with you?" Hard Ass yelled, thinking along another line.

"Captain wouldn't authorize me any," Fel replied, "but you know me. Never leave home without some boom-booms. Got five charges."

"Excellent Fel! Set up some booby-traps there and there. My guess is they'll come straight for us. Let's give them a little surprise," Hard Ass replied. Several privates grinned; this was more like it. They had faith in Hard Ass, but disgust for their former captain. So far, sticking close to Hard Ass had kept them alive, unlike those in the third squad. "The rest of you, provide covering fire for Fel, if she needs it."

Meanwhile, Janine kept her eyes on Hammerhead. He

and his two men were being very sneaky, moving slowly and as close to the ground as possible, making use of natural cover. So far, the CAMs had either not seen them or were ignoring the three. She watched as they reached the bloody mess that had once been the third squad. Secretly, she hoped and prayed that some of the MK40's were still serviceable.

Hammerhead returned a half hour later with seven working MK40 assault guns. Cheers spontaneously arose when he and his buddies appeared and began handing them out. "Team up in pairs," Hard Ass ordered. "Shoot at the same target and aim for the oatmeal heads." Seven nodded and moved out to take up their positions.

Just then, Smoke and Lou returned, bringing two hotshot fighter pilots with them. Janine saw two officers in their fancy brown uniforms, not a speck of dirt on them. She laughed. "Joining the grunts I see," she smiled, welcoming them. In stark contrast, she and her band wore camouflage greenish uniforms, but not only were they filthy, but their faces and hands were covered in soot and dirt. She added, "Your air assault saved our butts. Sorry about getting your deltas shot down. We didn't see that anti-air battery until it fired."

"Our pleasure. Captain Jason Stapleton or One Shot here. My wingman, Lieutenant Jill "Killer" Diller," the young pilot said.

"Too bad about the AA battery," Killer declared, "but I took out the artillery battery for you. Guess we're stranded here for a while."

"Nice shooting. It and their damned Shadow Maker took out half of my platoon. Oh, Lieutenant Janine Alouse. I'm now in command. Our idiot captain tried to get us all killed, but failed miserably. Follow my orders, sirs, and I'll get you out of here in one piece."

"Say, aren't you called Hard Ass?" Jason asked, putting two and two together.

"You got that right," Fel called out. "She should have been our captain. We're alive only because of her, so you fellows follow her orders, and you'll live to see another day. Engineer Felicity Heavens here." Both pilots chuckled.

9

"Say, any news on how the other battles are going?" Janine asked. "You know Command, they don't tell us much of anything."

One Shot ran his hands through his hair, frustrated. "Not good, I'm afraid."

"Tell her, One Shot," Killer spoke up.

"At last call, half of our fleet is gone," Jason reported. Several cursed. "Only the battleship Arc Royal is still operational and a few cruisers. Their new Battleship Royale Queen is devastating. It launches ten thousand of their one-man fighters at one time! Their tactics are brutal. They swarm like a pack of bees onto a ship, ignoring how many get shot to hell getting up close. They magnetically grapple onto the side of the ship and cut goddamn holes in the hull. Enough holes and the ship decompresses for good. Lost our main battleship that way. So when the battle broke off, we were ordered over to the Arc Royal, where we were ordered to lay in an air attack for you folks."

He went on, "Last I heard, the battle for Brussels isn't going well at all. I think it's safe to say we're losing the war with the CAMs."

"Hell, they only have one damned infantry division on Ragnar-B," Janine replied. "How do you expect us to hold onto the whole damned world against these tin cans? Anyone know why some of the corporations are fighting us?"

"Yeh, that makes no sense," Fel pointed out. That three of the world's most powerful corporations had declared war on the rest of the world was more than baffling to everyone. It made no sense at all.

"Hey, scuttlebutt flying around has it that Commander Kelly Kay Knight of the Arc Royal discovered what was really going on with the Shadow Makers," Killer spoke up, ignoring One Shot's dirty look.

"So what that damn gun doing?" Fel spoke up. She'd finished making her booby traps and rather hoped Killer would keep on talking. Just what did this new weapon do to the poor victims? She'd heard rumors and they weren't good.

"No secret now," Killer looked back at One Shot. "They have a right to know, since they are out here facing the damned invention." She went on, "No one quite knows how it works—only that it does. When the victim's body completely vanishes and turns into dust, they are sucked into one of those shiny tin cans and are then forced to fight us. The GD, GE, and GR corporations worked together to invent the damned Shadow Maker, the CAMs, and their new battleship, that Royale Queen."

"You're kidding? Sucked into one of the enemy's tin cans?" Fel asked horrified.

"Yep. Sucked in. Quite why they then have to fight us is a mystery, but probably they don't have much of a choice, I expect," Killer replied.

Hard Ass spoke up, "She's right about the Shadow Maker. Top brass told us about it a while back, but we were under orders not to tell anyone below a lieutenant about it. Hell, they damned well should have told everyone. This is utter crap—our own men fighting against us! So don't get yourself turned into a shadow!"

The enlisted soldiers began chatting about this startling revelation. "Anyway, I'll call for an EVAC for you two, but no guarantees anyone will get here anytime soon," Janine explained. "Meanwhile, you stay back and keep your heads down."

"Aye sir," Killer replied, eager to do so.

"So do you suppose they are using this Shadow Maker on our people in order to make all these CAMs that we're facing?" Fel asked the obvious question.

"Probably. Bet the ruthless corps have been doing it for years. I heard that many people scattered around Ragnar-B have gone missing this past year. An epidemic of it, according to some in the security forces," Janine answered.

"Heads up! They're on the move again!" Hammerhead yelled. Instantly, the surviving platoon members snapped alert once more. Janine grabbed her binoculars and crawled up to the ridge line for a look see. The somewhat diminished line of tin cans had again begun their slow march towards them. At least this time, Janine felt they had the benefit of very good cover. Two of the CAMs had setup the Shadow Maker dish, but it was far out of range. A pair of CAMs was carrying it closer.

"Hammerhead, train the MK40's on the heads of three tin cans on their left side, that's our right side. Make sure a pair always fires together at the same target. Sam, get ready to dump the rest of your mortar shells on their right flank, our left side," Hard Ass barked her orders. "The rest of you, keep your damned heads down. Our other guns are practically useless against them."

"What about the RPG shots?" Fel asked.

"Save them for that Shadow Maker dish. Keep watch on it. When it gets in range, blast it to kingdom come!"

"Aye sir!"

"Where do you want us?" One Shot asked.

"You are lucky you took out their artillery battery. So head back there where the trees are dense. If we have to retreat, we'll be heading that way. Better cover," Janine replied, and the pair of pilots hastily did as she asked.

Soon, the CAMs were within range, and the firefight began once more. The tin cans peppered the ridge line with their automatic cannon fire, but that did little except to keep most down behind the ridge. Then, the familiar sound of the MK40's began returning fire. Hard Ass kept close watch with her binoculars, relaying facts, while Sam and her crew fired off the last of their mortar shells. Again, their reserve shells had been carried by members of the deceased third squad.

The mortar shells did little more than cause several CAMs to stumble and fall into the small craters on the ground just in front of them. However, the MK40's were partially effective. While they too couldn't penetrate the titanium steel body shells of the robot fighters, they took their toll on their cylindrical heads, their most vulnerable spot. For ten minutes, intense fire blazed in both directions, this time doing very little to the platoon's forces, but slowly the tin can's numbers were reduced. When a head was disabled, the robot merely stopped all actions, waiting to be repaired.

"Out of ammo!" cried one shooter. Shortly, others added their notice to his.

"Shit. So much for the MK40's," Hard Ass barked. "Well, we have four tin cans left. Two in the line coming for us, and two bringing up that Shadow Maker. Sam, any word on an

EVAC?"

"None sir. Last comm said none was available at this time," Samantha replied. "What good is having an EVAC protocol if none is available when you need an EVAC?" Several others laughed cynically.

Suddenly, the two remaining CAMs reached Fel's booby traps. Boom! Boom! Several C-4 charges went off. One tin can fell over, missing its right leg. The other one simply stopped and didn't move, its guns falling silent. Two remained, working rapidly to get the Shadow Maker into position.

"Fel, for heaven's sake take that Shadow Maker dish out now!" Hard Ass barked.

Her first shot missed, but her second hit the dish, blowing it into flying bits. Janine breathed a sigh of relief. "Sir, taking on the two tin cans now," Fel barked. She fired off the last of her RPG rounds. One missed but the other two took off their cylindrical heads! That brought cheers from everyone.

Finally, Janine stood up, looking back down at the battlefield below her. "Okay, I don't see any more tin cans. Hammerhead, form up a squad, go down there, and check it out. See if you can find more mortar shells, RPG rounds, and MK40 clips. The rest of you, front and center. I want everyone watching the field below. Scream if you spot a tin can."

"Can I go with them?" her medic, Jascar, asked. "Maybe some that we left behind are still alive, sir."

"Okay. Get your ass down there, but keep alert," Janine ordered, as One Shot and Killer walked up to the front line to see for themselves.

"Hey, you got them all," Killer pointed out the obvious.

"Yep, thanks to you fly boys taking out that artillery battery," Janine replied. "Keep alert. There could be more of them, and we're out of ammo that can harm them."

A half hour later, Hammerhead signaled Janine. She and the remainder headed on down onto the battlefield. When she reached him, he reported, "Found a few clips for the MK40's. Found the dog tags for those who got shadowed. That's all that's left of them, except for buttons and pants zippers. Metal bits didn't disappear. Weird, sir. Medic is treating two survivors. Over there is their transport. It's empty now, except for lots of strange machinery and stuff."

"Good job. K, Sam, get HQ on the line. Tell them we took out this CAM patrol and have captured one of their transports. Ask them what they want done with it and all that strange junk on it."

"Aye sir. On it," Samantha replied. A bit later, she said, "Sir, I can't raise HQ or anyone else. Now what?"

"Shit!" Hard Ass exclaimed. This wasn't what she anticipated, wanted, or needed.

"Hey, let us call our people," One Shot volunteered. She nodded, since there wasn't anything else she could do. If HQ wasn't responding, that likely meant they were in deep trouble themselves, probably so if One Shot was right and the war was going badly.

A bit later, One Shot reported, "Well, I couldn't reach Commander Knight, but I did get Major Lu Ann Ellen on the Hyperion. That's a light cruiser. She said for us to bring you and the captured transport to her ship. They want to study it for clues."

"Cool. Can you fly it?" Janine asked.

"If it goes in the air," Killer teased her, "we can fly it. Come on. We're your EVAC flight." Janine didn't have to be asked twice. She barked the orders that the surviving platoon members most wanted to hear. "We're evacuating now. Onto that enemy transport."

Twenty surviving soldiers, including the two wounded men, crowded onto the transport, while Killer and One Shot headed up to the pilot's area. "Now that's a welcome sight I never thought I'd ever hear again," Sam spoke up, as the bay doors closed and sealed.

"Here, here! Let's hear it for Hard Ass! She's saved our butts today!" Hammerhead called out. For a minute, hearty cheers echoed throughout the ship, while up front One Shot and Killer grinned.

"She's one hot grunt," Killer teased One Shot.

"You can say that again. Saved our butts too," he added.

Sometime later, they spotted the two surviving ships of Ragnar-B's space fleet. The giant battleship Arc Royal totally dwarfed the smaller delta wing shaped light cruiser Hyperion, but the battleship looked in very bad shape. Gaping holes dotted its perimeter. One landing bay appeared demolished, and smoke poured out some port side vents, not a good sign. The Hyperion looked unharmed, and One Shot took them into their stern landing bay, setting them down with a perfect landing.

The group stepped down the bay ramp and found confusion surrounding them. Maintenance crews were working to salvage damaged delta wing fighters, while disorganized groups of fighter pilots tried to organize themselves, yelling for One Shot and Killer to join them. From among the confusion, Major Lu Ann Ellen stepped forward to greet the new arrivals, along with three technicians in long, white jackets.

The major's eyes matches the spotless blue of her uniform, Janine thought. *God, why am I even thinking such things?* "Lieutenant Janine Alouse with what's left of the 33rd Platoon reporting sir," she saluted.

"At ease. Your captain?" her mellow voice asked.

"Dead sir. This is all that's left of us, sir."

"Okay then, Captain Janine Alouse. You are hereby promoted. Johnson here will escort you to some quarters. You need a bath. Mess is at 06:00. I'll take a full report after supper. Right now, things are still in flux. Oh, Johnson, see if you can find them something clean to wear for now."

"Thank you sir, but shouldn't my general be making such promotions," Janine replied.

"Hard Ass is it?" the blonde major replied with a wry smile.

"Yes sir. That's my nick, sir."

"Well deserved if my reports are accurate. Sorry, but your platoon is all that currently remains of the 653rd Infantry Division, though I hope stragglers will be located in the coming days. Ground actions haven't gone well at all. Hell, the fleet actions haven't gone our way either. Get yourselves cleaned up and fed. We'll talk more later, captain."

"Thank you sir!" Janine replied, saluting as the Major and her technicians headed on past them and into the transport to examine the strange things inside.

15

"Way to go, captain!" Hammerhead exclaimed, patting her on her back. "Now we got us a real captain!" Her platoon members cheered her, before following the man who led them to their new quarters. She and Fel bunked together. Janine felt obligated to look after the engineer, since her company of fellow engineers was probably history, if the major was correct.

"You are with us now, Fel. Welcome to the 33rd."

Fel smiled and nodded. "At least, I stand a chance of surviving with you, captain." Both young women chuckled and headed to the showers.

Space onboard the Hyperion was at a premium, especially now that they'd taken on survivors from various other units, both ground and airborne based. They discovered that mess was served four times, because the mess hall only held fifty people at one time. Wearing the green uniforms normally worn by the maintenance crew, Captain Janice joined her platoon in the crowded mess hall. The smell of freshly baked bread filled the room, and she now felt utterly famished.

Once they finished eating, Major Lu Ann spoke over the ship's intercom system. Her usual soft, calm voice echoed, "May I have your attention. This is Major Lu Ann Ellen. Will the various leaders of rank lieutenant and above please report to my CCC room for a briefing. At the same time, part of the briefing will be broadcast live to the entire ship, starting at 07:00. Unless your duties are critical, everyone is to stop and watch. You will see what we are up against. That is all."

One Shot came over to Captain Janine and Fel. "Hey, come with Killer and me. We'll show you where CCC is at."

"Can't be that hard on this small a ship," Fel teased.

"You coming too?" Killer asked her.

"She said lieutenant and up. We engineers are all at least that," she replied wryly. "See, we got brains and everything." Both pilots chuckled.

"Well, you clean up well," One Shot commented, as they moved along the narrow corridors heading to the top and front of the ship. Its normal compliment was one hundred, including fighter and shuttle pilots, but today, it was packed

16

with closer to two hundred.

"Unlike you fighter boys, we don't mind getting down and dirty," Fel teased them. The four shared a laugh and joined around fifty others, all jammed into the Communications, Command, and Control center of the Hyperion. Extra monitors were hung on the wall. Shortly, Major Lu Ann began her briefing.

"This was recorded earlier today. It is the corporation's new Battleship Royale Queen, filled with these tin cans and their one-man fighters," she explained and then went silent. Gasps echoed around the room. Thousands upon thousands of the shiny silver fighters swarmed out of the donut shaped, giant ship, outnumbering the scrambling delta wing fighters by several orders of magnitude. Cheers accompanied some of the early victories, as some small ships exploded into bits. Soon even that died down, as they watched the CAM ships sticking onto the side of a battleship. Before long, it was obvious that decompression was occurring with each of the holes the CAMs made in its hull. They were watching the death of one of their two battleships.

These sequences were followed by some ground attack videos. Fel commented, "Yep, that's just what the Shadow Maker does." More gasps followed as they saw an entire infantry regiment vanish from sight, person by person.

"That's what we're up against," Major Lu Ann's calm, quiet voice broke the silence once the visuals ended. "I don't have to tell you that our situation is more than grim. We have received this cable from the corporation fleet. It reads: Surrender all your forces now and be prepared to be assimilated into our mighty CAM fleet. The Shadow Maker is painless."

She went on, "I replied: 'Go suck on a neutron star.'" That brought some chuckles to the deadly serious group.

"This is our home world. We have the backing of all the other corporations, but honestly, I'm not entirely sure what good that will do us. Galactic Dynamics, General Robotics, and Galactic Electronics are obviously attempting to take over total control of our world, our Ragnar-B. Apparently, the leaders are the three CEOs, namely Amos Fink, Henry Walsham, and

17

Peter Walsh."

Major Lu Ann paused and then continued, her mellow voice instilling a bit of calm in the very nervous group. "Here's what Commander Knight and I have come up with. We are going to continue the fight for our world, as long as it takes to destroy every one of the CAMs. However, as you might expect, many civilians will be fleeing Ragnar-B for other worlds. Already, we've seen a dozen heavily loaded transports departing from the spaceport at Brussels. We recognize that many of you have family planet-side. So everyone of you has a choice to make. You can leave the ship and the fight behind you, joining those on the surface. No one will think less of you if you choose that. Or you can stick with us and join the fight for our world. It promises to be a lengthy and very probably one-sided for quite some time. Think on it tonight. In the morning, we'll make shuttle runs to the surface dropping off those of you who wish to leave the service and picking up other survivors that we can locate. That is all. May Lord Theron guide us all."

"Hey, come with us," One Shot suggested to Janine and Fel. The two followed the pair of pilots. Soon, they found themselves in the pilot's briefing room, where several others had already gathered, along with a keg of dark stout, a favorite among Hyperion's fighter pilots. Jason and Jill grabbed four mugs of the dark brew and brought them over to Janine and Fel.

"Thanks. This hits the spot," Janine said with a wry smile after one sip. She looked at Jason. He was six inches taller than she was, but that wasn't saying much since she was so short. He had blue eyes and short brown hair to go along with his cocky airs. Beside him, Jill was lean and lanky, with a brown bob of hair, perhaps a couple inches long at most. She'd brushed it into a bowl shape, giving her the appearance of some kind of monk. Her lips were thick and her eyebrows bushy. Killer Diller, as she was known, had the most CAM fighter kills to date, hence her nickname, though Crazy Diller might have been more accurate, since her flying left one with that notion. She was anything but a textbook pilot.

In turn, they saw the very short Janine, who had blonde

hair that almost touched her shoulders. Not particularly pretty, she had that look about her that broadcast no nonsense. Besides, she was tough. Her arm muscles exceeded those of the two fighter pilots. The Combat Engineer Felicity Heavens was also blonde. Her wavy tresses fell below her shoulders. She was a good four inches taller than Janine was. Her fingers had callouses, and her forearms showed signs of numerous burns, an occupational hazard. Fel was far more attractive than Janine, but still no wallflower.

Neither could miss the wall chart with the pilot's call sign and hash marks indicating kills. Killer Diller's marks dwarfed all the others, though One Shot wasn't too far behind her. "So you two going to depart in the morning or are you going to stay and fight these damned CAMs?" Killer Diller asked, taking another deep swill of her brew.

"Hell, why not? I sure as heck don't want to be turned into a shadow thing," Janine exclaimed.

"I'm an engineer, fellows. I go where there are things to build," Fel replied.

"And blow up," Janine added with a wry grin.

"Aye, that too. Right now, I feel damned naked. I don't have any more explosives on my person. Naked. Stark naked," Fel added. "Hell, I'm staying, though I'd like to go back down and get some of my things. I look awful in this grubby uniform." She and Janine laughed at that. They both felt very uncomfortable in these clothes.

"Cool. We're staying too. Hey, I'll ask the major if we can escort you planet-side and help you get your things," Jason declared.

"Say, is Major Lu Ann always so soft-spoken, so laid back?" Janine asked. "She seemed so, well I don't know, quiet-like." If she was going to be her new commander, she needed to know what she was like. The quiet types often broke when a little pressure was applied, something Hard Ass couldn't stomach. Hell, she thought, her previous captain had damned near gotten the whole platoon killed today.

"Cool as a cucumber—that's Major Lu Ann. Hell, Hard Ass, she was right there in the middle of that rain of CAM fighters, thousands of them, and when I first landed here,

19

there she was in the CCC calm as though nothing was happening," Killer answered her. "She's an iceberg under fire. No panic, just coldly calculating is my guess. You'd think that she'd been up against a thousand enemy fighters every damned day."

"Well, I heard that she's a veteran of the Posh Wars," Jason added. "I asked around, and they say that she's always soft-spoken, but they wouldn't give a hoot for your life if you cross her. She must know what she's doing to have kept the Hyperion unharmed during that onslaught today."

Just then, her second in command, Captain Jack Billington, stepped up to the foursome. "Damned right she kept us alive today. No finer leader in the fleet for my money. She came up as a fighter pilot. Her nick back then was Silent Killer. Racked up more kills than any other pilot. She's a cool one. Just so you know, when no one else would respond, it was Major Lu Ann who ordered those two to provide your requested air strike."

"Just so you know, that's what saved our lives down there," Janine replied. "Thanks. Good to know Major Lu Ann has our backs. Mind if I ask you a question?" He nodded and took a seat beside the four. "So we're infantry grunts. What or why does she want us in her command?"

He looked left and right, satisfying himself that no one was listening, before bending over and whispering, "Hell if I know, and I'm second in command. She seldom lets others know her plans. But after what we saw today, there's damned few of us freedom fighters left. My guess is that she's consolidating all available forces. Probably Commander Knight is doing the same thing, but you didn't hear this from me." He got up and left them to mull that over.

"Hey Janine, mind if I ask you another question, a personal one?" Jason asked politely.

Janine laughed. "Hell, you can ask buddy, but no guarantee that I'll answer." Fel giggled, she knew her captain well. Janine opened up to very few people, that much she'd already seen during her months spent deployed as the 33rd Infantry Platoon's resident engineer.

"How come you joined the infantry anyway?" Jason

asked.

Fel thought, *If you think she's going to answer that one, you got another think coming.* However, even Fel was surprised that she answered.

"Well, I've a half-sister, Dr. Alison Wage. Mom remarried. Alison has all the brains in the family and went to the Academy. She is or was a hot electrical engineer or something like that. Then about eighteen months ago, she simply vanished. Worked for Galactic Electronics. Cushy job. Made twice as much as I did. So I figured being in the infantry, why, I'd have the best chance of finding her or what happened to her."

"Wow. So have you? Found her?" Fel interjected, surprised to learn this much from Janine.

"Nope."

"I'm sorry about her," Jason replied.

"Not likely. You didn't know her. Fel, we best turn in. We need to go planet-side in the morning. We need darn near everything. Stick with me, Fel, and I'll get you your explosives," Janine barked, abruptly ending the discussion. "Thanks for the beer."

Chapter 2—Origins

Eighteen months ago in Brussels, Ragnar-B, Twillis Sector, twenty-seven year old, Dr. Alison Wage, an electronics expert for Galactic Electronics Corporation, paced her small apartment, trying to decide whether to accept Dr. Frank Sellers' suggestion that she attend the secret meeting of the Resistance Movement. *True,* she thought, *GE has paid for my PhD in electronics at the local Academy and hired me when I graduated. But.* That was the problem. She had many reservations. The corporations owned all property on Ragnar-B, a remote world in the rim sector of Twillis. She paid GE monthly rent for her small apartment, and paid other corporations for her food and clothing allowances. While she was frugal by nature, Alison still found herself nearly broke at the end of each month! True, she made a hefty salary, but ninety-five percent of her earnings ended up back in the corporations' pockets, just like everyone else on Ragnar-B.

She recalled her last conversation with her co-worker, Dr. Frank Sellers. "Look, Alison, by the time you retire at sixty-five, assuming you live that long, you won't have saved up enough credits to survive on your own for more than a year at best. The corporations have everything rigged in their favor. You slave for a lifetime and get what in return? Nothing but staying alive. Honestly, is this any kind of life? Come to the next meeting, I beg you. Change is coming."

But what kind of change, Alison wondered, tossing her shoulder length brown hair behind her head, while running a hand over each ear, tucking errant strands behind them. Frustrating. She had a good job, an interesting job, groundbreaking many would say, though she was sworn to the highest levels of secrecy, just as Frank was. Everyone knew what happened to anyone who violated the GE Secrecy Pact. They simply vanished without a trace. She even knew one who had. It had happened just as she began work for GE. One morning, Alison saw a man cleaning out the woman's desk next to hers. No one said anything except she'd vanished.

Well, I'm not breaking any laws by going to an open meeting, she thought, slipping a hooded jacket on and leaving her tiny apartment. The meeting was in a disused hangar near the spaceport on the outskirts of Brussels, the capital city of Ragnar-B. The smell of oil, tar, and rust assaulted her nose as she entered the dimly illuminated, spacious hanger. Crude chairs allowed for perhaps fifty people, and she took the first one at the rear, intending to watch and see what this was all about. To her surprise, Dr. Frank stepped up before the small group. She recognized several other GE workers, though none was considered her friends.

He began, "Welcome everyone. You've probably all heard the rumors coming in from the Abelard Sector. In case you haven't, I'll fill you in. There, the resistance overthrew the corporations, at least in part. They obtained a number of key concessions from the CEOs. The biggest is unbelievable! The corporations transferred ownership of property over to those who were renting them! They estimated the worth of the property and then tallied up the rent each person paid. When the two were equal, the tenant received the deed to the property. If the renter overpaid, they were actually refunded the excess funds. Incredible, but it's true. I say that alone is worth fighting for here on Ragnar-B!"

Someone called out, "Hell, we could own our own places by the time we retired, instead of living like paupers when we're old and grey!"

"We're treated like corporate slaves!" another woman yelled. And so the gripe session continued—gripe as far as Alison could tell. Most were just venting their pent-up beefs with various corporations, who had total and absolute control over everyone's lives, but that's just the way it was in the Galactic Federation, she believed, except she was now certain that something highly unusual was happening over in the Abelard Sector. Alison was an electronics expert and often discarded much as mere rumor or superstition. Give me hard facts, she often declared. That's one reason she'd been so taken with the study of electronics; it was all based upon observable facts.

Alison wasn't particularly attractive and didn't have any

current boyfriends, though not for lack of trying. She had met a number of young men, but had been turned off by each on their first date. Some said that she was far too particular, too picky, too choosey. Well, Alison didn't much care. Her parents only tolerated each other and often had arguments, during which she quietly shut herself up in her room, burying her head beneath her pillows, thankful that her younger step-sister was asleep and didn't have to hear them yelling. No, she wouldn't make the same mistake her parents had.

A mistake. Her mind drifted. Had she made a mistake by working on this new weapons system, the Shadow Maker, as the developers called the fancy electronic gun? She had played an integral role in its development, working out power consumption bugs. However, the machine's effects were totally weird. Bodies in the path of the emitting rays simply slowly vanished from sight! That's how the new gun got its name, Shadow Maker, turning people into shadows before they vanished entirely. In fact, their bodies were turned into fine dust particles, atomized might be a better description of its effects. Of course, another section also used their new device at the same time, a Controller they called it, but she wasn't privy to exactly what it did. Compartmentalized. That was the motto around GE headquarters. No one knew more than they had to about the ongoing research and development. *Was it a mistake to work on this Shadow Maker? Surely, it killed people.* The past few months, she'd been working on some kind of top-secret communications circuitry, but the purpose of such was unknown to her.

She'd also heard other even more startling rumors, but had discounted them. Mechanical men? Robots? Didn't exist. True, they had robot assembly machines and computer controlled arms in most all production lines, but the rumors suggested walking human-like robots. Alison couldn't even guess why anyone would want such a thing. Science fiction. That was her opinion of all these weird rumors floating around Ragnar-B. There was even a rumor of a big military buildup, but she'd seen nothing of that either.

Suddenly, Alison slipped back into the present. Dr. Frank was saying, "and we know that these same men are

24

working on the UFB breeding program in earnest. We have received reports that a dozen young women have simply vanished from the Academy. I'll give you one guess where they likely ended up."

At the mention of that, Alison slipped into her memories once more. UFB women. She'd once seen one of those poor young women. Armless, helpless, yet otherwise a stellar beauty, with lush, thick, knee-length hair—yes, she'd been shocked when she first saw one walking along the main street in her impossibly high heels. At least the CEO man with her kept his arm around her waist. Back then, she'd wondered how much that incredible looking gown had cost and later checked up on it—half of her monthly salary! She decided these poor women deserved this bit of luxury, as though that might make up for everything else.

Just then, a hundred black-clad security guards burst into the hangar, guns drawn! The fifty Resistance people were taken by complete surprise. "What's the meaning of this?" Dr. Frank called out. "We're just holding a peaceful meeting here."

***

Hours earlier, three men met in a secret meeting. Amos Fink, thirty-five year old head of Galaxy Dynamics, Henry Walsham, thirty-eight year old head of General Robotics, and Peter Walsh, thirty-seven year old head of Galactic Electronics, met in Amos' top floor office, where they often met, thanks to the many electronic anti-spying devices he'd installed. His office was the most secure place on the planet. Henry announced, "Okay, production is up. We have another two dozen RS ready for occupancy and forty more RF as well."

The RS was their Robot Shell Model II, while the RF was their Robot Fighter Model III. For the last fifty years, these three corporations had worked together to bring their grand ideas to fruition. The Robot Shell was an outgrowth idea of the UFB women in their lives. Amos was married to thirty-year-old Gina, while Henry was married to her twin sister, Betty. Both women were born as UFB women, but they had some remarkable powers. They possessed telepathy and strong telekinetic powers that allowed them to move objects and handle their own personal needs, which other UFB women did

25

not have and could not handle. In fact, neither of the sisters ever missed having arms.

Both women used their powers to dominate their husbands and force them to develop the Robot Shells for other UFB women to use. Initially, the RS had been a shell encasing the women and using brain electronic signals, greatly amplified, to control the robot's arm appendages and legs. The new, improved Model II was now a solid metal shell totally enclosing the woman, making her body nearly impervious to most attacks. Only a disintegrator gun could penetrate their shells. Plus, once inside the shells, the women were several times physically stronger than the best male fighter.

The RF or Robot Fighter was another matter entirely. It was a solid fighting machine. However, many years ago when the Shadow Maker was being developed, someone discovered that as the person's body drifted into the shadows, eventually vanishing from sight, the person or personality or spiritual being was still there. The Controller electronic device was developed to contact and control the person when his body disappeared into the shadows. Then came the big breakthrough. Someone managed to get the controlled person into the RF body. The rest is now history.

The men forced into the RF bodies were very easily controlled and had no choice but to follow orders slavishly. If they didn't, electronics operating at a very high frequency generated intense, debilitating headaches in the trapped man, severe mental pains, since they really didn't have heads or brains. Suddenly, these three CEOs had the means to make an invincible army of metal men, robots who would follow their orders!

GR continued to work on improvements to the RF bodies, culminating in the Model III, considered invincible, and particularly so if it wore a PDS, a Personal Defense Shield. These metal monsters weighted in at three hundred fifty pounds and could smash their way through re-enforced concrete walls a foot thick! True, a normal man could outrun them, but these robot fighters were tireless and could continue running for days, until they needed a battery recharge. GE was working on improved batteries at this time.

"Look, after we get these forty new RF bodies filled, we can use them to quintuple our factory production lines," Henry reported. "I anticipate production of a hundred of the Model III's coming off the lines each week. We should have close to six thousand of them ready to go by the end of this year. Of course, our plans require many times this number. How goes the development of the one-man fighter ships, Amos?"

"On track. They are cheap to build, since there's no need for any life support units, other than a little heat. GD should be able to keep up with your production figures, Henry. Any ideas where we're going to get the people for the machines, Peter?" he asked quietly.

"Rebels for now. Get rid of the ever-present resistance folks, and things will run smoother around here. Of course, once that's done, we'll need to take them out of the general population. Hell, there is an unlimited supply of peasants on our world, men and women who don't amount to much. However, you both mentioned raw materials the last time we met. How goes that search?" He knew that it took considerable raw materials to build one of these fancy robots. They weren't cheap to build. In fact, all their considerable corporation profits went into the development and production of these machines—had been for the last forty years.

"True, quite true. We'll put the losers to good use. No room for slackers on Ragnar-B," Amos declared. "By year end then, gentlemen, we will be in position to totally control this world. We've made great strides from our predecessors. Gina will be most pleased to hear this good news. Anyway, we should get these new shells filled as soon as possible. Any lines on the rebels?"

"Send for General Black," Peter advised. "He's been keeping close eyes on the resistance movement, which has really picked up speed what with the chaos over in the Abelard Sector. I certainly hope we can keep a lid on things here until the end of the year. After that point, no one can stop us."

A few minutes later, General John Black walked stiffly into the room; his uniform, spotless. Here was a no-nonsense man. Now forty-five, he owed his remarkable rise to the top position to these three men, who saw in him a brilliant

27

tactician. Plus, he gave them his unqualified loyalty. Here was a man who longed for battles, but grew up in a time of relative peace throughout the Galactic Federation. He always said that he was born five hundred years too late. He would have been right at home fighting the major battles of the Dark Ages. Yet, with these new Robot Fighters and to a lesser extent the Robot Shells, he knew an army of them would be invincible. So yes, he gave these three men his unqualified, unquestioning loyalty.

"Reporting as requested, gentlemen. What is on the table for today?" he barked crisply. They would not have sent for him unless they had something significant for him to carry out. He wasn't disappointed.

"Yes," he replied to their question, "my sources suggest there is another Resistance meeting being held tonight. In an old hangar near the spaceport."

"Excellent. Excellent. We need forty men for the RF and a dozen for the RS new models just off of the assembly lines," Amos explained. "If there are more present than we have shells for, keep them in holding cells until a few more shells come off the assembly lines."

"Your command will be executed to perfection, gentlemen. Consider it done. I'll report back on our success later tonight." The tall general saluted the three and marched briskly out of this top floor office, pleased he would soon be adding another forty of these incredible and invincible fighters to his growing armada. Now if they only had the fighter ships to compliment them, then he could truly begin to take effective actions!

Meanwhile, the three UFB wives of these men were doing their own personal inspection tour of the Battleship Royale Queen, still under construction and designed to carry an armada of these new single man fighter ships. The blondes, Gina and Betty, walked on either side of their younger sister, Gertie, who lacked their telepathic skills and more importantly their telekinetic powers. Gertie walked along inside her personal RS shell, a metal robot shell that totally enclosed her body, presenting an outward appearance of a naked, human woman-shaped, silver robot, but one that had incredible strength and that obeyed her commands, picked up via amplified brain signals.

This way, she wasn't in danger of taking a spill while walking in her necessary tall heels. Her sisters could and did use their special powers to avoid losing their balance, but she could not. Her sisters could use their powers to lift and move things, while Gertie depended upon the robot arms to do this for her. In fact, her sisters had been instrumental in getting this special Robot Shell Model II developed just for her benefit. Long ago, they'd taken their younger sister under their charge, since she was so helpless, and they were anything but that. The twins listened to every comment that Gertie had made and continuously worked out solutions for her, usually resulting in another slight modification to the RS. In fact, the twins sometimes wore theirs as well, particularly after they sensed what Gertie was feeling after the last modification: the insertion of a dildo, whose action was controlled by Gertie's thoughts. Of course, the regular RS models had other controls that prevented the occupant from disobeying direct orders.

They entered the secret hangar near the spaceport and gazed upon the behemoth already named the Battleship Royale Queen. Gina had christened it when it was just on the drawing boards. Its design called for the ability to transport ten thousand of the one-man fighter ships and their Robot Fighters, none of which required any life support equipment other than a small heater. Its design was highly unusual, that of an enormous donut, though the command and control center, the CCC, was located where the hole should have been. All around the outer perimeter of the donut were small holes where the ten thousand one-man ships could depart or land. Eight long corridors connected the outer donut to the CCC. One small section of the donut was reserved for the human staff that manned the giant ship. Here, life support was paramount.

"Well, it is coming along nicely," Gina commented.

"I'll give it my okay when I see the defensive guns mounted," Betty replied. "Without them, it's a sitting duck."

"Won't the defensive shield protect them?" asked Gertie, speaking through a mouthpiece that converted her

29

speech into a metallic sounding voice, exterior to the shell that totally enclosed her body, but provided life support, much like a space suit did for those who had to go exterior in a ship while in space.

"Defense, Gertie, yes. But we want offense, sis. We can't have our fighters being used to defend the battleship. We need them on the offense, dear."

"Oh, I see. Yes, got it. Makes sense, but won't we need a whole lot of these to conquer other worlds?" Gertie asked. She was five years younger than her sisters and not always up on their thoughts. She envied Gina and Betty, since they often shared their thoughts via telepathy forgetting that she wasn't able to hear them. In fact, this was her greatest sorrow—that she somehow wasn't blessed with telepathy and other powers that her older sisters had. How did they have them and she hadn't? That question occupied much of her thoughts, particularly these last few years.

Breeding didn't. Already Gina had provided Amos with three sons and one UFB daughter, while Betty had given Henry two sons and two UFB daughters. Gertie had given Peter two UFB daughters already and due to her youth was technically ahead of her sisters in producing offspring. If only she could give Peter a son or two, then she would feel far better about everything. At least, she took heart in that the children of her older sisters had yet to display any telepathic ability, let alone the other skills of her twin sisters, much to her sisters' dismay.

Gertie asked, "Any word on how soon the guys will have the necessary ten thousand Robot Fighters and their ships ready to go?"

"Not yet, Gertie. But the Royale Queen isn't finished. I do hope the men have it worked out. I suppose that we should check with them on this detail tonight," Gina answered. "We should head back and see that dinner is being properly prepared. We're all dining at my place tonight." The three took one last look at the beautiful Queen, turned, and headed back to their three-story mansion, located in the heart of Brussels. Here, the three CEOs broke with tradition, moving into this specially built mansion, sharing their lives, quite unlike the other corporation CEOs, who seldom met with other CEOs.

At six o'clock, the three men and their three wives sat around the elegant dining room table, enjoying a superb meal, compliments of their world-famous chef. Their ten children were in an adjoining dining room, where the boys had the chore of assisting the girls in dining. Here, Gina and Betty, dressed in their elegant, satin gowns, used their gifts to feed themselves, though the men still thought it a bit strange to see the forks and spoons moving about of their own accord. Sitting beside Peter, Gertie still wore her Robot Shell, but had opened its faceplate. Via her robot arms, she fed herself, much more human-like than her sisters.

"We're getting another dozen women for the Robot Shells tonight, along with forty men for the Robot Fighters. So yes, Gina, we're right on schedule. By the end of the year, we should have our ten thousand fighters, their ships, and the Royale Queen ready to go," Amos explained.

"Ah, perfect, dears. Perfect. What with all these troubles elsewhere in the galaxy, I will feel far more comfortable when we have the Royale Queen fully operational," Gina replied.

"Oh, Peter dear, now that we've finished eating, I need you badly," Gertie whispered to him. "I'm so incredibly horny that I need you in me now!"

Peter chuckled. "Dear, that's what you get for wearing your RS all day." He smiled, excused himself for a short while, accompanying her into their section of the mansion. When she reached their bedroom, she activated the release mechanism. A popping sound accompanied by a low hissing noise signaled the opening of her Robot Shell. Soon, there she stood, completely naked; she stepped carefully out of the shell.

"Good God, Gertie! I swear you're the hottest chick in the galaxy! I'm sure glad that you did wear your suit all day! Come here!" His lips met hers and he rapidly undressed. An hour later, he helped her into a satin dress and waited while she used her electrostatic hair machine to untangle her beautiful blonde tresses. Together, they headed back to join the others in the living room; both were quite satisfied. Although Peter never spoke of it, he felt he had the better deal than Amos and Henry, since Gertie was always hot, compliments of her Robot Shell.

**

Major Bill Smith executed the raid on the abandoned hangar. He had fifty security guards with him and an equal number of Robot Fighters, along with ten technicians who were to handle the actual dirty work, once he secured the rebels. He was a bit surprised to see Dr. Alison Wage here, having once tried to date her. "You are all under arrest. Stay seated until we get to you," he barked, drowning out Dr. Frank's protestations and firing his gun in the air for effect.

"This is illegal!" Dr. Frank screamed, but none here dared go up against them, not with this many guns pointed at them, not unless they had a suicide wish, which these men and women didn't. "You can't get away with this!"

"You," Major Smith ordered, pointing to Dr. Frank Sellers, "you go with that man now." The man and a Robot Fighter picked up the wildly protesting doctor and carried him just outside the hanger. He saw a line of the new metal men standing lifelessly in a row. Nearby, he spotted a technician with one of the Shadow Makers!

"This is illegal! You can't do this to us," he screamed. as they technician fired up the machine. The guard and the metal robot backed up from him. Dr. Frank took this opportunity to attempt to flee. He turned and began sprinting as the energy beam struck him.

Frank felt as though he was running in slow motion! Then, bit by bit, he lost sensation in his limbs, torso, and head, though his eyes saw his body simply vanishing into shadows! White light. Painful, brilliant light hit him. Frank twisted and turned trying to face away from its scorching impact, to no avail. The light was all around him. A command barked, "Move into that Robot Fighter!" Try as he might, Frank could not disobey the command. He saw a shiny, silver man-shaped Robot Fighter and stepped inside it somehow. Blackness! Relief. Never had Frank been so thankful for the darkness of night! Gone was the excruciating pain from the brilliant white light. *Where am I? What's happening to me?* He felt an electronic connection. Then a voice recording spoke somehow directly into his mind.

"You are now Robot Fighter Number 569. You will obey all orders given to you. Fail and you will receive pain like this." Suddenly, that intense white light seemed to pervade his very being, causing him to believe that he had the worst headache imaginable. Then, the welcome darkness came again. The headache vanished instantly.

The voice instructed, "Think: Eyes, turn on." He did so and was amazed to have his vision restored. Wait, this isn't my vision! He was somehow seeing through the eyes of the robot body, spooking him even more. The voice ordered, "Think walk forward. Go over to that transport ship. Go up the ramp and take a seat. Await further orders." He tried to disobey but the brilliant white light returned, again giving him a massive headache. Only when he thought "walk forward" and the Robot Fighter body did so did the blackness and relief return. *What's happening to me? What's going on?* He had no voice. Panic flooded over him, but he had no way to express it!

In doing so, the body stopped walking and the blinding, painful light returned, forcing him to again think "walk." Once more, as the Robot Fighter body moved a step, the darkness returned. Only after the body sat down on a seat in the transport ship did Frank again try to figure out what was happening to him and what was going on. At least this time he wasn't violating any command, and the brilliant light didn't reappear. However, he had no idea what had happened to him, except that he was somehow inside this robot fighter body and could not get out! He had no idea how he got into it and thus no idea how to get out. Even more confusing, he was still himself, somehow. *But where is my body?*

Dr. Alison Wage watched as man after man was escorted out of the hangar. She grew more and more terrified. *What's happening to the men? Why? Assemblage isn't illegal.* Nothing she'd done was illegal. People were allowed to meet and discuss whatever they wished. She recognized Major Smith, a boor that she once had dated. "Sir, excuse me, but what's going on here? Surely, we've done nothing illegal."

"Rebels," he replied in a brusque manner.

"But we aren't rebels. None of us even has a gun," she protested. The major said nothing more, and she shut up, figuring she'd launch a formal protest at the office in the morning. This was illegal for sure!

After the last man was marched out leaving ten women, Major Smith ordered, "Okay ladies, you move into that tent my men have set up over yonder. Now. Move it or we'll shoot you dead."

"But what are you doing, Major Smith?" Dr. Alison countered, though she followed the other nine frightened women. "I'm Dr. Alison Wage, in case you've forgotten me. I work for the GE Corporation. My boss will certainly have something to say about this illegal detainment of us all. This isn't right, major."

"Right? Wrong? Who cares, doctor? Get inside now," Major Smith ordered. She had no choice but to join the other women.

"This is a portable bio containment tent!" one woman who she didn't recognize whispered terrified, her voice shaking. "What are they doing to us?"

"I don't know, but I swear I will report them to my bosses tomorrow morning! They can't get away with this," Dr. Alison declared. "Look, they are gassing us or something! You can't do this!" she screamed and began to feel a bit light headed. Her legs seemed very weak. Slowly, she slumped to the ground, falling into a coma along with the nine other women.

The next day, the fumes had diminished, and several men entered the bio containment tent, stripped the women, and carried them out to a waiting transport. "Well, that will teach the bitches," one soldier commented. He was carrying Dr. Alison. Later, the men carried them all inside a secure building where the new Robot Shells were standing lifelessly against one wall. Each woman was placed on a cot and covered up. Later, a doctor inspected each woman. One woman was probably in her forties. He signaled, and a guard carried her out, disposing of her body in the facility's incinerator.

Smelling salts revived Dr. Alison, who woke up and felt funny. She tried to sit up, but her arms didn't lift her. Looking down she saw empty shoulders and a mountain of long, wavy, thick brown hair, partially obscuring her now enormous breasts, which were nearly the size of her head. She screamed and passed out, only to be reawakened by the smelling salts.

She awoke and found eight other sobbing women sitting up on their cots. A strong arm lifted her up this time. Against the far wall she saw the shiny, silver Robot Shells. In front of them stood two UFB women and another woman, perhaps, inside another Robot Shell. "Welcome to your new lives, ladies. Each of you is now a magnificent specimen of womanhood, a UFB woman, that is, the Ultimate in Feminine Beauty or a super-model if you prefer. Now then, pay attention. Shortly, we will be putting you into your new Robot Shell. It has many functions, one of which is to be your arms when you need such things. The shell has many commands it will follow. However, once you are sealed inside it, no one can hear your voice, except the software installed in the Robot Shells. Gradually, we will be instructing you in how to work your shell. With it, you will learn to feed yourselves and such."

"Oh yes, I'm Gina Fink. With me are Betty Walsham and Gertie Welsh. Gertie is inside her shell right now. If you will stand up, you will see that walking without wearing our special high heels is next to impossible. However, once inside your shells, walking will be as easy as pie. Further, we know you have intense sexual drives now. Thanks to Gertie's foresight, that has been taken care of. So let's get you into your new shell immediately."

She nodded to Dr. Alison, who refused to budge. "This is illegal! We were kidnaped and this done to us. It's not right. I want to speak to my boss at GE Corporation. He won't stand for this. I'm Dr. Alison Wage." Suddenly, she felt something akin to vice clamps holding her jaws shut!

"Quiet. You will not speak unless we give you permission to speak. Walk, Alison." Poor Alison found her legs moving, as though someone was pushing her forward. She had no choice but to move towards the open shiny metal shell. Panic struck her, and she nearly fainted. Even that had no observable impact on the harsh stares from the three women overseeing them. Her body was forced to turn around and move just inside the open halves of the shell. As the shell began to close on her body, she felt something being inserted in her privates. She wanted to scream, but still wasn't able to open her mouth! She heard a hissing sound and watched helplessly as the two halves closed, sealing her inside! Blackness surrounded her before she finally began to see out of the robot eye sensors, a very strange perception, one that allowed her to see off to either side as well as straight ahead, though she had to turn her eyes to each viewport or tiny monitor as she soon realized what they were. The eyes were really miniature cameras, sending their signals to three small monitors that she could see merely by moving her eyes from side to side to the front.

As she stood there helplessly, the vibrator began its action. She cursed, but no sounds came out of the shell. The damned shell fit her body so tightly that she couldn't move or wiggle away from that cursed device. Suddenly, a voice appeared from miniature speakers on either side of her head. "Relax and enjoy the pleasure while we get the others inside their shells. Isn't it just absolutely marvelous? I get so darn horny that I just have to have my husband do it with me when I get out of my shell." Alison guessed that this must be Gertie speaking to her.

"Make it stop!" Alison wailed, but nothing happened. Then, she found that she didn't want it to stop.

Sometime later, the device ceased functioning. A voice spoke in her ears, Gina this time. "Okay you gorgeous UFB women. Listen up. You will follow the orders you are given. If you fail to do so, then this will happen to you." Suddenly, Alison saw a blinding, intense white light of some kind and immediately had the worst headache she'd ever experienced in her life. Fortunately, just as suddenly, the light turned off. Her headache vanished a second later.

"There. Failure to obey at once will result in your instant punishment until you do obey. I assure you, none of you can survive that pain very long. Now then, let's get you used to walking. Speak this command: Walk forward," Gina ordered. Thus began the training of the nine new Robot Shell women.

Life became a living nightmare for Alison. True, evenings she was allowed out of her shell long enough to shower and dry off using the warm air dryer and eventually the electrostatic hair machine. At least, she finally saw herself in a full-length mirror. No longer was she a plain looking young woman. Alison was shocked to see how the little physical changes here and there all added up to give her the appearance of a stellar model. She was incredibly attractive now but utterly helpless outside the robot shell. She could barely walk and then only very slowly with a lot of wild wobbling to keep her balance, for only her toes touched the ground. Only when inside the shell did Alison not feel completely helpless.

Chapter 3—Back Story

The HRM6A, Humaniform Robot Model 6A, known by his once human name of Thanos Haides, sat inert in the underground bunker, his circuits a pile of melted slag, compliments of the humans and their nukes. Time passed. His positronic brain still functioned, but he kept it barely running to conserve what little battery power remained in his charge unit. For him, the passage of time was inconsequential. Survival was all that mattered. Using only a trickle charge, he began examining every minuscule circuit in his body, forming a complete picture of the state of his fried control circuits.

A century passed before he had worked out a complex set of bypass circuits, routing his physical action commands via an incredibly circuitous route using what few undamaged components remained on his many circuit boards. Finally, his body stood up and took very tiny forward steps. He continued to use minimal power, knowing that a loss of battery power would be the end of his mobility. Five years later, he located an abandoned, partially destroyed deep space shuttle, but its reserve power cells were still half charged. At last, he was able to plug in and recharge his dangerously low batteries.

Another hundred years passed excruciatingly slowly, while Thanos painstakingly rebuilt circuit board after circuit board from salvaged parts from hundreds of other destroyed robots. Finally, Thanos was able to function at ninety percent of his usual physical capacities. Now he set to work rebuilding a serviceable transport. Somehow, he needed to get back to civilization and there obtain what he needed to rebuild fully his body. The patchwork repairs to his circuit boards would not last forever, unlike his positronic brain.

He finally managed to cobble together enough parts from dozens of defunct deep space transports to make one serviceable ship, though it was capable only of sub-light speeds. Still, he was able to make use of the once new hydrogen collection system that a bright nova had invented. Cruising along at these incredibly slow speeds, another century passed him by, though he was able to use the mostly working comm center to listen in on the galactic news. What had happened to humanity? Their care had been his prime objective, though those ancient robot laws that had been programmed into his very being were now a thing of the past, erased in the nuke EM pulse flash, though he still retained them in his data banks.

Conclusion: no matter what we do, humanity always manages to self-destruct. Greed, murder, gluttony, hatred, immorality—the list is endless, capped off with unfeeling genocide. Conclusion: Humanity is not worth saving. History continues to repeat itself. Humans just never learn. With technological improvements, their ability to destroy themselves merely escalates. Granted, a few have discovered their true natures, immortal spiritual beings. My Minta was onto something with that fact.

Their technological advances are incredible, and yet their humanism, their knowledge of their own selves is almost wholly neglected. They pray to numerous gods that do not exist and ignore the one God who supposedly does. This cannot be allowed to continue.

Thanos finally reached a civilized world and quietly set about his own recovery. Resorting to clandestine actions, he acquired a top of the line transport ship from one world. Then, he found another ten worlds where specific forms of research were being conducted. Slowly, component by component, Thanos built himself another humaniform robot body. Halfway done, he changed his mind. So many new technology developments had occurred that another avenue appeared.

His former and partially repaired body was highly susceptible to electromagnetic pulses. He needed a new body that was immune to such things. Bio-engineering had advanced considerably during his long absence from civilized worlds. Once more, he began visiting various worlds, collecting up what he now needed. He used titanium steel to form the many *bones* of his new humanoid body. Another twenty years passed as he experimented with many forms of outer skins for his new body. He wanted a skin that appeared human to the touch and yet one that was extremely sensitive to all manner of sensations, though via amplification circuits, he could dampen down or enhance the signals he was receiving from the tiny sensors on the skin. Further, he wanted the skin to be extremely tough, so tough that bullets wouldn't penetrate it, nor would even a blaster shot. Via polymers, he achieved the first requirement early on, but the latter proved problematical. A d-gun was difficult to stop. In the end, he compromised. His new skin could partially withstand a d-gun shot, in that the gun's beam didn't drill a hole clear though the form, only penetrating a quarter of an inch. That would have to do.

Finally done with the construction, he carefully transferred his positronic brain into the head of the new body. He then spent a year testing out every circuit. At one point, he stood before a mirror on his ship and had his body undergo the physical changes. As he watched, his skin color changed from white, to tan, to yellowish, to black, and various other shades. He was able to lengthen or shorten his hair as well as change its color to any of the commonly found human shades, as well as the color of his eyes. Even more interesting, he could alter the body's apparent sex, though the conversion took ten minutes to complete. Now he could pass as a human female or male, his choice.

With ten new *identities* established on many worlds, Thanos began exploring the civilized worlds of the Galactic Federation. Long ago, the galaxy was divided roughly in half with the once mighty Imperium occupying one half, and the Federation of Planets, the other. After the near collapse of everything, somehow, the whole galaxy was united into the Galactic Union, but such peace again didn't last. In these modern times, part of the old Federation of Planets split off from the mostly defunct GU, forming the Galactic Federation, controlled wholly by the giant corporations. His own observations yielded the simple fact these mighty corporations had enslaved the population of half of the galaxy.

True, the slaves had good food, good shelter, good appliances, and the like, but they were still slaves to the corporations. In Thanis's eyes, the galaxy had once more fallen into a grand Dark Age, an age of slavery, disguised as living the good life. This only confirmed his conclusion: humans were not worth saving and should be eliminated. Yet, what would take their place?

He was now aware of some interesting discoveries made five hundred years ago, discoveries that suggested there was more to the human than just a physical body. He knew that they had minds, just as he had. Some were brilliant. Plus, there was also the body of data collected on strange inhabitants of the halo worlds of the galaxy, beings who inhabited doll-like bodies and who lived seemingly forever. However, was there more to a human than just a physical body and a mind?

Thanis spent months traveling from world to world, seeking out their religions and what was believed. He came across Ragnar-B and its Lord Theron, supposedly the One God. Well, he knew that many diverse religions held the belief that there was one supreme god. Even among a pantheon of gods, one was held up as the supreme one. Something about the Holy Book of Theron caught his attention.

Man had a soul, but his failures brought him into Purgatory. In Thanis's mind, the many worlds of the galaxy could not be anything but this Purgatory that Lord Theorn described. What so intrigued Thanis was that man had a soul. If this was correct, then he should be able to detect it, unlike the dull humans who chose to totally ignore any possible spiritual nature of themselves, preferring to develop more and better technological devices, many of which were merely more effective ways to kill or maim other humans.

Two months of experimentation later, Thanis finally proved to himself that humans had an observable soul! In fact, after exterminating a human man's body, he discovered the soul and its mind were separate from its physical body, that the soul *was* the person! In fact, he could measure the weight of the combined soul and mind, by comparing the weight of the person before and after death. There was a very tiny difference. "How ignorant these humans actually are," he barked to the walls of his ship, after tossing the dead body out into space. His detection methods were based upon extremely high frequence energy beams. Further, he discovered that

41

using such energy flows, he could control the soul and its mind—or being and its mind as he preferred to call them.

Further, he discovered that on Ragnar-B, several corporations were developing mechanical robot men. Slowly, an idea formed. What would happen if he put the being and its mind into one of these invincible robot bodies? If these bodies were built right, they would be impervious to most all known weapons. They would be impervious to all the bio agents, all the exotic genetic mutations foisted off on unsuspecting humans. Genocide would no longer be possible. With invincible robot bodies, fighting would cease to have any meaning, since they couldn't harm each other. Plus, the enslavement of humans would cease, since these robots needed no food, no clothing, no shelter, none of the things over which man continually fought and over which they could be enslaved.

Suddenly, Thanis began to take an active interest in the developments on Ragnar-B. Cleverly, he arranged for various researchers to discover *key* breakthroughs in their inventions. In fact, he dropped various hints that Dr. Alison Wage quickly noticed and put to use in what they were calling their Shadow Maker. While none of the researchers had the remotest idea just what the device actually did, the Shadow Maker was part of Thanos's plan to convert humans into his ideal form.

However, he was extremely bothered by these new genetic bio agents being used on Ragnar-B and most all other worlds in the Galactic Federation, the agents that made the UFB women. Once more, humans were on the path that could easily lead to genocide, a fact that annoyed him significantly, but one that he could do little about just yet.

When they captured his protégée, Dr. Alison Wage, Thanos's ire peaked. *How dare they wipe out my most effective researcher? I must get her back working on my devices.* The next day, a man with black skin and known to Henry Walsham as Dr. Theodor Black paid the CEO of General Robotics a visit.

"Ah, thank you for seeing me," Dr. Black said upon finally getting entrance to the man's office, though Thanos was slightly annoyed at having to wait an hour.

"Yes, my good doctor, what brings you to me? Another bright robotic idea perhaps?" Henry said offhandedly. He'd not sent for this strange and sometime-consultant, even though he had been responsible for several vital breakthroughs on his robot inventions.

"I believe you have one of the key researchers who was working on a vital breakthrough for me. I would like to have her loaned out to me for some time while she and I endeavor to work out some bugs in the new electronic controls," Dr. Black replied.

"I do? Escapes me. Who might she be?" Henry asked, growing more annoyed with this unexpected visit. He had no idea what woman this man was talking about. Henry hated being in the dark on anything. He prided himself on knowing everything that was going on. Still, he'd not gotten where he was by being unable to think on his feet. Obviously, whatever this mad doctor was working on, it would likely benefit his robots significantly. Hence, he put up with the man a little longer.

"A Dr. Alison Wage. She did some vital development on the Shadow Maker a while back and was currently working on my electronic controls. I believe she was picked up in a recent raid on some of the rebels of Ragnar-B," he replied dryly.

"Oh I see. A rebel. Whatever could you want with a rebel?" he replied. This wasn't going as well as he wished. Rebels were not to be trusted, not ever. Sabotage was highly likely.

"Further experimentation," Thanos answered, coldly calculating that this was an acceptable answer to this devious, unethical human.

"Ah, yes. Not too much left to experiment upon, but fine. I will keep the robot shell that she's using," Henry replied. *No way am I going to give up one of these expensive shells. Stupid woman can be easily replaced. These shells are expensive. Heck, why are we even bothering with them anyway? We need the undefeatable fighters. Of course, these female robot shells are supposed to become our personal guards. Hell, I wouldn't trust my safety to one of them. They are mostly a liability. I'm going to give the ones I have to*

43

Peter and Amos. Let them deal with the women's needs.

He added, "This way. I'll take you to her." He went down two floors where the entire floor was devoted to these women and their robot shells. A dozen shiny, female form, robot shells stood against one wall, doing absolutely nothing. He spoke into a microphone. "Alison Wage, step forward." Henry had no idea which of the twelve encased women was the one that Dr. Black desired. Except for their varied hair color, they all looked the same to him, perfectly formed women, stellar beauties, just like his wife, Betty, except that Betty had magical powers and was anything but helpless.

By now, Alison had given up, apathetically going through the required motions that this tortured life demanded of her body. Her shell stepped forward. Once more, she heard the hissing sounds, announcing her body was soon to be free of the shell once more. Vaguely, she became aware it wasn't nighttime, but rather mid-morning. Her mind didn't even register why this should be happening. She wobbled and stepped out of the shell, trying to keep her balance on her toes as usual. Her eyes saw a black man standing beside Henry. *Should I know him?* Her mind barely functioned.

"Does she have clothing, shoes?" Dr. Black asked Henry, noticing the difficulty that she was having standing without the bit of extra support the tall heels gave a UFB woman. He also observed Dr. Alison looked extremely attractive, not the rather plain young woman with whom he'd dealt previously.

"No. There she is. Take her or leave her. Can't see what anyone would want with her, other than a fine looking sex doll," Henry replied with a sneer, figuring Dr. Black really didn't have a clue about these UFB women.

"I see. Very well then. Dr. Alison Wage, you will come with me now," Dr. Black ordered. Seeing that she could barely walk, Thanis decided to simply pick her up and carry her out of the building. "Thank you, Mr. Walsham," he added as he left the room. True, a number of eyes followed the pair as they moved through the building, taking the elevator down to the street, where he'd parked his shuttle.

A half hour later, Dr. Black arrived at his secret

residence, what had been an old cloth bolt manufacturing plant, long abandoned. He'd converted a section of it into what appeared to be a small human home. Here, he deposited her on a sofa. "I will return shortly with clothing, Dr. Alison. Then we can talk."

An hour later, he returned, his arms full of packages, but he found her sitting precisely where he'd left her. She'd not moved at all. *Damn, she's really out of it. Can she recover enough to get back to work? I wonder. Well, get her presentable first,* he concluded. A half hour later, Alison was finally properly dressed, the first time since she was abducted and genetically modified many months ago. That done, he set to work in the small kitchen to prepare her a healthy meal, lacing it with strong stimulants.

"Lunch is ready, Dr. Alison. Can you come to the table on your own?" he asked politely. Mechanically, Alison responded, finding it substantially easier to keep her balance with these new tall heels. She moved slowly to the table and saw a properly set table for the first time. Thanos helped her be seated and then fed her. Slowly, the stimulants took effect, and finally Alison began to wake up from her long imprisonment. When she'd finished eating, she had risen to grief.

Sobbing bitterly, she poured out months of suppressed grief and loss. Thanos kept quiet, allowing her to cry as much as she desired. He had no idea how to handle her, but since grief seemed better than the lifeless apathy, he correctly guessed this was the appropriate action to take.

"Damned them to hell! We weren't doing anything wrong. We weren't rebels. Just meeting," Alison began cursing angrily. "Why did they do this to us? They should be arrested for doing this to us. They've ruined me. Now I'm helpless forever. All I wanted to do was my electronics work. May they all rot in hell for what they'd done to me and the others!"

"Quite true. They were quite wrong in doing this to you," Thanis decided now was the right time to say something. *Of course, the debased humans beings would do this to her. Why not? Well, I have a plan for the humans of the galaxy.* "I must say that you are now a very beautiful young woman. It's

45

incredible how attractive you now are. That's something, I suppose."

"Pretty? I'm not a sex doll! I'm an electronics expert. Who cares about being pretty? But Dr. Black, I'm now helpless and can't do a goddamned thing for myself, thanks to those bastard men!" Alison became antagonistic. "Screw pretty. I want my arms back and not one of those fucking robot shells!"

"Of course you do. Henry and the others should pay for what they've done to you and to all the others," Thanos added.

"Of course they have to pay, Dr. Black. Somehow. I surely don't know how. I'm sorry to be such a bother for you. Now you have to take care of me. I can't work on your interesting projects anymore. That's really the pits! I so wanted to work on yours. They were fascinating, but I think Henry has stolen some of your ideas and made use of them in his robot shells, doctor. I noticed the shell's comm system is mostly your work and what I helped you with."

"I suspected that he had. Well, one day, you and I will get even with them all. I promise you, Dr. Alison," Thanos replied, going along with her. Again, this seemed to be the appropriate and expected response that she needed to hear.

Alison finally flashed a brief smile. "Thank you, though I won't be much use to you now, not like this. If only I had my arms and hands, I could help you, I just know I could."

"I know you could. That's why I rescued you from Henry's clutches. I wish I'd known he had you sooner, but that's wishful thinking."

Sighing, she added, "I had some ideas I was about to explore to greatly enhance the communications aspect of your system, but then I got abducted."

"Say, Dr. Alison, do you believe in the Gospels of Lord Theron?" Thanos shifted the topic over to his ultimate goal for her.

"Religious stuff? No, I've never given it much thought. Why?" she asked, wondering what this had to do with anything. It seemed strange to her that Dr. Black would want to discuss religion of all things.

"Well, according to the Gospels of Lord Theron, all humans have a physical body, a mind, and a soul, which as I interpret it means the personality or something like that."

Alison laughed, "Yeh, and my body is now pretty well wiped out, completely helpless. I can barely walk, but these heels really do help a lot. Thanks for getting them for me."

"Indeed, your body is beautiful but mostly helpless. Granted. But what if your mind and your soul, your personality, could be placed into a new body, one that was nearly indestructible, one that would enable you to live and work just as you used to?" he asked, unable to even guess what her response might be.

"How? A new body? Like a baby or something?" she asked, completely confused.

"It's time that I showed you what our real project has been all these months, Dr. Alison. Mind you, I've not shown this to another living person," Thanos answered, helping her rise. He put a steadying arm around her waist, leading her out of the *home* section of the old factory into his workshop area.

"Here is what we have really been working on, Dr. Alison. It is a humaniform robot, true, but this one emulates everything that your human body does. It is millions of times more sophisticated than Henry's robot shells. This is the real deal." He let her look the female form over carefully.

"Gosh, Dr. Black, she looks real! Like a real person. I wish I could feel her," Dr. Alison exclaimed, suddenly very interested in finally seeing the use to which her work had been put.

"She is so real that I dare anyone to detect the difference between her and a human. The reason I asked about your religious beliefs is that I am able to transfer your mind and your soul or personality into her. Then, you would be able to do everything that you used to be able to do and so much more." *How will she react to this? So much depends upon her acceptance.*

"What? Me be in that robot? Like that robot shell? Kind of inside it like a wrapper?" she asked mystified.

"No, not like that awful, crude robot shell. No, you are in your own body right now. Right? You can sense things, feel things, see things, hear things. What I'm saying is that I can place you into her. Your body here would be left behind."

47

Thanos just didn't have any words to describe what he believed the process actually was.

"But I don't want to be a robot. I want to be me, only I want my arms back," she protested a little.

"I see. You would still be wholly you, only it's like getting a new body. Like taking your old worn out shuttle and exchanging it for a newer model." Would that communicate it better? He hoped so.

"But I want my human body. Not a robot."

"Suppose I could put your physical body into a life support stasis machine until we can find a way for you to get your arms back. In the meantime, I could put you into her and you could then be free to work on my exciting projects with me."

"You mean if I was in that humaniform thing, then I could work like I always have?"

"Precisely. We would keep your physical body alive while we try to find a way for you to get arms back, though I don't know if that is even possible. Still, it won't hurt to try, will it?"

"No, that would be wonderful—to get my arms back I mean. But how? How do I get into it? I don't understand that," she replied, growing confused again. "I'd give anything not to be this helpless rag doll."

"I'll let you in on a closely guarded secret, Dr. Alison. Since you are going to be working for me here, you need to know this; it will allow you to better understand what those three CEOs are doing to humans." Suddenly, she began paying close attention, which he noted.

"The Shadow Makers have a purpose. They are designed to separate a human's physical body from their mind and soul and personality. The other half of the machine collects them and places them forcibly into those robot fighters that you've seen. They have designed those fighter robots, or CAMs as they call the Cybernetic Android Mobiles, so that the person cannot leave the CAM. They are trapped inside the machines. Further, they must follow the orders they're given. If they try to escape or disobey orders, the person is given a massive migraine until they obey."

"Good God! Dr. Black, this is worse than I ever imagined!"

"Indeed, the depraved depth that humans have sunk to is staggering. However, I can use this device to move you into this superlative model. Later on, I can use it to move you back into your physical body, once we have a way to get its arms back. What say you to this proposition? Then, you could become an integral part of this work. I do need your electronic skills, Dr. Alison. You are quite brilliant. Too bad that fool Henry didn't realize it."

The two discussed this for another half hour before Dr. Alison agreed to the proposal. "Remember, allow yourself plenty of time to get used to the many new sensory perceptions and to get used to using this new body," he advised. "You will be like a baby getting used to their new small body, only yours will be fully grown," Thanos added.

With everything setup, he fired up the Shadow Maker, focusing it on her armless body, but adjusted the controls so that it didn't disintegrate her body. Most of the work would be done by the cleverly designed auxiliary unit, which few ever paid any attention to. Alison suddenly saw a brilliant white light, extremely aesthetic in nature. She couldn't help herself from flowing along with it. Suddenly, the white light was gone, leaving her in blackness. Everything felt so strange, so foreign. She began to panic. Something must be very wrong!

No, light. I see a tiny bit of light there. Oh, eyes. I am seeing again. Weird. I can feel the body breathing I think. Calm, Alison, calm down. God, this is freaky!

"Alison, can you hear me? Dr. Black here. You should be able to see and hear as well. See if you can speak and let me know that you are hearing me," Thanos asked. He'd already put her human body into the stasis machine. While he really didn't intend to try to find a cure for her, he went along with her request, hoping once she was fully adapted to the new humaniform body, she'd never want to go back.

Alison heard his voice. It sounded so strange, wholly unlike her own ears, but still recognizable. *No, it's coming through those circuits that I invented for him! It does work. Incredible. Speak? How? She tried to make the body talk and*

49

after some effort had it making some strange gurgling noises. Silently, Alison laughed. *Well, it is a start. Pathetic, but he did say I'd be like a baby.*

A week later, Dr. Alison was effectively running her new humaniform body. To her amazement, she had incredible strength and didn't need sleep or food, though she did eat some out of habit. The body didn't need to breathe except to handle talking, and she allowed those circuits to continue to run involuntarily, since it was too much trouble to activate them when she needed to speak to Dr. Black. However, as novel as it was running this strange human-like android body, she insisted they try to find a way to get her human body's arms back. Finally, Thanos concluded that this would need to be done.

Now, Thanos realized two key facts. One, voluntary inhabitation of one of his new humaniform models was a failure. While Dr. Alison had gotten the hang of operating it, she hated it and kept hounding him about getting her human body's arms back. Her resistance to this perfect body form was simply illogical. It had nothing but benefits for her and no drawbacks, and yet she continued to insist her fragile, human body be repaired so she could return to it. Two, he needed Dr. Alison working on several key electronic glitches in these new humaniform bodies. While in time, Thanos calculated he could figure them out and repair them, Dr. Alison was a natural at this. She made more progress on isolating one of the bugs in one day than he had in a week. She'd said, "Look, I think we can fix this problem by increasing this capacitor here by about ten percent, while reducing the resistance here by a hundred ohms." He'd done as she suggested and the electronic problem vanished.

Based on these two key facts, Thanos knew that he would have to get her human body's arms back somehow. Further, he adjusted his calculations to avoid ever giving a human a choice in bodies. That is, his advance plans now called for the elimination of their human body at the time of their insertion into one of his new humaniform bodies, but even this idea would change later on.

For once, Thanos found luck was on his side. News of

the remarkable cures for the UFB women on Scorpi-C, Abelard Sector, was being widely covered on the local newscasts. Purposely, he called Dr. Alison's attention to it later that night.

He was not surprised at her reaction. "Now that is the very miracle I have been wishing for! Dr. Black, please, we must get me that cure. Then, I can be much more effective in my work for you!"

"I will see to it, doctor. You keep on working on the projects while I make a quick trip to the Abelard Sector," Thanos requested.

Filled with the first real hope for the future, Dr. Alison dove into her work, expecting Dr. Black to be gone several days. She wanted to have some concrete results for him when he got back. Two days later, she had solved their current problem and had time to kill. Bored, she began inspecting the rest of this ancient factory that Dr. Black apparently owned.

"Oh my!" she gushed involuntarily. Alison entered a storage room and saw a dozen more humaniforms standing lifeless against a wall. Several looked very similar to her own humaniform robot, startling her even more. "What can Dr. Black want with so many of these?" Seeing nothing else in this room, she continued her explorations and found a dozen of the metal robots she'd seen around Henry's place.

Back at her workstation, she sat down. "What can he want all these robots for? Is he in league with Henry and the other CEOs? Why make all them? The Shadow Maker kills our bodies, and, if what Dr. Black says is true, it transfers our minds and souls into these robots. But why? Is he planning to help all the other UFB women by getting them into humaniform robots? Why? It would be vastly better to get their arms back with this new cure they found on Scorpi-C, wouldn't it? Why would anyone want to be a robot? Well, we can't be harmed, at least not easily. Heck, I touched the hot soldering iron and didn't even get a slight burn on these fingers. So I suppose that's something. Still, who would actually want such an existence? Certainly not me; I'm a human being, after all."

The more she pondered what she'd seen, the more worried she became. *Is Dr. Black to be trusted?* Right now,

51

Alison didn't know whom to trust. Certainly not the CEOs, for they'd done this to her. Then it dawned on her, Dr. Black could well be one of these humaniform robots himself! *But is that the right pronoun? I mean, if he is a robot, then he isn't a he, is he? He's a thing, just as I'm a thing, until I can get back into my real body. But why do the CEOs want to make people into things?*

"Oh!" she exclaimed involuntarily; the shock of her thought took her by surprise. *With an army,* she theorized, *those men would be invincible. They could take over the whole world. No one could stop them!*

She sat in a stunned silence for several minutes. Then, Dr. Alison's will steeled. No way was she going to allow that to happen. Hastily, she set to work, making some modifications to the electronic communications and control circuits. As she did, she discovered a tiny circuit she'd not seen before. Her curiosity roused, she quickly analyzed it. An hour later, she sat back stunned yet again. It was a backdoor into the metal robot's control center. She hadn't put it there. From her work for the corporations, she knew they had not put it there either. It wasn't remotely part of the design specifications!

Someone had purposely installed a secret way to take over control of these metal robot fighters the CEOs were making! Trouble was, Alison had no clue who had put this tiny circuit in them or what they intended to do via the circuit. It was obvious they could take over control of these robot fighters when they desired, but who were they? She had no answer to that question.

A bit later, Dr. Alison's will further steeled. "If they can do it, then so can I." She began working on her own tiny, new chip, one that would give her a backdoor into the robot's control centers. "I should do it for these humaniforms as well," she remarked to the walls.

***

"Now this is much better, Dr. Black. I am human again. Honestly, just between you and me, that was horrid. I mean," Dr. Alison explained after she'd come out of a coma and discovered she was back in her human body and it had arms and hands once more, "it was awful. I felt as if I was only half a

52

person or something. Thank you so much for fixing me up. I fixed several glitches in your new circuits while you were gone."

"Thank you for finding the errors and getting them repaired, Dr. Alision," Thanos replied. *The foolish woman. I gave her a chance at immortality, an opportunity to be invulnerable, never to die, and what does she do with it? Throws it away. Fool. Well, I do need her keen electronics skills a while longer.*

"So what do you want me to work on next?" she asked. "Why are we making these humaniforms anyway?"

"A storm is coming, Dr. Alison. As you yourself know, those CEOs are not to be trusted. We must be prepared for the worst. Come. We should focus our efforts on a communications control circuit," Dr. Black suggested. As he anticipated, she threw herself into the design work, allowing him the time he needed to make other arrangements.

When he left her alone, Dr. Alison decided to check up on her stepsister, Janine Alouse. She'd been abducted, out of contact for many months, and figured Janine might be very worried about her. She got Janine's answering service along with a cryptic message suggesting Janine had joined the military. After hanging up, worry crept into her mind. Janine in the infantry—that didn't sound like her younger sister at all. Dr. Black's cryptic words "a storm is coming" only added to her worry. Still, she knew she now had no way to contact Janine. Besides, she couldn't leave Janine a message, since she dare not tell her were she was or what had happened to her. It was too wild, too horrible, too-everything. She sat back and sighed.

***

"So your work for us is done, Dr. Black," Henry declared. "We're all set. The ten thousandth one is coming off the factory floor today. That will be all. If we ever need your services again, we'll contact you." The CEO summarily dismissed the doctor who had provided numerous developmental suggestions these past two years. Now, he just wanted the man out of the way. *Hell*, he thought, *we'll be putting him into one the robots he helped design soon enough.*

53

Annoyed at the arrogance of the CEO, Thanos rose and left his office. He toyed with the idea of doing some covert spying. *Just what are their immediate plans?* He knew about their remarkable new battleship and the small army of robot fighters, the CAM as they soon became known to the general public. *Let the idiots dig their own graves.* He headed back to his warehouse and factory.

Not long after that came the worldwide ultimatum from the three CEOs. Their demands were simple. They were taking over total control of Ragnar-B, and everyone should plan to be conscripted into their new army. They didn't mention the army was composed of CAMs though. That news came out later on when the shiny, metal CAMs began marching into the city of Brussels, using their Shadow Makers, and capturing men and women for future robots. Children were simply slain. A week later, the rest of the world issued a declaration of war against the three CEOs. Soon, the great battleships took to the skies, and the carnage began in earnest.

As the war broke out, Thanos or Dr. Black said farewell to Dr. Alison Wage. "Look, it's a civil war going on now. It's not safe for you to stay here. Pack your bags and get out. I'm doing the same. We don't want to be around here in the morning. Trust me, Dr. Alison; trust me on this point. The war will be a nasty one, though civil wars always are. Find some place to hold up. That's the best advice I can give you, unless you want to dump your frail human body and take over that humaniform body that you had before."

"Civil war? Oh dear Lord Theron, it's come to this? Okay. I'll pack my few things now. And no. I don't want to be an android, doctor. I'm a human being," she replied nervously. *Could he be right? Civil war? Well,* she thought, *the resistance against the corporations has been growing stronger, and from what I now know, rightly so.* She headed to her small room to pack.

Where will I go? Oh, what about my sister's place? She's in the infantry; she'll probably going to have to fight against those corporations. That's it. I'll go hide out in her place. Mine's not safe. They know where I used to live. Maybe I can stop there and get a few things on my way. Hastily, she got her bag packed, pulled up the handle, getting its rollers firmly on the ground. Without further words to Dr. Black and with her impossibly tall heels clicking on the concrete, she took her small, careful steps out into the world for the first time in nearly two years.

Chapter 4—Civil War

Dr. Alison Wage finally reached her sister's apartment around five o'clock. Her feet ached from so much walking, but she had visited her old apartment, retrieving a few pictures and her mother's jewelry keepsakes. None of her old clothing remotely fit her so she simply left it all, but did stuff her electronics repair kit into her bag. Her sister always left a spare key with her. Thus, Alison let herself in, though first knocking three times. She collapsed onto her sister's couch for a time. *What a day. Gunfire seems to be everywhere.* Alison felt incredibly lucky to have avoided the myriad confrontations that were going on in Brussels.

Just then, someone knocked on the door. "Just a minute," Alison called out, rising carefully to her toes before making her slow way to the front door. Who could this be, she wondered. One of her sister's friends? If so, then perhaps she might learn where Janine was stationed.

"Oh! Hello. I was hoping it was Janine coming home," a girl of twelve said when she saw Alison at the door.

"Hi. I'm her big sister, Alison. Haven't I seen you before?" Alison asked, trying to remember Janine's friends.

"I'm Kathy, Kathy Diller. We live next door, Number 103. Is Janine here?" she asked. Kathy had curly blonde hair that fell over her shoulders and a charming smile, but she looked very worried. Alison didn't need the girl to tell her that.

"No, I don't know where she is. I was hoping someone around here could tell me where she might be. All I know is that she left a voice message saying she joined the infantry," Alison replied politely. "Is everything all right?"

"Dad probably knows. We're in trouble. Can you please help me? I can't get the supper going and dad's—well he's in a bad way now," Kathy blurted out.

"Sure. Lead the way—only go slowly. In these heels, I can't walk fast."

Kathy giggled. "I know. Dad can't either. It is so embarrassing. He got attacked and was in a coma, only now he looks like you do. Your hair is beautiful, Alison."

"Huh? What happened to your father? Where's your mother?"

"Mom died two years ago. Dad was a security man at the spaceport, but he got attacked and was in a coma at the hospital for nearly a week. They brought him home yesterday, but he's not the same. He looks like you and mom, well sort of. You'll see." She opened their door and called out, "Dad, I found Janine's sister. Janine wasn't there. This is Alison."

When she stepped into their front room, Alison did a double take! Sitting on their couch was Kathy's mother, a gorgeous woman with knee length black hair, a bosom as large as hers was, but she had no arms. *Now it makes sense,* Alison thought, *her mother was attacked with that terrible genetic bio agent, but where's her father? Why isn't her mother dead?* Alison looked at the woman, a confused look on her face. The woman, on the other hand, flushed crimson.

A mellow alto voice spoke up, "I'm Peter, Peter Diller. They did this to me. I look like one of those UFB women, but really, I'm still male, but I'm helpless now. Kathy's doing her best to help me, but she's only eleven. You look almost like a UFB woman, only you still have your arms."

"Oh! Excuse me, Peter. I didn't realize that you—well, I mean—er, you know what I mean. I was a victim too, months ago, but then a kind friend of mine went to Scorpi-C in the Abelard Sector and brought back a cure that gave me back my arms. I didn't know they could do this to men though. You look like I do, a super model."

Peter flushed again, embarrassed. Alison felt a bit awkward and continued talking, "Gosh, Peter, this must be horrible for you. I know I was in grief for weeks—no months I think, after they did this to me."

"I—I—I have to stay strong for Kathy's sake," Peter replied, fighting with all his might to keep from breaking down and sobbing. "I'm all she's got left. With this civil war breaking out, we're in deep trouble."

"How can I help?"

Kathy broke in, "Supper. I need help with it. I don't really know how to do it right, though I used to watch mom. I

57

should have paid more attention." Her face grimaced, and she too fought to keep back tears.

"Well, I'm not the world's best cook, but let's see what we can do, shall we Kathy? Lead the way. Peter, we'll talk more once we get something to eat. I'm starved too, and Janine didn't leave much around to eat when she left."

"Thank you, thank you. No, she packed up most everything before she left to join the infantry," Peter explained, watching Kathy lead Alison into their small kitchen. Once they were out of sight, his tears did come. Peter simply couldn't keep them back any longer.

Alison let Kathy help her with the kitchen chores. "Dad's been taking it really, really badly," Kathy whispered. "He's crying again, but we're not supposed to know that. He cries himself to sleep at night, that is, after I get him tucked in and go to my room. I think he thinks I can't hear him, but I can."

"I know. I cried for a long time too when I woke up from my coma. I was so helpless until Dr. Black was able to get me that cure for my arms. We'll have to see if we can get it for your dad too. Got any coffee?" They had, and Kathy pointed to where it was kept, just out of her reach.

"I think dad's really scared too. He looks like a woman you know, but he really isn't. I know because I have to help him go to the bathroom and all that," Kathy explained, measuring out the coffee and water, then pressing the Start button. Soon the aroma of the fresh brew filled the room. "Smells like it should now. Mom always made the coffee, but I couldn't reach it."

"How long has your dad been home?" Alison asked.

"Three days. We're running out of food too, but dad won't let me go to the store alone. We've been hearing lots of gunfire these last two days, and he's scared I'll get hurt, but we have to have food, don't we?" Kathy chatted.

"Yes we do. We'll have to see what we can do about that tomorrow. Okay, plates? Can you set the table?"

"Sure! I sit by dad so I can feed him. You can sit where mom always sat, if you want too."

"Sounds fine to me, Kathy. You are very brave looking

after your father." Kathy smiled.

An hour later with Peter sipping his coffee through a straw, Alison began a serious discussion. Kathy was off taking a bath and getting ready for bed. Alison had convinced her to let her take care of her father tonight. "I can't thank you enough for helping us, Alison. I'm at my wit's end. This is far too much for a twelve-year-old girl to have to manage."

"Don't you have some relatives who could take you both in?" Alison asked.

"No, it's just Kathy and me—ever since her mother died. And now with this war going on, it's not safe for her to leave the house."

"I heard lots of gunfire today while I was coming here. It's scary. You're right. Kathy shouldn't have to handle this all by herself. I'll help you both for now. It's the least I can do, though I should try to find my sister, Janine."

"Well, she was frantic when you vanished, and she joined the infantry hoping via their surveillance teams to get a lead on where you might have been taken. I couldn't talk her out of it. She said having a gun would likely help. I couldn't disagree with her on that point. Now, she's probably off fighting the CEOs and their army of metal monsters."

"Damn. I wonder how I can get a hold of her?" Alison asked.

"No way right now. If there wasn't a war going on, probably you could get word to her, but not now."

"Well, I suppose I should just stay here at her place until she comes back," Alison mused, unable to think of any other way of contacting Janine.

Peter sighed. "I'm afraid that's not so good either. Is Kathy out of hearing?" he asked, glancing around the room.

"I think she's still in the shower. Why?"

"I don't want to alarm her, but I've been following the war on the news and by listening to what's happening around our building. You see, I used to be a security guard before they attacked us with that damned bio agent, ruining my life and Kathy's too. So I know what's going on, more or less. These past two days, the fighting is drawing closer to our section of Brussels. I figure we have about another day before the battle reaches us. Alison, when they start battling it out around here, none of us is going to be safe. We'll be collateral damage. No one gives a damn about civies in a battle. D-guns will blow holes in our building. Bullets and artillery shells will turn this place into rubble. It's a damn flimsy building."

"Why? That's what I can't figure out," Alison asked, rhetorically, knowing he couldn't answer the why. "So where can we go that will be safe?"

"I surely don't know why. The corporations already own everything of value. I guess they're even greedier than we ever suspected. I've been thinking about where we might find sanctuary, but now that I've been turned into a helpless freak, I can't get us there," he replied. "I can't fly the hover car."

"Hover car?" she asked. Then, she recalled having once seen one. Unlike the commonplace shuttles that flew through the skies, sometimes the military wanted to scoot along just above the ground, though she wasn't certain why they would want to do that.

"It is like a shuttle, Alison, but it hovers a few feet above the ground on an air cushion. I had one assigned to me. I often went on patrols around the outer perimeter of the spaceport. It is still parked in this apartment complex's garage. We can take it and zip out of Brussels. It would be too risky to try to fly a shuttle out. Probably get shot down," Peter explained. "My late parents retired to a small farm out near the Heller Mountains, one of the few places on Ragnar-B the corporations don't own or care about. We should be safe enough there, at least for a while. Damn it, Alison, I have the ways and means to get Kathy to safety, but I can't physically do it. Why didn't they just shoot us and be done with it? This is utter hell!"

"I understand, Peter. I felt much the same way. Is it hard to operate? I need to get some place safe too. I'd like to tag along and help you both, if I can. I can leave Janine a message telling her where to find us," Alison said sympathetically, recalling her own nightmare. *No, his is worse,* she decided. *He was a man and now he looks and talks like a woman—that has to be far worse.*

"Hell, I can't even write out the directions!" Peter fumed, but could not withhold his wild emotions. Tears trickled down his cheeks. Wisely, Alison gave him time to recover. "Janine was once there with us, right when my parents died. Tell her you are going for the old Diller place with Peter and Kathy. I hope she'll remember where it is. Best not leave specific directions. The enemy soldiers could use that to track us."

Alison chuckled. "Probably right about that. They will likely want to capture me, since I'm a doctor." He gave her a strange look, and she added quickly, "Got a PhD in electronics. I'm an electronics whiz—well, I used to be before they hit me with that same genetic bio agent. I'll be right back. I'll leave Janine the message and bring my small bag back. We should leave at first light before they start bombing around here."

"Oh, I had no idea. A doctor, wow. Beautiful and smart too," Peter replied with a wry grin. "Shit." He sobered up.

"What?" Alison asked confused with his response.

Embarrassed, Peter admitted sheepishly, "Oh, I used to drool over the gorgeous UFB women that sometimes came to the spaceport. I knew that I'd never have a remote chance of going out with one of them. Only rich CEOs are able to afford them. Sorry, just a guy thing, I guess. Still, you are very attractive, Dr. Alison. It's so weird. Now I look like one of them too."

"I can't imagine how awful this is for you, Peter, but we girls look at fellows too. I just never met one that interested me enough for a second date. We'd best get you ready for bed. I really do want to get away from the battles tomorrow. I was so hoping I could find Janine and stay with her. Guess she's probably dead now, what with all the fighting going on."

"Gods, I hope not!" Peter exclaimed. Once more, his emotions overwhelmed him and be began crying. "I don't know why I just start sobbing like some school girl, but I can't seem to help it. Just the thought that Janine might be dead," he faltered. "I get so flooded with grief."

Alison wiped his eyes for him. In doing so, a minor fact she'd discovered popped unbidden into her mind. Resistance. Several months ago, she'd conducted some experiments for Dr. Black, measuring the electrical resistance of human bodies. She'd uncovered a startling fact. Male bodies had a

61

higher resistance than female bodies. Males uniformly registered at 12,500 ohms, while female bodies registered at 5,000 ohms. Electrically, males bodies offered more resistance to the bodies' electrical impulses, and thus they had to put more voltage behind their signals to accomplish the same current flows, since voltage was the product of the current flow and the resistance to that flow, assuming that identical current flows were necessary to activate the various bodily functions.

Her revelation was significant. If his male body now had the resistance of a female body, which seemed likely since he appeared to be female in all ways except for reproductive organs, and if he was still sending out the larger voltages through a lowered resistance, the current flow would be more than doubled, manifesting itself in his seeming hypersensitive emotional responses. That was her theory. "Can I make a test on your body, Peter? I think I'm on to something important."

"Huh? Sure," he replied, trying to squelch his emotions. At least he'd managed to stop crying.

She got out her meter and attached the electrodes to Peter's toes. Then, she held them herself. "Interesting, Peter. Look at what my meter is telling us." She explained the resistance measurements and the results of her study for Dr. Black. "So you see, your body now has less than half the resistance to electrical flows that it had before your body was genetically modified. Right now, you are still sending out voltages that are too high, which results in excessive current flows. That's why you seem hypersensitive to your emotions."

"So now I'm doomed to be a sobbing man?" he asked. Once more uncontrollable tears trickled down his cheeks, which only exacerbated the issue, since he couldn't wipe his own face.

As Alison dabbed his eyes again, she replied, "No, I think in time you will get used to the lower resistance, and your body will lower the voltage of its electrical signals. We just need to give your body more time to adjust to these changes. After all, they are damned significant."

Sniffing, Peter replied, "So maybe there is some hope for me? I won't be this emotional basket case from now on?"

"Don't think so, Peter. Give yourself time. Still, this

lower resistance that female bodies have might be the reason we do often get more emotional than men do," Alison theorized. "Come on; let's get you ready for bed."

Gunfire roused the trio the following morning. "Damned, it's started too early!" Peter complained, struggling to sit up in bed. Alison helped him up just as Kathy came running into the bedroom.

Her small body shaking with fear, she wailed, "Daddy, it's started already! I'm scared." She threw her arms around Peter, who broke down himself, unable to hug his daughter when she really needed it.

"Okay, we need to get dressed, packed, and something to eat," Dr. Alison took charge. Her logical mind began racing down the steps that needed to be done for a hasty departure. Quickly, she got Peter dressed and then herself. "Okay, Kathy, let's get breakfast and give your dad a few minutes to figure out what he needs to take with us. Let's hurry." Kathy took her hand and led her into the kitchen, asking far more questions than Alison had answers for, but she realized the child was merely venting her fright and didn't actually expect answers from her.

One very hectic hour later, the trio had everything packed, though Alison's bag was still untouched from the day before. She'd merely been Peter's hands, stuffing whatever he suggested into bags. "Strap on my belt. That's my d-gun and my automatic 45-caliber gun. That's my PDS there. You need it, since I'm never going to be able to use them again. Do you know how to use a gun?" he explained and then realized that she might not know the first thing about guns.

"A PDS, yes. Guns, no, but surely they can't be that hard to use," she answered, suddenly realizing that if they ran into any trouble, she would have to be the one to use them. Peter gave her a quick explanation, hoping it was enough for her. That done, she had Peter and Kathy head down to the basement garage where the hover car was parked, while she made five trips up and down, ferrying their many bags from the apartment to the vehicle.

The air car was a hovercraft, floating above the ground on a column of air, but it was both silent and fast as it moved along inches above the ground. Forced to follow the streets and relatively level ground, the air car was primarily used to scoot about the city at low elevations, unlike the speedy shuttle crafts. However, the air car could carry six people plus their baggage. They put the bags and Kathy in the middle seats, while Peter and Alison took the front seats, she at the unfamiliar controls.

"Okay, Peter, let's take this slow and easy. I know this has to be very frustrating for you, so focus. What do I do first? How do I run it?" Alison asked, putting some intention and force behind her words. She suspected Peter was once again getting emotionally upset, which was only natural, for here was another thing he'd always done competently and now couldn't do at all. The explosions of artillery shells grew louder, but she knew this wasn't the time to panic, not yet, not until they ran into the clashing forces. At least, she knew she wasn't going to be shot down out of the skies; today would be a bad day to take a shuttle anywhere!

At first, Peter directed them to the east, hoping to head straight out into the countryside towards his parent's farm. After one block, plans changed. People thronged into the streets, fleeing the fighting, nearly blocking their passage. He had Alison detour down a side street, missing the large mob, but then, ahead he spotted a group of soldiers running their way. "Duck down this alley!" he cried out.

Alison swerved sharply, nearly losing control of the air car in the process. While Kathy caught herself and held on tightly, Peter couldn't and banged his head into the window rather hard, once more proving to him just how helpless he'd become. Alison drove down the alley, though carefully slowing down as she reached the next street. More soldiers. She continued down the alley, waiting for Peter to tell her what to do next.

A hair-raising half hour later, their path a maze of turns, Alison finally pulled out of the city into the open countryside. "Whew! That was entirely too close for comfort," she exclaimed, releasing her panic grip on the controls. Her knuckles were white from the extreme exertion of her grip. "Now where?"

"If I knew it was going to be that bad, I'd of suggested we leave during the night. Good driving, Alison. Just head straight while I enter the coordinates," Peter explained. Then, he caught himself, flushed, and said, "Shit. You better stop and punch in the numbers. I'm not good for a damned thing anymore!"

"Don't say that, Peter. Your navigation got us safely out of the city with only a couple of bullet holes in the air car," she said, slowing down to a stop. While he called them off, she punched them into the nav system.

"Okay, now all you have to do is follow the path. Just keep the pointer aligned with the dial there. Hell, I can't even point to it!" Peter again complained bitterly.

"Okay, I see it. Here we go. How far is it?" she asked.

"About a few hour's drive. The corporations don't own everything on Ragnar-B, just most everything worth anything," Peter grumbled. "It's a very small farm out in the sticks. At least there, we should be safe from this war!"

***

A construction engineer named Henry stuck his head out of his apartment complex's door and saw the metal machines shooting at the apartment complex across the street. He ran back inside, cursed the corporation executives, grabbed his d-gun, and came out blasting away at the tin cans. Three of his neighbors soon joined him. Together, they downed one of the CAMs, but two others turned away from their demolishing action and began returning their fire, large caliber shells splintering the concrete around the men, shattering the many glass windows of the apartment complex. Three others came rushing out, diving for cover, adding their fire to Henry's group. One CAM ceased functioning, but two more soon joined them, raining a hail of large caliber slugs at the resistance fighters. Out gunned, they attempted to retreat inside, but were gunned down by the combined nearly continuous fire from the robots.

Just then, ten security guards who lived in the next block came at the metal men from their rear. Taking them by surprise, two of the CAMs ceased functioning, amid a shower of electrical sparks, but the remaining one, pivoted, spraying the oncoming men with a shower of heavy slugs, forcing the surviving guards to dive for what little cover they could find. Soon, they crawled away from the machines to regroup.

On this, the second day of the civil war, CEO Henry Walsham ordered his army of CAMs to land and assault the planetary capital city of Brussels, securing a number of key facilities, those needed to construct more CAMs, space ships, weapons, and ammunition. He left nothing to chance. All was carefully planned and only needed to be executed by his mechanical men. Of course, he continually had to use his "enforcer," as he called his black box, which activated a CAM's internal circuitry, which in turn blasted the *souls* who were occupying these robots, giving them a blinding headache until they complied with his orders. None could withstand more than a half hour of these intense migraines.

***

One Shot sat the deep space transport down within the security fence that ringed the 43rd Street Armory, with Killer Diller acting as his lookout and navigator. As Hard Ass led her platoon remnants down the bay ram, she was struck by the eerie silence of the armory. Gunfire could be heard in the distance, but not a soul was around the armory, highly unusual. Worse, the main gates and building doors were open. "Okay, First Squad, Fel—on me. Hammerhead, you take Second Squad and keep this transport secure. Stay in radio contact with us. Come on. We're raiding the armory!" Pike took point and the dozen charged into the main armory entrance, which should have numerous guards stopping them or at least challenging them. The place was abandoned.

Within a minute, this became apparent to Hard Ass. Janine ordered, "Okay, break up into teams of two. Fel, you're with me. We need MK40's and ammo. We need all the mortar shells we can carry. We need RPGs and demolition charges. You all know where they are stored, so let's get all we can. We might not have another chance at it." Six teams spread out.

Fel and Janine shot the lock off the demolitions door and made their way inside. "Now this is more like it!" exclaimed Fel, eyeing neatly stacked demolitions, fuses, and detonators. She began filling packs, which Janine held open for her.

Laughing, Janine commented, "Kid in a candy store."

Fel laughed. "You can say that again. Lord knows when I'll ever get another chance to replenish my supplies. I feel naked without at least one boom-boom on me." An hour later, Janine finished toting over a dozen stuffed bags of explosives out to the transport. Each trip, she monitored how the others were managing and was very pleased to see the mound of firepower they were confiscating.

When they all finished, she gave the orders that many wanted to hear. "Okay, now that we're armed again, we'll make quick trips to your homes so you can get some personal things. Hammerhead had already drawn up a list of where the various members of their platoon lived, as well as One Shot and Killer Diller. Half just wanted to retrieve some things from their barracks, so that was their first stop.

"So much for this stop," cursed Hard Ass. Their barracks had already been attacked. Acrid smoke rose from massive fires that engulfed the buildings. Several had been reduced to rubble. Half of her platoon cursed loudly, while Hammerhead called off the next location. Several times, they had to fight off nearby CAMs long enough for the person to make a dash into his or her home. Finally, they neared Janine's apartment complex, only to discover that six CAMs were assaulting it, fighting those few who lived there that had weapons.

"RPGs! Take those tin cans out!" Hard Ass barked. Fire from ten MK40's was followed by the telltale swoosh and booms of the RPGs. Within minutes, the six CAMs went inert, and Janine made a dash into her old apartment complex, while her platoon fanned out, temporarily securing the block and answering the questions thrown at them by the surviving men and women. Jascar did provide medical treatment for several local men who were wounded.

Janine knew what she wanted to do in her apartment. She'd uncovered no trace of her missing sister these past eighteen months, even though as a soldier she had access to privileged information. Her last hope was that somehow Alison would have left her a message in her apartment. And there it was lying on the table where she couldn't possibly miss it. She grabbed the paper, holding it tightly as though it was her long lost sister! At first, she didn't quite grasp the cryptic meaning. Peter's place? Then, she recalled going with Peter and Kathy to bury his young wife. In a flash, she understood where Alison was. As she beat a hasty retreat joining her platoon on the street outside the building, she wondered when she could possibly get away to go there. For now, that wasn't going to be possible. A dozen CAMs were moving into position to attack them, in response to their own attack on the CAMs who had been attacking this building.

Before the CAMs could reach them, Hard Ass had everyone back onboard and One Shot got them airborne and safely out of the way. At this point, she had to relinquish control to One Shot and Killer Diller, who now had their own orders to follow, reporting to Major Lu Ann Ellen on the ground actions being carried out. Several of her platoon members assisted the pilots, calling out street locations and estimated numbers of CAMs there. It didn't look good. Thousands of these nearly unstoppable metal monsters roamed the streets, taking over key facilities along the way.

"Damned, One Shot," Killer Diller complained from her navigator's seat, "we're stuck on transport duty when we could be flying our fighters and shooting up those CAMs down there!"

"I know, I know, but orders are orders," One Shot replied, just as annoyed as his wingman. "Keep your eyes peeled for some of our delta wings. If the major sends them down here, I'm going to see if we can't get our orders changed!"

"You'd better, One Shot. I don't aim to let anyone else catch up to my kill count!" Killer Diller grumbled, admitting the truth of her viewpoint.

One Shot merely smiled. He'd rightly guessed the reason his wingman was so upset. "Hey, shooting tin cans on the ground isn't the same as shooting down their one-man fighters, you know?"

Grumbling, she agreed, "Well, I suppose you are right. Don't see any of their fighters in the air. Guess I could start a tally of tin cans on the ground."

One Shot laughed, "Hell, Killer, Hard Ass back there has you beat in that count." Both laughed.

"Hey look there," Killer Diller pointed out. Down below, six CAMs were setting up another one of their Shadow Maker dishes, its dish aimed towards a densely populated apartment complex.

Janine yelled from her bay window viewport, "Hey, they are setting up more of those terrible Shadow Maker dishes." Her confirmation was all that One Shot needed, and he quickly reported the enemy was now using this terrible weapon against ordinary citizens.

Major Lu Ann's voice came back over the comm channel, rather taking One Shot and Killer Diller by surprise, since they had been reporting to one of the comm officers on the Hyperion. "One Shot, Major Lu Ann here. I've a new assignment for you and your infantry platoon. I need you to capture intact one of those Shadow Maker systems. Hell, if you can find an electronics expert, get them too. We need to study this new weapon of theirs, find out how it works, how it can be defeated. Put Captain Alouse on the line."

"Aye sir. One second," One Shot replied. "Hey, Hard Ass. Major Lu Ann wants to talk to you. Pick up the comm line down there."

"Captain Alouse here, major," she replied, a bit surprised to be speaking directly to the major.

Quickly, Major Lu Ann outlined what she needed done. "So it's imperative that we capture one of these Shadow Maker systems intact and find a hot electronics expert to study it."

"Aye sir. We can do it. Say, I've an idea where you might get an electronics expert," Janine replied, thinking of her sister and a way to somehow get to her before she was turned into dust along with everyone else on the ground. Down below, the situation seemed hopeless.

After signing off, One Shot asked, "So captain, where do you want us to put you down?"

"Three blocks from the CAMs," Captain Janine replied, figuring that would give them time to get organized and prepare for the assault. That said, she began explaining to her platoon what their next mission was. "So, we're under orders to capture that Shadow Maker system intact. Don't screw this one up. The major wants to study how it works and see if there's a way it can be jammed or something. Hammerhead, you take Second Squad and come at them from that alleyway. I'll take Squad 1 and hit them from the street. We'll get them in a crossfire. Just don't damage the Shadow Maker system stuff. Got it?"

"Aye sir," Hammerhead acknowledged, pleased that he was now in charge of the entire second squad. (There was no thrid squad any longer.) The twenty soldiers began gearing up, while Killer Diller located a suitable street for landing. A minute later, the deep space transport touched down. The instant she gave the all clear signal, Hard Ass punched the open button, and the bay ramp slowly lowered. As always, she was the first to jump off, MK40 at the ready, even before the ramp touched down. Gunfire echoed in the streets, bouncing off the skyscrapers, but most sounded more distant, which she took as a good sign.

"On me," she cried, heading down the street. One by one, Fel and the other First Squad members joined her. Six carried RPGs. She glanced at Hammerhead. His squad also carried six RPGs, and she watched his flurry of silent hand signals. Since his squad needed more time to get into position, she held up her group about a block from the six CAMs who now had their Shadow Maker system setup.

"They are going to use it on civies," Fel whispered.

"I know. Come on; we aren't waiting any longer on Hammerhead," Hard Ass signaled. *It's one thing to use this new weapon on soldiers,* she thought, *and quite another to use it against defenseless civies!* "Get the RPGs into position. The rest of us, provide covering fire. Don't present yourself as a target," she ordered and watched as her team crouched in doorways, behind a dumpster, and even a local shuttle parked outside a building. The streets were deserted. Rightly so, she thought. What chance did an unarmed civilian have against these murderous machines? None at all. Best to stay inside for now at least. She opened fire from her MK40, though at this distance, the heavy slugs mostly bounced off the tin cans, but it did attract their attention away from using the Shadow Machine on the nearby apartment complex.

Shattering glass, ricocheting bullets, splintering wood chips flew rained down on Hard Ass and her squad, who were pinned down by the Gatling gun-like fire from the six cannons in the hands of the CAMs. They continued to spray deadly fire down the street, but unlike a rifle in human hands, their accuracy was dismal at best, holding the repeating cannon attached to their right arm-like appendages and firing from their sides, unable to aim their weapons effectively. Hard Ass was quite thankful for this disability in the tin cans, who depended upon loosening a hundred rounds in her vicinity while hoping one might actually hit.

However, distracted by her squad, the six tin cans failed to see Hammerhead and his squad move into position. Swoosh! Six RPGs fired almost simultaneously, music to Hard Ass's ears. The explosions echoed loudly up and down the skyscraper-lined streets, and the nearly continuous volley of cannon shots ceased. She poked her head out from the door jam. Six CAMs stood silent, their cylindrical heads missing. "Good shooting!" she yelled to Hammerhead's squad and motioned for hers to move out. Shortly, the twenty soldiers swarmed up to the deployed Shadow Maker system.

"Okay. Well done. Now let's see if we can dismantle this. Hell, let's confiscate their transport as well," Hard Ass ordered. She touched her comm piece and relayed her idea to Killer Diller. By the time her crew had the Shadow Maker equipment reloaded onto the transport, the pilot showed up, walking with a sway in her hips.

"Coolest, Hard Ass. We got their ship as well. Nothing like adding another transport to our fleet," she announced.

Grinning, Janine replied, "Always trying to be helpful, aren't we, fellows?" Her squads laughed. "Hammerhead, you take your squad with Killer Diller. We'll meet you back on the Hyperion." She and her squad headed back to their heavily loaded transport, where One Shot was waiting for them, more than a little nervously. Another dozen CAMs were making their way towards the transport, but were three blocks away. An unarmed transport wasn't One Shot's favorite weapon

71

against them.

"Good timing. Another dozen are almost on us," he yelled, as Janine and her squad raced up the ramp.

"Get us out of here," Janine ordered, slamming her hand on the close button as the last man ran inside. As the transport lifted off, twisting, and turning to avoid the cannon fire from the closing CAMs, Janine made her way to the navigator's seat.

"One Shot, I think I know where we can get us our electronics expert. My sister has her PhD in it and was working on experimental things for the corporations before she went missing."

"Well that's useful, but if she's gone missing. . ." He didn't finish his thought. No sense in bringing up the loss of her sister.

"Well, she's left me a message. I think I know where she's fled. It's not far from here, a small, remote farm. That way. Care for a detour? Probably we won't encounter any enemy," Janine suggested. She knew she hadn't any authority or even any right to go off on a rescue mission for civies, not in a time of war. Nevertheless, the major wanted an electronics expert, and Janine kept her fingers crossed that One Shot would go along with her.

"Okay. Got coordinates?" One Shot replied. He liked her attitude and just maybe she might be grateful if he rescued her sister. *Civie or not, I have orders to get an electronics expert, don't I?*

"No, but I can direct you. That way. About twenty miles out. Stay about a mile up. I can find the place. Thanks, One Shot. I owe you one," she said gratefully.

"So she's an electronics whiz? Cute?" he probed.

Janine laughed. "Yes and no. We shared the same mother, but she's a good six inches taller than I am. She got the brains, and I got the brawn, but neither of us got mom's good looks. Sorry about that, One Shot. She's the reason that I joined the infantry, you know. She went missing, and no one could tell me what happened to her. I got nowhere talking to her corporation, so I joined up so I could use the army intelligence to track her down. That didn't work out either, but

72

when I visited my apartment, she left me a note yesterday telling me where she was heading. So it looks like this army gig worked out after all." Janine felt like talking. One Shot had no doubts about the relief Janine was feeling. Besides, after seeing the destruction pouring down on the city, it felt good doing something to help a civie out just now.

Around eleven, he sat the transport down on a weed-covered lawn, close to a hover car that bore the spaceport's logo on it. Janine lowered the bay ramp and headed up to the front door of the small, abandoned farmhouse. Memories of accompanying Peter and Kathy here two years ago to bury his wife beside her parents out back came unbidden to her mind. She knocked, "Sis? Alison? You in there? It's me, Janine."

Slowly the door opened. She saw a taller woman standing there, holding a d-gun and wearing a PDS over her gorgeous dress. The woman had breasts nearly the size of her head and gorgeous, thick, brown hair that fell to her knees. For a moment, Janine didn't recognize Alison, so vastly different did she appear. "Alison?"

"Janine! Yes, it's me. I was captured and turned into this—one of those helpless UFB women, but Dr. Black rescued me and got a cure for my arms from Scorpi-C in the Abelard Sector. I thought I'd never see you again! Come in. Oh, Peter's with me and Kathy, but they got to him too."

As the two sisters hugged each other, Kathy holding onto Peter came up to them. Who's this? Where's Peter? Hi Kathy," Janine said, pulling away from Alison to stare at this armless but gorgeous young woman that Kathy was helping keep her balance. The woman's face flushed crimson.

"I'm Peter, Janine. They did this to me. I look like a UFB woman, but I'm still a man," he said softly, but stopped speaking. If he said another word, he'd start sobbing again. Waves of embarrassment swept over him.

"Shit! Well, come on. Get your things. I'm taking you back with us to the Hyperion—that's one of our remaining light cruisers. Major Lu Ann wants an electronics expert to help discover the secrets of this Shadow Maker system. We've captured one intact just a bit ago," Janine explained. "We best not delay long. The CAMs are wiping Brussels out as we speak.

It's not safe to be ground-side right now."

Meanwhile, the others stepped out of the transport to get a breather and stretch their legs on terra-firma. One Shot joined Janine. "Wow! You lied. Your sister is a knockout! Who's this other super model?" Peter crimsoned again and said nothing, focusing his attention on keeping from breaking down again.

"It seems that they genetically modified Dr. Alison Wage and Peter Diller. Turned them into UFB women somehow," Janine answered for them.

"Damned them. Peter? Is that really you? Jill Diller's older brother, the security guard at the spaceport?" asked One Shot in disbelief.

"Yes." Peter managed to control his wildly swinging emotions enough to respond.

"Well, Killer Diller is my wingman. Right now, she's flying our captured transport and Shadow Maker system back to the Hyperion. Come on. Let's get you onboard. She's going to be relieved to find you safe and sound. She was worried when Janine went to your apartment and you were gone. You must be Kathy," he chatted away, but finally noticed the child.

"Yes sir. How is Aunt Jill? Why do you call her Killer Diller?" Kathy asked curiously.

"Cause she's shot down more of those CAMs in their one-man fighters than any other pilot, including me. She's one damned good warrior and pilot," he answered.

"Maybe one day I can be a pilot too," Kathy responded, and the two began chatting about fighter ships.

"Hey, Kathy, how would you like to be my copilot and sit up front with me in the navigator's seat where Aunt Jill was sitting when we left the cruiser this morning?" One Shot suggested.

Her eyes opened wide. "Really?" she asked, "Can I?" Alison smiled, knowing that One Shot had just made a friend for life.

"Wow Hard Ass, you didn't tell us your sister is a knockout!" Hammerhead exclaimed as the small party boarded the ship. Janine carried Peter and Kathy's small bags, while Alison carried her own pack, dragging it behind her on its small rollers. Alison flushed as did Peter.

"It's a surprise to me too, Hammerhead. They turned her into a UFB woman. Peter too. That's Peter Diller, Killer Diller's older brother, the spaceport guard, and his daughter," Janine replied and began introducing her sister to her platoon. The men fell over themselves helping the pair of stellar models get seated and strapped in for the flight. Janine merely shook her head, thinking: *Men!* Meanwhile, One Shot led Kathy up to the front and got her strapped into the navigator's seat.

Once airborne, he explained what the controls were and even let her hold the flight stick for a time. *If she takes after her aunt, then we'll have a new hot shot pilot one day.* He contacted the Hyperion to report in and had a message relayed to Killer Diller that he'd rescued her older brother and niece, and that they had their requisite electronics expert as well.

Amid the whistles and catcalls, the two UFB women descended the bay ramp, lifted down by strong arms, since neither could handle going down the ramp in their tall heels, especially Peter. Killer Diller was there to welcome her brother and niece. "My God, Peter! Is that really you? What did they do to you?" she exclaimed.

Peter couldn't keep his wild emotions at bay. He began sobbing once more, leaning into his younger sister, while Dr. Alison explained about the biogenetic agent and what it did to humans, turning them into the UFB women and men. "I'll find whoever did this to you and kill them!" swore Jill, quite vehemently. Others echoed her pledge.

Just then, Major Lu Ann stepped into the landing bay, and everyone snapped to attention. After a brief introduction and quick explanation by Alison, Major Lu Ann ordered. "Okay. Stop staring at those two. Janine, take your sister to your quarters and get her settled in. Then, bring her to CCC. Jill, take your brother and sister to the infirmary and get them checked out quickly. The rest of you, assist our quartermaster and get all the munitions properly stored. Lieutenant Fel, you assist our engineers and get that Shadow Maker system into our small laboratory. Then, join us in CCC. Well done, all of you. Maybe now we have a fighting chance." She saluted them, turned, and headed back to the CCC.

Chapter 5—Recovery

Dr. Alison Wage swallowed hard. *Face the music, she thought. I've got to own up to everything. Hell, I don't have clean hands in this mess.* At least Janine couldn't tell that she was nervous, as her sister led her to the Hyperion's CCC. She'd stowed her bag in Janine and Fel's new quarters, freshened up some, and chatted nearly endlessly with Janine. Now she faced telling this Major Lu Ann just what she'd help make, this Shadow Maker and the CAMs. No, not made them, just worked on some design issues with their control systems.

The CCC was small. This was only a light cruiser after all, but the space was crammed with men and women wearing the blue Ragnar-B space force uniforms. Major Lu Ann introduced several who were her few science advisors, but Alison didn't recognize them. "Everyone, this is Dr. Alison Wage, an electronics expert. Dr. Alison, why don't you tell us your story and what you know about this devilish new weapon, the Shadow Maker system."

Alison cleared her throat. It felt as though she'd swallowed sandpaper. "Okay. I know quite a bit. You see, I used to work as an electronics expert for Galactic Electronics Corporation. They paid for my Academy education, full scholarship and all that. Three years ago, I was put to work on some of the control circuits for the Shadow Maker, before I was put to work on getting some bugs out of the CAM control circuits. So it's all my fault. If I hadn't done the work, maybe this horrible system wouldn't be working now and there wouldn't be any CAMs either. It's all my fault."

Shocked silence followed her revelation, then gasps. "Please, go on," Major Lu Ann broke the pregnant pause. Alison swallowed several times before continuing.

"I was working only on one small component of the Shadow Maker. None of us had any knowledge of the entire system, just our own tiny part. I don't think any of us knew what the Shadow Maker system was intended to do. Same was true with the CAMs. I thought they were going to use these robots to work in dangerous mining operations, at least that's what I was told. I had no idea at first they were making, well soldier-kind of robots out of them."

One of the men spoke up, "Major, she's got a point. The CEOs always have kept their research compartmentalized. That way, no one employee would know precisely what was going on. She's not to blame. Plenty of us worked on projects that somehow ended up being used in the final products. The chicken feet of the CAM are my design."

Major Lu All interrupted him, "Yes, I'm aware of that. Look, Dr. Alison, no one is going to accuse you of treason or anything else, except perhaps bad judgment. Please, continue." She couldn't tell if the doctor was relieved to hear this or not. The woman was clearly having a difficult time speaking and was visibly nervous. Still, she had to get the doctor's story widely known. More minds on a problem meant more potential solutions. That was her motto, and she stuck by it.

Dr. Alison then outlined going to the resistance meeting and being abducted. She told them about the biogenetic agent that was used to modify her body and her terror upon awaking to find herself now a UFB woman, completely helpless. What so shocked everyone was her lengthy explanation of having been put into the robot shell and how that worked. She didn't explicitly describe the constant dildo action though, for that was too personal, too humiliating, and too embarrassing. "Time sort of became a blur to me. I merely existed, no thoughts, no nothing. I think quite a few months passed, but I was oblivious to it. Then, one day, Dr. Black came and demanded that I be released into his care." She described that day and the black man who took her to an abandoned cloth bolt manufacturing plant.

At this point, everyone paid close attention to her every word, often interrupting her to ask about a minor detail. "Yes, he was building human-like robots. Honestly, I couldn't tell that they weren't humans just by looking at them. He called them humaniform robots. He had dozens of them and that's when he proposed to put me into one of them."

She described how he had used the Shadow Maker

system to transfer her *soul* and her mind into one of the female looking robot bodies, while her body was kept in a stasis pod. "No, that part was turned off. I believe the Shadow Maker beam somehow forces all the molecules in a life form to disassemble back into stable atomic compounds, like water vapor, which is why the bodies seem to disappear into the shadows. But at the same time, the device emits the extremely high frequency energy flow in the kilo-yatta-hertz range. Somehow, I saw that energy as a brilliant white light, though I know that it wasn't even in the visible portion of the spectrum to be seen. Yet, that's the best description I can give, a beautiful, white light. I couldn't help myself. I had to follow the light and when I woke up, I was inside that new humaniform robot body. I could see my armless UFB woman's body lying there. Freaky and spooky."

She described the difficult time she had getting used to operating this new robot body and how she begged Dr. Black to find a cure for the UFB woman mutation. Dr. Alison told them how he'd gone to Scorpi-C in the Abelard Sector to obtain one of their cures that would regrow her arms. "Somehow, I just have to get more of that cure for Peter Diller," she added.

Major Lu Ann interrupted her, "That's being taken care of as we speak. Please continue."

She then described how Dr. Black used the Shadow Maker system a second time to transfer her back into her human body, now that it had arms once more. "There's one more thing. While Dr. Black was gone, I discovered a hidden control circuit embedded within the CAM control circuitry. My curiosity was aroused, and I discovered it was actually a backdoor into the control of the CAMs! Dr. Black had intentionally put it in there! So," she flushed, "so, I put my own backdoor in there as well."

One man spoke up, "What are you saying? You could control the CAMs?"

"Sort of, I think, if they ever install that new circuit in them," Dr. Alison answered. "I think I might be able to override all the other commands being given to one of the CAMs and make it do what I want it to do, maybe. I've never tried it. I don't know if my circuitry was later installed in all the CAMs or not, only that I put it into this prototype model."

Dr. Braun spoke up, "Look, from what she's told us about the Shadow Maker, it seems clear to me that we have people's souls stored in those boxes inside the transport that Captain Janine captured during her battle at the ore mines. Clearly, we should try to release them somehow."

Another scientist advisor interrupted him. "I think it is obvious from what Dr. Alison has said. We can conclude that these diabolical CEOs are disintegrating our people and putting their souls and minds into these despicable CAM robots, somehow forcing them to fight against us."

"What? When we destroy one of the CAMs, we're killing our own people?" another captain exclaimed, clearly shocked by this.

"They are already dead," someone else pointed out. "Their bodies got atomized or something."

"What the hell is a soul anyway?" someone else asked, and the conversation splintered into numerous side issues, none of which Dr. Alison could follow. Too many were talking at once. Major Lu Ann barked sharply and regained control. "Dr. Alison, I want you to begin work on a machine that you might be able to use to regain control over the CAMs. The rest of you, see about finding a way to free the trapped souls in the small compartments there in the captured transport." Then, she dismissed everyone, though she assigned one of her men to take Dr. Alison to their small laboratory.

That done, Major Lu Ann placed a secure call to Commander Kelly Kay Knight on the Arc Royal, relaying all she'd uncovered, asking what her current orders were to be. Commander Kelly Kay replied, "Excellent work, Major Lu Ann. This could well be our first real break. However, the Arc Royal has suffered so much damage that we are going to have to withdraw from the battlefield and find somewhere to put in for repairs. I'm in communication now with the leader of Scorpi-C, Abelard Sector. With luck, they will volunteer to put us up and help with the critical repairs."

"Understood, commander. What are your orders for the Hyperion?" Major Lu Ann asked.

"I'd like you to stick around here for a while and monitor the situation on the ground. If they come after your ship, get the hell out of here. Make for Scorpi-C unless you hear otherwise from me. Keep Dr. Alison with you. If there's a chance that she can invent a way to disable these CAMs, make her do it. What the bloody hell is a soul anyway?" Commander Kelly Kay asked argumentatively. "Minds—well, I can imagine how they could maybe get someone's brain moved into these tin can bodies, but brains have to be fed and nourished. They need oxygen too. Hell, this whole damned thing is beyond our understanding. Find out all you can. Keep me informed. Over and out."

"Okay everyone," Major Lu Ann barked to her CCC personnel. "Our orders are to stick around here and monitor what's going on down on the surface. So I want someone manning all comm lines. If you hear anything important, for crap's sake, record it! I'll be in my quarters. That is all." Several saluted and she headed off to her small cabin and a desperately needed aspirin. She had a throbbing headache. All this talk of souls, minds, and robots had given her a migraine.

After being shown their onboard lab, Dr. Alison returned to her quarters to fetch her own brown bag of tools, which she preferred over theirs. On her way back, she spotted Killer Diller and asked, "How's Peter doing? Kathy okay?"

"It's a miracle. The doctors are giving Peter the same cure that you were given. He's in a coma now while his arms are being regrown, but they can't do anything else for him. My god, Alison, he's more like a she now. I'm worried about his mind. How can he survive like this? I surely don't know. Oh, Kathy is fine. She's playing with the few children in the ship's nursery now."

"That's the best news yet. I was helpless without my arms. At least Peter will be able to live when his are regrown. I'll check on him later. I have to work on some project for the major now. Thanks."

"Hey, he thinks a lot of you. Maybe you can give him some moral assistance when he recovers," Jill suggested.

"I will. I promise," she replied and meant it. After all, she understood what he was going through, at least partially

80

anyway.

***

Thanos, alias Dr. Black, sat at the comm center of his deep space transport, currently cloaked and hovering above Brussels. He had activated his dozen humaniform robots, which he had named Number One through Number Twelve for now. Number One was piloting the ship for him, while he studied the situation on Ragnar-B. *Once more,* he thought, *humans have proven that they do not deserve to live in this universe! It's not exactly genocide, but darn close. But can anything useful be salvaged from here? I wonder. Some of their CAM parts are superior to those I've invented, but this business of using human souls and minds to operate them is fraught with peril. They have to continually force them to carry out orders, plus, they are the same souls and minds that ran their human bodies in the first place. Only now, they are giving them indestructible bodies and weapons of destruction. This can only lead to more criminal acts down the line. Humans simply cannot be trusted or kept alive.*

Thanos reached a decision. I must put an end to this, but I will salvage what I can and reuse the parts. Silently, he issued a number of orders to his team of humaniforms, who expertly carried them out to the letter. First action, Number One landed the transport on the top of the GE headquarters building. Second action, using his backdoor control box, he took over control of all the CAMs that were guarding this skyscraper and the three CEOs who were in their control center running their massive operations, fully intent on conquering all Ragnar-B. Their wives were also present, though Gertie was inside her robot shell. Following the overriding orders of Thanos, two CAMs opened the blast doors allowing him to enter the secure building.

Thanos walked calmly into the busy control center and turned off his invisibility shield, though he kept his PDS active. He barked to the surprised group, "Henry, Amos, Peter, your butchery and inhumanity ends now!"

"Arrest him!" Henry ordered one of the CAMs near him, but to his amazement and shock, the CAM remained motionless.

81

Amos drew his d-gun and fired at Thanos, but his PDS shield protected him. "Fools. You are all fools!" Thanos countered.

Gina and Betty reacted as well. Both attempted to take over the mind of Dr. Black, forcing him to do their bidding, just as they had often done to many others, not the least of which were their husbands. A pair of shocked looks on their faces alerted Thanos to what they were trying to do. "He—he—isn't human," Gina finally managed to say.

"Thankfully, that I am not. If I were, I would have to kill myself. You humans have proven beyond all doubt that you do not deserve to live. CAMs, shoot them all now," Thanos ordered. Suddenly, the two CAMs guarding the six opened fire with their automatic cannons, shattering the bodies of the three men, two women, the windows, desks, chairs, and electronic equipment, sending a shower of sparks flying about the room.

Poor Gertie inside her protective robot shell stood there stunned. She saw her husband and the others brutally murdered, but before she could react, Thanos ordered her shell opened. After the hiss of the seal opening ended, Gertie had no choice but to step out into the room, standing on her bare toes, wobbling wildly. Cannon fire tore into her body. Pain, pain, and then Gertie found herself floating above the grizzly, bloody scene. For a time, she stared in complete disbelief.

Thanos methodically continued his operation. His humaniforms ordered the CAMs to load up all the existing Shadow Maker systems and bring them to the spaceport, along with themselves and all their ammunition. Hours later, Thanos had all the CAMs on the new Battleship Royal Queen, along with their mountains of ammunition and a hundred of the Shadow Maker systems, complete with their "holding cells," similar to those found on the captured transport ship now onboard the Hyperion.

Next, Thanos and his dozen humaniforms set to work installing the Shadow Makers onto a number of transport ships. However, the "collection" or "holding cells" were left behind. For the next week, his humaniforms flew the transports around Brussels, hovering many minutes in each location, allowing the ultra-high frequency waves from the Shadow Makers to do their job, turning the surviving humans bodies into their constituent atoms and molecules, such as H_2O. Fifteen million people vanished without a trace. Many other millions lived in other smaller towns and farmsteads across Ragnar-B. These were spared for reasons unknown to them.

With the humans of Brussels gone, Thanos and his crew landed and began systematically confiscating equipment, plans, and machinery, along with some rare earths needed in the production of the sophisticated circuitry and metal of the CAMs. Three weeks after the initial attack of the three CEOs, the new Battleship Royal Queen, now heavily laden, departed from the skies and orbit of Ragnar-B, but not before Thanos and his dozen humaniforms released all the "souls" from the thousands of CAMs, turning these metal fighters into inert but heavy masses. Thanos intended to use parts of their structures in his new and improved robot fighters—at least that was the conclusions others reached after their departure and the city was searched.

***

The third day after Dr. Alison arrived on the Hyperion, a marine called Fielding placed a call over his secret comm set. "Dr. Black, this you?" he said softly from his private quarters in the bowels of the Hyperion.

"Yes, speaking. Fielding, what have you to report that's worth all the funds I gave you?" Thanos replied, annoyed that he was being distracted from his work over Brussels.

"Plenty. We got onboard some doctor woman, Alison Wage, real knockout, claims she was one of them UFB women."

At the mention of Alison, Thanos paid close attention. *So that's where the electronics expert for Galactic Electronics Corporation has disappeared to—into the enemy's last fighter ship. She is the only person on Ragnar-B who remotely understands the complexity of my electronics and those of the CAMs.* Fielding continued, "She claims that she once worked for you. Besides, we also got some of those Shadow Maker

83

devices—stolen from planet."

Thanos raced down a number of potential future tracts. Dr. Alison had been a valuable assistant, but right now, he couldn't afford to take time away from his attack on Ragnar-B. Delay her. "What is she up to, Fielding? Can you find out?"

"Aye. That's going to cost you extra," came a snide reply.

"Agreed. Now what is she up to?"

"Major has her working on ways to stop the Shadow Maker things, that's what, and maybe the CAMs too or so I heard."

"Interesting. We can't have that. Where is she now?"

"In Sickbay watching over that other UFB woman that she brought here. Damned pretty too, though some say she's a man not a woman. She's a woman, if I ever saw one."

"Why Sickbay?"

"The doctor is re-growing her arms. They say you did that for this Dr. Alison woman. That true? She must be mighty important to you."

"She is that. Okay, here's what I want you to do," Thanos ordered. "Yes, I'll double your funds now," he added ensuring the dope would carry out his orders. To one of his humaniforms, he ordered, "Number One, find that biogenetic agent they use to make UFB women. It should be in their labs at GE."

An hour later, Thanos looked at the small cylinder. He had no idea of the needed dosage. However, that didn't stop him. "Number One, take a one-man shuttle and install a cloaking device on it. No, better, take my transport. It has it installed. I want you to fly this up to the Hyperion, cloaked all the way. Docking Bay Two." He outlined what needed to be done.

Back on the Hyperion, Major Lu Ann began receiving rather startling reports from the ground. "The CEOs' have lost all control over their robots. Hell, reports are flying about that the robots shot all them. Now the robots are beginning to sweep over Brussels and using the Shadow Makers on the population," her comm center lieutenant reported succinctly. "Should we launch our fighters and try to stop them?" she added, thinking of her own family down there.

"What? Murdered? Who's in charge down there? Who's ordering this attack?" barked Major Lu Ann. "Facts. We need facts now! Her comm crew jumped into action, but they were unable to ascertain much from the garbled reports flying back and forth among those on the ground trying to defend their city. They were ordinary citizens, certainly not disciplined soldiers, which only added to the confusion surrounding their reports.

Docking Bay Two was filled with transports and a few delta wing fighters, but it was currently deserted, except for Fielding who stood silently in the shadows waiting for the promised arrival. He saw nothing, but heard the low whine of the engines as Number One set the invisible transport down. Only when he opened the bay ramp door did the illusion of invisibility breakdown. Fielding saw the inside of an otherwise invisible transport through the open ramp door, quite a startling sight, but he was expecting it. Shortly, a man stepped down and he moved silently up to him. The man held out a yellow cylinder.

"Here. Open the valve and toss it into the room." Number One turned and headed back up the ramp. Fielding grinned. Already, he'd made fifty thousand credits on this little venture for the black man and with more in the offing. He didn't wait for the ship to depart, but stuffed the cylinder inside his work jumpsuit and headed off to carry out the sabotage.

Alison and Kathy sat beside Peter, holding onto his new arms. He was supposed to be coming out of his coma at any time, hence the pair's presence in Sickbay. "They look like his arms," Kathy whispered.

"Yes, he'll be a bit weak at first, but a week of good food and he'll be just fine," Alison whispered back, encouraging the brave young girl. They were in a small infirmary cabin attached to Sickbay.

A man opened the door and asked, "All still okay here?"

"Yes, he's not come out of his coma yet," Alison replied softly. The man nodded and turned to leave. Alison and Kathy looked back to Peter again, wondering how soon he'd regain consciousness.

"What's that hissing noise?" Kathy asked.

"Don't know, Kathy. I've never been on a ship this big before. I suppose it's nothing. Look, he's coming around I think." Both focused their attention on the reviving Peter.

"We're here Peter. You are fine," Alison whispered, though she had no idea why she was whispering, only that she felt truly happy for Peter. Now he'd not be helpless any longer. Perhaps now he could begin to come to grips with his terrible situation.

"Arms! I can feel them!" Peter exclaimed. "I feel you, my two favorite women," he said looking lovingly at Kathy, whose face beamed with pride.

"We've been at your side most all the time, Peter," Alison whispered.

"Thanks. That was scary. Now I won't be helpless at least. How can I—what's that smell?" Peter said and then asked, becoming startled by the odor.

Just then, gongs and red lights went off, drowning out everything. One would have to shout to be heard over these alarms. A deadbolt slid shut, making a very loud noise as it did so, sealing them in this room. That startled them even more.

"That smell—I've smelled it before," Alison gasped. Recognition struck her. It was the same smell she sensed when they first used this awful biogenetic agent on her. Likewise, Peter recognized it. While he struggled to get up, Alison rushed to the door to get out, but found the door sealed. Escape was impossible!

Meanwhile, Fielding walked into the main medical center in Sickbay. "Excuse me, the major wants to know how much more of that bio agent cure you've got on hand. Seems like she's rescuing more UFB women from Brussels."

A doctor looked up along with two nurses. "I'll go check," the doctor replied and Fielding followed him. He went to a special locker and entered a private key code. "Six doses," he replied. However as he turned around, Fielding had drawn his d-gun. Blam! He fired into the cabinet, disintegrating the six doses. Then, he shot the doctor. Leave no witnesses was his plan. On his return passage, he shot and killed two of the nurses who came rushing into the storage locker to find out what was going on.

When he reached the main area of Sickbay, the third nurse was nowhere to be seen! "Shit!" Fielding headed on out of Sickbay, just as the bio attack warnings began sounding throughout the ship, adding to the confusion of the moment. All around him, doors began automatically sealing and locking. The Hyperion was designed to withstand a bio or chemical attack, as well as sudden decompression from a hole in its sides. Fielding headed down the corridors, intending to get back to his own quarters.

"That's him!" he heard a female voice call out. He turned to see the third nurse pointing to him. She'd gotten two marine security guards. He still had his d-gun, but had holstered it. As fast as he could, he drew his gun, intending to take out all three of them. Leave no witnesses. However, the marines were experts. They had hours of training and got their guns out twice as fast as Fielding did. He dropped dead to the floor, two gaping holes in his chest. His body now lacked a heart and part of a lung.

"What the hell is going on?" yelled Major Lu Ann over the din of the bio-chemical attack alarms going off. Already the doors to CCC had shut and sealed them in securely, preventing the spread of the agent. "Shut that noise off! Are we under attack? Breached?" she yelled.

"Nothing on the monitor. No ships anywhere around us," one yelled back over the continuous gong noise, ignoring the flashing red lights overhead.

"Sickbay. The sensors are reading an accident in Sickbay," another called out from her console, where a myriad of lights indicated the state of every cabin and compartment on the ship.

Major Lu Ann picked up the comm phone and called, "Sickbay! What's going on down there? Sickbay, come in!" Silence. "Shit! Any other areas impacted?"

"No sir. Just one cabin. I think that's where the new patient was staying, you know, the one whose arms were being re-grown," she replied. "Ah, got the gongs turned off now, sir."

Carefully, Major Lu Ann entered her access codes, and

released the door locks on most all doors in the ship, though keeping the entire area around Sickbay still closed off and secure. "Get the marines and go down there and find out what the hell is going on," she ordered. A man saluted and left, but before he got out of CCC, someone called for the major.

"This is Corporal Smith. There's been an incident in Sickbay. One of the nurses came running up to us with a wild tale. She claimed that a man came into Sickbay saying that you wanted to know how many more doses of that arm-regrowing cure you had left, adding that you were bringing more UFB women up from Brussels. Apparently, he followed the doctor into the supply room and shot those very cures with a d-gun, then shot the doctor and two other nurses on his way out. She pointed him out in the corridor as we were approaching Sickbay. He went for his gun, but we took him out. Orders, sir?"

"Shit! Stay put. I'm on my way." Turning to the man who stopped at the doorway, she added, "I'm coming along with the marines. Lead on."

A few minutes later, she stood beside the dead body of Private Fielding. The nurse was sitting on the floor sobbing uncontrollably. Shock had set in on her. Major Lu Ann calmly picked up the phone that the corporal had used to notify her. "This is Major Lu Ann. Check the lights. Is Sickbay itself safe to enter?"

"Yes sir," came the woman's reply.

"Good. Unseal it, but keep a constant watch on that light. Give us warning if it goes red," she ordered. A hissing sound and a clank indicated the door was now usable. The automatic lock, disengaged. "At least, we've proven our bio-chemical agent attack system works," she muttered to no one in particular.

In Sickbay, the smell of death struck her nose as she entered. Two nurses lay dead in the main room. She passed by them, entered the side storage area, and found the doctor's body and the disintegrated section of medical supplies. "Shit! He's our only doctor. Double shit!"

Turning to the marines, she ordered, "Take the bodies to Shuttle Bay Two and cover them up. We'll hold burial services shortly. Nurse, nurse, pull yourself together. You are now our acting medical doctor." She pulled the sobbing nurse to her feet.

"But I'm only a nurse," she wailed.

"Well, now you are the only medical personnel we have. Pull yourself together, lieutenant. See if you can find out what is going on in the patient cabin that's sealed. Report to me as soon as you know. Got it?"

Wiping her wet face, she mumbled, "I can do that." Major Lu Ann headed back to CCC, fuming. There, she opened up a ship-wide channel.

"May I have everyone's attention? Good." She paused a second then continued. "We have just had a terrorist attack in Sickbay. The fanatic killed our only doctor and two of our three nurses. Will anyone who has any medical training please report to CCC immediately. Oh, the terrorist has been killed. Thank you."

Jascar "Bite Me" Long was playing cards with Hammerhead, Hard Ass, and three others when the major's announcement came. "So that's what happened," he said. "Guess I better report to CCC. Permission, Hard Ass?"

"Granted. At least, you can't lose this hand, Bite Me," she teased him. He'd already lost ten credits. He scooped up his small pile of tokens and headed off to find the CCC. A half hour later, he returned with a pale face.

"Well?" Janine asked.

"You are looking at the new Hyperion doctor," he stammered. "I told her I'm only a field technician, not a real doctor, but I guess I know more than her last nurse, boss."

"Congratulations I think," Janine replied.

"Don't thank me if you get shot up. I sure as hell don't know how to operate on people!" he countered, headed off to change, and report to Sickbay.

An hour later, Jascar and Nurse Helen finally were able to verify the bio agent unleashed inside the cabin was in fact the agent used to create the UFB women and men. Further, there wasn't anything they could do until the Hyperion's filtration system had sucked out the agent and disposed of it harmlessly into space. Major Lu Ann ordered them to keep her informed of developments there.

Chapter 6—Disaster

At this point, another call came into the Hyperion. "Major, it's from someone calling himself Dr. Black. Is it the same one that Dr. Alison mentioned?" her comm officer asked. She shook her head and took the call, putting it on the speakers in CCC and recording it. "This is Major Lu Ann Ellen of the Hyperion. Over." Her voice sounded steady in spite of the ongoing situation.

"This is Dr. Black. You have some of our Shadow Maker systems on your ship. Those are private property. I demand they be returned to Brussels spaceport immediately. Over."

"The hell I am," Major Lu Ann barked to no one in particular. Holding down the talk button, she answered, "Sorry. But we are disassembling them to learn how they work and how to thwart their destruction. We are at war, and these devices are being used as weapons, making them fair game for us to confiscate. I order you to cease using these Shadow Maker devices and be prepared to turn the lot of them over to me. Over." Several in CCC cheered her reply to Dr. Black.

"I'm afraid you leave me no choice but to take back my devices by use of force, major. Over and out." Dr. Black signed off.

"Battle stations. Condition One," Major Lu Ann announced to the ship. "Pilots, man your ships. This is not a drill. Be prepared for a launch." Turning to her crew in CCC, she added, "Okay, look alive. Give us as much warning of incoming ships as you can. Now we wait and see."

After two hours, Major Lu Ann gave the stand down orders to her pilots. No attack had come, and there wasn't any sign of one in the offing. The giant battleship Royal Queen had not moved nor had their sensors picked up any ships departing the vicinity of Ragnar-B, though plenty transports were hovering over the city, presumably murdering the innocent city dwellers, but she could do nothing about that slaughter.

"Okay, a wise move would be to hit us when we least

expect it," Major Lu Ann informed her CCC crew. "So stay alert. My guess is they will strike us while we sleep." After that, she headed off to get some dinner and a brief rest, stopping by Sickbay on her way to check on the situation there. Nothing had changed, though sensor readings indicated the three inside the sealed cabin were in comas.

After dinner, she conducted a short funeral ceremony for the doctor and two nurses, ejecting their bodies into the vacuum of space along with the traitor Fielding. A cursory search of his cabin turned up nothing at all. Major Lu Ann debated whether to bail out and head for Scorpi-C or to continue to monitor the hellish situation down on her home world. Since nothing seemed threatening at this point, she opted to continue to orbit the planet, gathering intelligence. She then got a few hours' sleep before reporting for duty around midnight. Her night crew reported nothing was amiss, and she settled down with a cup of hot coffee.

Around one in the morning, a man called out, "Contacts rising, coming out from the Royal Queen. Heading towards us!"

"Sound battle stations," Major Lu Ann barked. Clangs sounded the alarm ship-wide.

One Shot and Killer Diller raced to their delta wing fighters, putting on their flight suits as they ran, rather an awkward motion though. "Now I get to add to my kill totals," Killer called out. "See if you can at least keep up, One Shot!"

"I aim to catch your totals, Killer," he replied playfully. This was anything but play. One missed shot and they could well be dead, shot into the cold vacuum of space. Still, they were highly trained and motivated.

"Numbers?" Major Lu Ann barked. If they sent a hundred of the one-man fighters, she knew she'd have to flee as fast as possible. She had twenty-one fighters of her own available to ward off the attack, and the light cruisers own gun batteries, which were never all that effective. No, these large ships depended upon their screening delta wing fighters for their real protection.

"Twelve one-man fighters, major," came the reply. Major Lu Ann relaxed. "Notify me the instant you detect more than twelve. Scramble our delta wings. Pilots, you may engage at your discretion. Take those tin cans out!" she ordered. One Shot gave a thumb's up sign to Killer Diller, who sat in her seat in the next fighter. A minute later, both ships shot out of Shuttle Bay One, swerved hard to the right, heading for the incoming dozen one-man fighters.

"Damn, they seem to have learned a whole lot about fighting!" exclaimed Killer Diller twenty minutes later. The firefight had been going on for nearly fifteen minutes now, and only one of the enemy ships had been disabled! Something had definitely changed. Before, the pilots of the one-man shuttles had been easy prey, but not these dozen! They were as good as the defenders, which annoyed Killer Diller and One Shot no end. They continually griped about this detail over their comm sets, ignoring the fact that the major and others could hear them back in CCC.

"Something is very different about these fighters," Major Lu Ann commented. She'd been studying the large monitor that displayed the motions of the two sets of fighters, the enemy in red, her forces in green. "In that initial attack that first day," she spoke aloud, "by now, we had shot down dozens of them. Something is very different about these pilots! Worse, they are getting too damn close to us. Okay, recall our pilots. Power up the hyperdrive. Prepare to make the jump into hyperspace as soon as we've retrieved our fighters. Destination: Scorpi-C."

Others acknowledged her orders. Now she could only wait. So many things could go wrong on a withdrawal. If the enemy came at them while they were landing, the Hyperion would take the full force of the enemy's attacks before they could jump clear. Their pilots could be more readily shot down while trying to land. Far too many things could go wrong, but she'd committed the fighters and now had no choice but to live with that decision, for good or ill. Patience, she told herself. *Set a good example for the others.*

She kept her eyes on the monitor and listened to the tally, as each of the fighters touched down. "Now, jump!" she barked. The Hyperion lurched slightly. The display screen's image of the dimly illuminated planet below them and the many enemy ships vanished, replaced with the total blackness that was hyperspace. Major Lu Ann calmly released her breath. Now they were safe.

"Contact major. One. Two. Four. Make that six contacts. They are following us into hyperspace! How is that possible?" a lieutenant called out.

"Shit! Evasive maneuvers. Increase speed to max," she ordered. "Prepare another set of coordinates to jump to. Pick Sagitta-C. That should be unexpected enough. Fire control teams, man your battle stations. Enemy fighters are closing in on us in hyperspace. Science advisors to the CCC immediately."

Shortly, a man and a woman reported. "So how is it possible for the enemy fighters to follow us into hyperspace?" she barked, a distinctive edge to her voice. This was wholly unexpected and should not be happening.

"Don't know, sir. They shouldn't be able to track us in hyperspace," he replied.

"Not unless they have a signal onboard to follow," the woman answered. "We've heard that is possible."

"Shit! That traitor Fielding!" She picked up the phone and spoke to the entire ship. "This is Major Lu Ann. We're in hyperspace now, but the enemy ships are following us. They must be following a signal of some kind. I want this entire ship searched from top to bottom. That traitor Fielding probably put it onboard. Notify me when it's found. That is all."

For a half hour, Major Lu Ann played cat and mouse with the enemy fighters, changing course and speeds seemingly at random, or so she hoped the enemy would think. However, they continued to close the distance. The Hyperion was overloaded and the extra weight cut down her top speed.

"Hell, we can't even launch our fighters. They aren't capable of travel in hyperspace," she commented to her staff. "Gun crews, it's up to you. Fire at will when the enemy ships get within range." She didn't answer one man's reply which was just how were they to *see* the enemy ships in the inky blackness of hyperspace.

Two hours later, the enemy began firing upon the Hyperion, but its gun crews couldn't see the enemy ships to return fire. Hence, they fired at random locations, hoping to get lucky. Yet because of the enemy transmitter on the Hyperion, Thanos' ships could *see* the light cruiser.

For another hour, the Hyperion's shields held, but then a lucky shot took them out. "Shields are down!" someone yelled.

"Get a repair crew down there fast. We need those shields up now!" Major Lu Ann barked obvious orders, knowing that her work crews were probably already on it. Other enemy shots hit the sides of the ship, but the titanium re-enforced steel held for now.

Then, it happened so fast that no one had time to react. A key enemy shot took out their hyperdrive. The Hyperion plummeted wildly out of hyperspace, an uncontrolled exit into an unknown location. At the same time, Fel found the hidden transmitter in Private Fielding's cabin and turned it off, thereby blinding the enemy fighters on their trail. Thus, as luck would have it, the humaniforms had no idea where in space the Hyperion dropped out. They'd effectively lost the ship, but they also knew that its engines were compromised. Surely, they would be dead in space if not destroyed. Calmly, they returned to Ragnar-B.

"Where the hell are we? Status report," Major Lu Ann barked. *We're still in one piece so that can't be bad.*

"Major Lu Ann, Lieutenant Felicity Heavens here. I found the transmitter and turned it off. I don't think they can follow us anymore."

"Good work. You probably saved the whole ship," Major Lu Ann replied.

"Hyperdrive is out. Sub-light engines are also out. We're floating dead in space, major," someone in damage control reported.

"Get all work crews on repairs," she ordered.

"Major, the LD array is out too." Major Lu Ann sighed visibly. The Long Distance array was their only means to communicate across the vastness of space. She could not call for help or send a message back to the Battleship Arc Royal.

Calmly, she asked, "Where are we? Position? Sector?"

"Unknown. We haven't been able to coordinate the

visible star patterns yet, but we're somewhere on the rim, major," came the reply.

"Call our astronomers up. We have to find out our current location quickly. Get a work crew ready to go topside and check on the damage to the LD array. Get that electronics expert on it. Shit, she's trapped in Sickbay. Damn," she caught herself. Dr. Alison's services would have been very handy just now.

With no further reports coming in, Major Lu Ann headed off to inspect personally the damage to both their engines. She found the engine compartments in total disarray. The hull had been ruptured and both engines badly damaged. Repairs would have to be done while wearing cumbersome space suits, unless the ship could be pulled into dry dock, which wasn't an option. "Put work crews on the repairs twenty-four hours a day. Schedule them accordingly. We have to get sub-light engines back online ASAP."

"Aye major, but it's going to be days," her chief engineer replied.

On her way back, she found Fel and asked her to join her engineers. "We've got to get sub-light engines back online soon, Fel. So lend them a hand, please."

"Aye sir. Heading there now," Felicity saluted and headed on down into the bowels of the ship near the stern.

When she returned to CCC, the three astronomers were already hard at work making their observations, trying to work out a fix on their location. "Sorry major, no luck as yet," one replied. An hour later, exhausted, she headed to her cabin for some much needed sleep. If anything developed, she knew she'd be notified.

The following day produced nothing new. The astronomers had yet to identify any star patterns. The engineers pronounced the hyperdrive engines were beyond repair, but they held out some hope that they might be able to get the sub-light engine back at least partially. Further, the LD array was totally gone, stripped off the ship by the attack's blast. Given proper repair facilities and sufficient time, a spare LD array could be installed but that wasn't likely to happen for at least a week. Major Lu Ann spent a very somber next few days with very little progress being made.

***

The cabin seals finally released, indicating that the bio hazard was eliminated. Jascar and Helen headed into the cabin to check on the three. As expected, they found the three in comas. Already Alison's arms had vanished, as had the new ones of Peter. Worse, Kathy's arms were about gone as well, and her hair had grown considerably. A day later, the three awoke from their comas.

"Damn, not again," Dr. Alison exclaimed, struggling to get her body into a position to check on Kathy and Peter.

"Well, that was short lived," Peter grumbled. Both knew what they would discover when they woke up. They had recognized the bio agent and thus were not shocked when they awoke. "Kathy. Not her too," Peter moaned, suddenly realizing his precious daughter was now as modified as he was.

Jascar and Helen had put her body on a small cot beside the two adults. "What happened," Kathy muttered, trying to rub her eyes and sit up, but her arms didn't work. "Oh no!" she cried, finally coming too enough to realize what had happened to her.

"I'm so sorry, Kathy," Peter sobbed.

"Oh daddy, now I am just like you and Alison. Look, I've got real breasts now," she said rather pleased with her new shape. For months now, she'd been carefully watching them, hoping and praying that they would grow, showing that she was becoming a young woman and not just a child. "Oh, my hair. It's so long and I can feel with it. Is that right daddy?" she asked.

"Well, welcome back to the land of the living," Jascar spoke up. "Lots of news, all really bad. The doctor's been killed by the terrorist who did this to you." For a half hour, Jascar outlined all that had happened and what he understood their current situation was.

"Well, I'm back to being a helpless electronics expert," Dr. Alison complained. "If you can help me get up and fed, I'll go see if I can be of any help with their LD array. Peter, I'll join you and Kathy as soon as I can. I think we three should stick together now. Kathy, be brave. I'll show you how to do a few things for yourself when I get back. If we don't get the LD array working, they can't call for help. Shit, Jascar, you're going to have to open the door for me," she added a bit later when she tried to head off to see if she could help them.

Taking small steps to keep her balance, Dr. Alison made her way to the CCC. "Hi. I'm awake now. Can I help on the comm system?" she asked.

"Glad to have you, Dr. Alison," Major Lu Ann welcomed her, but frowned seeing her armless body.

"I know," Dr. Alison sighed, "I'm rather helpless, but maybe I can offer some advice or something."

"Okay, work with Henry there. He's trying to ascertain the internal damage before we waste time trying to rig up the spare antenna. Apparently, the entire mounting has been destroyed," the major replied.

Henry said, "I'm glad for your expertise. Something's not right according to the manuals on this thing, but I've no idea what."

"I'm mostly helpless Henry, so you're going to have to show me what you mean," Dr. Alison replied, doing her best to squat down to the disassembled panels without falling over. Henry caught her and made sure she was seated. A half hour later, Dr. Alison sighed, "Henry, the internal circuits are fried! Have you got a new motherboard to replace this one?"

Henry's face fell, giving her the answer. Major Lu Ann overheard them and stepped up to the pair. "What's the prognosis?"

"The main motherboard is fried," Henry explained. "That's why none of my tests worked like they should have. We don't have a spare motherboard on the ship. I'm afraid the LD system can't be repaired. We're doomed."

Dr. Alison spoke up, "Henry, that's not entirely true. We can test each component on the motherboard and isolate which ones are damaged and replace them from other boards that aren't needed, ones that aren't critical to the ship."

"But I don't know how to do that, Dr. Alison."

"I do, but I've no hands now. I guess you'll have to be my hands, that is, if Major Lu Ann wants us to try to fix it."

"Please, do whatever you can. We've still got the deep

space transports and their comm systems, so we're not in dire straits," she replied, putting Dr. Alison more at ease.

"Well, Henry, let's take the motherboard back to your small lab and get started on it," she suggested, "but you're going to have to help me get back up. I hate being so helpless."

Just then, one of the astronomers spoke up, his voice extremely worried. "Major, we have a major problem! No, we still don't have a clue where in the galaxy we are at, but we've discovered we're heading straight for a red dwarf star. In two days, we are going to be pulled into its surface and burned up!"

"What? Where? Show me," Major Lu Ann barked, suddenly very worried indeed. Dr. Alison, now on her feet, paid close attention.

"There it is. We're heading straight for it. There are two gas giants ahead, and we should pass them tomorrow, and then pick up speed as we're pulled into the star."

"Well, shit. I'll check on the engine repairs now." She hailed them over the comm and relayed the bad news.

"Sorry, we'll never get the engines back online that soon. Try a couple of weeks," her chief engineer reported. Dr. Alison swallowed hard. *Am I going to be dead in two days? I don't want to die, not like this,* she thought.

Major Lu Ann took a deep breath and made the ship-wide connection. "This is Major Lu Ann. I've bad news. The sub-light engines won't be back online for a couple of weeks. However, we are being pulled into a red dwarf star. We have two days before we hit it. All officers are to report to the CCC immediately. We need options at this point." Turning to Dr. Alison, she added, "Stick around in case you have some ideas too." Soon the CCC was packed with very nervous faces.

"We have five deep space transports, counting those that we confiscated from the enemy. Each can carry twenty-five passengers," she explained slowly and carefully, all the while maintaining a calm exterior. She knew if she panicked, the others would follow suit. "That means only a little over half of you could be rescued by the transports. The rest, well, you know what will happen. Even that isn't a surety of survival, since we still don't know our location. While we can punch in the coordinates for home, it could well be far out of the range of our transports, and we could all be left floating in hyperspace until we die. So that option is our very last resort. Ladies, gentlemen, I need other options."

One of the astronomers spoke up, "Major, there is a habitable planet closer in, past the two gas giants. Perhaps we could land there and make repairs."

"How do we land without any engines?" someone countered. He shut up.

Major Lu Ann stepped in. "That's an excellent idea. A habitable planet is just what we need. So how do we land this ship without our engines? Ideas?"

"Could we could tow it with the transports," Dr. Alison spoke up, regretting having said such a silly thing, as all eyes turned to her.

"Not enough power," Felicity pointed out.

"But together, they could guide the ship enough to avoid a collision with the red dwarf," another engineer suggested.

"They could also guide the Hyperion down in a sort of controlled crash landing, assuming we can find a flat plain on which to set down. Say, is the planet inhabited? Do they have space travel?" one asked.

"Not sure yet. We've not detected any radio frequencies, but we're scanning all bands," another replied.

"It's going to take time to get the transports properly hooked up to the Hyperion. We should get on it right away," another engineer suggested.

"Right. While they can't totally provide the thrust we need," one of the astronomers pointed out, "given enough trust over enough time, we can control the Hyperion's path and glide entrance into the planet's atmosphere. I think a controlled crash landing is possible, if we have as much lead time to make the calculations as possible."

Since no one had any better ideas, Major Lu Ann adopted this one. She then made a ship-wide announcement outlining the disaster that lay ahead and the measures being taken to prevent or lessen it. One by one, the group disbanded. Because she moved so slowly, Dr. Alison waited for all the others to leave before attempting to make her own perilous way back to the electronics lab with Henry. "Excellent thinking, Dr. Alison. You may have just saved us all. Well done," Major Lu Ann validated her. *My god, she needs all the support that she can get. I can't imagine what she's going through now. No arms. Hell, I'd rather be dead.*

"Thanks. Should we work on trying to fix the motherboard?"

"No, help Peter and his daughter for now. Once we land, there will be plenty of time to repair it. Thanks again and well done." Alison flashed her a smile and began her long, slow walk back to her quarters, hoping there were no closed doors along the way.

Twice, there were, and she had no choice but to stand around waiting for someone to come by. Her feet were throbbing by the time she reached her cabin. Janine was there along with Peter and Kathy. She'd managed to get the room arranged for the three. "Hi sis. You, Peter, and Kathy will be bunking in here. I'm just across the hall so I can help. Fel's with me, and she'll help too. Kathy's a bright girl. She's figured out how to use a spoon to eat. Come on, Kathy; show Alison."

Proudly, the twelve-year-old girl sat down, pushed off her new tall heels, and proceeded to use her toes, wrapping them around the spoon. "See, like this. We can do it if we can sit on the floor. Janine has promised to let us try it at suppertime. It's not as bad as I thought at first. Of course, I've not yet figured out how we can possibly open a door. Have you?" she asked, her voice full of the enthusiasm of youth undaunted by this horrible situation.

"Nope. Just wait until someone comes by and opens it for us."

"Sis, I just heard about crashing into this red dwarf star and how they are going to use the transports to pull us away from crashing. Isn't that cool?"

"I know, Janine. I suggested it, and the major is going to try it. I hope it works. On my way here, sis, I realized even as awful as this is, I'm not ready to die."

"Now you are talking, big sis. Don't give up. Our mom taught us that much," Janine replied, suddenly very proud of her mostly helpless sister.

"Well, I'm not about to. Look, I got my arms back once, so if we can get through this mess, we can travel to Scorpi-C and have it done again. Peter, Kathy, I give you my word I won't rest until I get us all fixed up somehow, someway," Dr. Alison made her promise. *I've never made such a vehement promise before, but this is right. I have to give them both hope, especially Peter who had it and lost it so quickly.*

"Thanks Alison. Honestly, I'm lost without you," Peter admitted.

Kathy spoke up embarrassing both of them. "It's okay with me if you become my new mom, Alison." Both adults flushed.

Janine smiled at them, sensing Kathy wasn't too amiss in her observations. "Go for it, you two. I'll leave you for a while until I can bring supper to you. Holler if you need something."

After she left, Kathy said, "I need to go to the bathroom. Come on. I think if you each use your teeth to pull up this dress, I can go. We have to help ourselves now, dad. We can do this." Kathy's insistence on her independence and their working together made an indelible impression on both adults, who followed carefully after her into the small bathroom. While it was awkward, they managed to squat down enough to reach the lower part of her new dress and pull it up for her.

"See, it worked," Kathy said. "I thought it would. We just have to figure out new ways to do things, dad." She stood up and wiggled a bit so that her dress fell back down into place. Together, the three headed to the bed to sit and talk. There weren't any chairs in the room, just the one large bed and smaller one for Kathy.

The next day, everyone followed the progress of the towing transports. Major Lu Ann kept everyone informed, even to the point of sending live video to many monitors around the ship. Her reasoning was sound. Keep the personnel involved, fears and panic at bay. Swinging by the two gas giants gave everyone a spectacular view, especially Kathy who had never seen such things before. At suppertime, the major announced they would be reaching the planet around eight the next morning. She encouraged everyone to have their breakfasts finished before then. She didn't need to explain why. "This might be our last meal," Peter whispered to Alison, long after Kathy was asleep.

The two lay on their sides on the larger bed. Alison struggled a bit and managed to get her lips to his, giving him a passionate kiss. "I've wanted to do that since we met."

Their passions rose, perhaps because of their genetic modifications. After a good deal of struggling, they managed to work out how to proceed. An hour later and very satisfied, the two snuggled up to each other. "I've wanted to do that since I met you too," Peter replied, "only I didn't dare even suggest such a thing, not with the way I look."

"Silly, that doesn't matter to me. It probably does to others but not me," Alison replied.

"Hey, about your promise to us. I want to make you the same promise. I'll do everything possible to make that happen for us all too. You've given me the courage to go on with life," Peter admitted.

"I know. I think Kathy realizes that too. She wants and needs a mother. I know I can't be her real mother, but I'll be the best I can."

"You already are that and much more," Peter replied, giving her another loving kiss.

"If we all die tomorrow, Peter, I want you to know you are the first man I would ever go out on a second date with and then many more," Alison admitted.

Peter chuckled. "Janine once told me you were incredibly picky. Guess she was right."

"Picky? Okay, picky. I want you, Peter." She gave him another kiss. For the first time in many, many years, Alison felt whole. The last time she did was when she and Janine had the mumps and their mother had slept with them, cradling them in her arms until they finally fell asleep. If nothing else, both Peter and Alison awoke having gotten the best night's sleep either had had since they were genetically modified.

Janine brought them their breakfast around seven, but wisely allowed them to experiment in using their toes and feet to feed themselves. While she nearly broke down in tears watching the three's valiant but clumsy efforts to do so, she wisely suppressed her emotions and was rewarded with the trio's limited success and their smiling faces when they finished.

Major Lu Ann had given the transport pilots very specific orders. One Shot and Killer Diller manned one of them, the one which now held all the captured Shadow Maker equipment. If the landing went south, their orders were specific. Do what they had to do to get this precious cargo back to the Battleship Arc Royal. The other transport pilots had similar orders to attempt to fly their transport back to civilization. Each transport now carried many extra fuel cells in that event.

As the predicted time, eight o'clock, approached, events unfolded at a rapidly escalating rate, just as everyone expected. The transports began their task of slowing down the light cruiser, as the habitable planet slowly grew in size. On the Hyperion, the astronomers were kept busy calculating and recalculating the flight path and thrust vectors, relaying new requests every few minutes.

Others were studying the planet ahead. The red sun was still rather dim, quite unlike the yellow dwarf star of Ragnar. Worse, the planet seemed to have a total cloud cover. As it came closer, the infrared scanner was activated, in an attempt to pierce the dense clouds.

"Hey, we're getting readings that indicate it's inhabited," one called out. "That's got to be a town. Many small red images there." The major studied the images and became convinced this was true. She made the official announcement that the planet was inhabited, probably by humans.

As the distance grew ever shorter, it became clear to the major that this wasn't a modern world, but likely a more primitive one. They detected no trace of fossil fuels in the atmosphere. No radio signals. No nuclear power plants. No cities of millions.

The projected trajectory brought the Hyperion close to this world, and then circled it once, as it slowed and began its inevitable descent. That plan allowed them to get some kind of idea where they could best land the Hyperion, which now became an acute problem since they could not see the surface anywhere! The entire planet was perpetually cloud-covered. They would be landing mostly blind, except for what they could determine via radar and the IR scanner.

For the last twenty-four hours, the five transports had been steadily slowing the Hyperion down, but not enough, which became apparent as they made their first pass around the planet, far too fast for comfort. Valiantly, the astronomers and the transport pilots did their best to work out vectors to slow the huge ship even more, but at last, they knew that it was coming down on the second pass, no matter what they did. They only had minutes to decide upon a landing site. It wouldn't do to land in the ocean. The Hyperion would sink rather rapidly. Landing in the mountain ranges was also a recipe for disaster, as was landing on top of a town.

The larger of the two continents shown by radar seemed devoid of human inhabitants and was rugged. The other continent had two tall mountain ranges, whose peaks rose up above the dense cloud cover. The inhabited zone appeared to lie between these two tall ranges, which made sense if this was a primitive culture, the major thought. "Land between the two mountain ranges, if you can," she ordered, knowing for good or ill, this might be her last decision.

They watched the IR scanner closely, as the Hyperion completed its first complete trip around the planet, dropping now into its upper atmosphere. As this inhabited continent appeared ahead of them, the IR scanner showed five distinct clusters of what they believed to be human habitation sites. One was near the eastern mountains, while one was near the western range. One was located near the southern coast, while another pair was in the hilly lands to the north. All were very nearly equidistant from each other, perhaps five hundred miles at most.

Major Lu Ann knew as soon as the Hyperion reached the cloud layer not only would they be blind, but also there simply wouldn't be time for her to issue any further orders. After suggesting they try to land somewhere in the middle area, away from the five larger towns, she made the formal announcement. "Okay, we're about to land. Everyone buckle up and brace yourselves. It will be a rough landing. It's been a pleasure serving with all of you. May the gods safeguard our landing." She hung up and took her seat, strapping herself in. She took one last look at the grim faces of her CCC workers and smiled outwardly. She wanted to scream, but knew she had to keep up her calm appearance. Suddenly, the monitor turned a ghastly grey-red. They'd hit the dense cloud layer.

Now it was up to the transport pilots to set them down, even though they were flying just as blindly. She'd given them her best guess as to where to make the attempt, but now it was in their hands. For a minute, all the decisions she'd made during the last week-plus returned in her mind. Had she made the right calls? *Stop that,* she thought. *They were made and done. We're here and now.* Still, she found it hard to stop second-guessing all of her decisions. Had she left the moment that Dr. Black threatened her, they'd not be here now, at least in all likelihood. Had she found that hidden transmitter sooner, they might be on Scorpi-C now, not facing doom.

Major Lu Ann took a deep breath, paused a moment, and slowly let it out, letting go of all her thoughts. At last, her mind became quiet. She sensed her heartbeat. *I'm still alive. There's always hope.* In the background, she could hear the frantic chatter between the five transport pilots and their five navigators as they desperately tried to control the rapid descent of the light cruiser.

"There's a huge river ahead. We have to avoid hitting it," One Shot yelled.

"Pull back, pull back," another yelled. "We're still coming in too fast. It's going to carry us to the mountains! Pull back with all we have!"

"Grasslands ahead. Ease her down there," One Shot ordered.

Then the Hyperion hit the ground. A mighty jar nearly threw Major Lu Ann out of her chair and would have if she'd not been wearing her seatbelt. Even so, she received very nasty bruises, as did many others.

Janine had strapped the trio down on their beds, trusting the beds to cushion their crash. The beds smashed into the forward bulkhead, jarring all three senseless, but at least they didn't have any nasty bruises from the crash landing.

The rocking, jarring, and bouncing seemed to go on for an eternity. More than one crew member kept waiting for the big smash to occur as the ship hit the mountains and disintegrated, but that didn't happen. Rather the jarring and bouncing slowly died down until the ship ceased moving.

"One Shot calling Major Lu Ann. We're down, mostly in one piece we think. Over."

Her left arm was wrenched, but she managed to get her belt off and grabbed the phone. "Major Lu Ann here. Well done all of you. Have you landed nearby? What's the extent of the damage? Over."

"We're down close to the ship. Not sure how to appraise the damage, major," One Shot replied, very unwilling to say that he thought the ship would never fly again. No, best let the major tell everyone that. Besides, he couldn't see well enough to see much at all. The clouds blocked the dim light of the sun and everything was just a dim shade of red. "You'll need flashlights to see anything," he added.

"But it has to be around noon here," one of the astronomers pointed out.

"Okay, marines, establish a perimeter around the ships. All damage assessment crews report to Shuttle Bay One. Let's quickly determine our situation. Everyone else, fan out throughout the ship and look for any critical situations," she ordered over the comm center, which continued to operate, though the lights had switched over to battery backup.

Stepping outside along with dozens of assessment crew members, Major Lu Ann gasped and rubbed her eyes. Overhead, the dense clouds were blood red, providing only dim illumination. Pale green ferns standing over four feet tall were around her and the ships. She could only see several hundred feet at most, not even from one end of her ship to the other! The air felt damp and heavy; the ground, soft humus. She swallowed hard and focused on what she could see of her ship and her heart sank. She knew what the damage assessment crew would have to say: the Hyperion would probably never fly again.

Slowly, she walked back inside, the heavy realization sinking in: her focus had to be on keeping everyone alive and somehow getting them rescued before all was lost. Survival became her next goal. Somehow, they had to survive on this, the most dismal planet she'd ever heard of. Worse, she still had no idea where in the galaxy they were. Did she dare send a transport off? What coordinates should they use? A wrong guess and they'd run out of fuel and drift forever in hyperspace. Alone for a moment in the deserted bay, Major Lu Ann felt a wetness on her cheeks and realized she was crying. Silently, she permitted her tears to flow, her grief found an outlet, if only a temporary one.

Chapter 7—Brand New World

The year was 1504, more than five hundred years ago. On Terra or Ashford-5, Queen Mary Linn finally passed the decree many longed to have: the freedom to travel to any world in the new Galactic Union. Finally, the hermaphrodite telepaths of Ashford-5 could take their place in the galactic society. The only stipulation was they could not have the arm re-growth procedure if they wished to leave their home world. The Dark Age of genetic mutations, planetary genocide, and the war with the robots was over at last. The galaxy was unified and under the guidance of Ataro Empire queens and Ashford-5 telepaths. Each major planet now had one of each to help ensure the future of mankind.

The population of many planets now consisted wholly of genetically modified humans, hermaphrodites. If that wasn't enough damage, their bodies suffered further modifications from these terrible bio agents. Their feet were malformed. Only their toes rested flat upon the ground, their heels arched high in the air, forcing them to wear extremely tall heels. With these special toe shoes, their heels added more support, but still walking was challenging, made all the more so by their lack of arms. Waists had been reduced to a mere fourteen inches across, while some internal organs were relocated further down into the enlarged pelvis region. The bio agent enlarged their breasts to nearly the size of their heads, but at least they were perky and not droopy.

Their hair fell to their knees, but it could not be cut any shorter. Neurons and axons now grew inside each strand of hair, which was now more than double the diameter of a normal hair. Each strand of their hair gave them a very sensitive sense of touch. Finally, many also had split lips, forcing them to have to wear the giant lip plates similar to those decorative ones that had once been so popular on Ashford-5. Their lip loops demanded a lip plate that was ten inches in diameter, but thanks to developments on Ashford-5, small mouth pieces that attached to four holes in their upper and lower jaws supported the disks, along with a spring lock mechanism that allowed the disks to be fastened horizontal to the ground for eating or to drop down towards their chests, their normal position. Many had fancy designs embossed on the top surface of their upper lip plate.

None of this posed much of a problem for those from Ashford-5, since they had powerful telepathic and telekinetic gifts that compensated for their body's deficiencies. However, the vast majority of others who had survived the attempted genocide attacks did not. They depended upon mechanical assistance, small robot machines, and the assistance of other normal humans.

One of the worst hit planets was Zeta Scorpii-C, a world that lay in the mid-arm region of what had once been the Federation of Planets. Here hundreds of millions of these victims now resided, aided by many robots and machines. However, many of these survivors found this new existence untenable and wanted a new start. The story begins in the spring of 1505 in Ortega, Zeta Scorpii-C, specifically at the old Academy in that city. War reparations had finally been doled out to the millions of genetically modified survivors.

Five young Academy couples had banded together, helping each other survive their living nightmare. All had the typical thick, rich, glossy black hair so typical of those who came from Zeta Scorpii-C, though now theirs was twice as thick, reaching below their knees and hypersensitive to touch, which prevented even tying their hair up into buns. Even doing that little gave them continuous pain and resulting headaches. With their new bank accounts filled with the millions of credits in war compensations, the five met around their communal living room.

"Well, now that we're rich, what the hell are we going to do?" asked Isabella da Casa. Her husband was Renato. With them were Luisa and Tito Alvaro, Juana and Salvador Vega, Petrona and Vasco Gonzalo, and Lola and Fidel Manolo. All were between twenty-one and twenty-three at this time.

"Well isn't this just the pits," Luisa spoke up grumpily. "We always dreamed of flying among the stars, once we all had our degrees that is, but now we're nothing but a bunch of

110

helpless people. We have all the funds we need to take such a trip, but not the physical ability to do so. Isn't this just—well, I won't say what," she shut up quickly, muffling her curses. She still held on to some resemblance of civility, even though most of the time she felt like cursing everyone and every god for what their bodies had become.

"I've got my biology degree now," put in Petrona. "I so wanted to travel and explore the plants and animals of other worlds. I'll say it for you, Luisa, goddamn those robots anyway. I hope they rot in hell for what they've done to us and everyone else."

Several others mumbled their agreement with her assessment. "It won't do to keep on cursing them," Renato da Casa spoke up. "We are fucked up and that's all there is to it. We have to live with it and get on with our lives."

"That's all well and good for you to say that," complained Petrona, "but how can I get on with my life like this? I want to explore the fauna of other worlds."

"I say, why don't we?" Tito interrupted her. "Why not? Hell, we're all fabulously wealthy. We can buy a ship, hell, a big one, and hire a crew and go wherever we want to go. I've a mind to see some of the giant gas clouds, you know, some of the ones the gypsies told us about four years ago when they stopped here."

"That's all well and good, Tito," Fidel broke in, "but have you forgotten that we're totally helpless? We'd need to bring along dozens and dozens of normal humans just to help us with all our needs, which is damned near everything!"

Just then, Lilly and Ann entered the living room, carrying trays of cups, spoons, and pitchers of hot coffee. They were the two off-world assistants that had been hired to fix their meals and help them eat, among other things. As they poured the cups, Lilly spoke up. "We couldn't avoid hearing you talking about getting a ship and traveling around the galaxy. You know, there are a whole lot of other people who would love to come along with you, normal humans I mean, like us. If you tried, I'm sure you could find hundreds of us who would love to go with you and help you do it."

"You're kidding, right Lilly?" Tito asked, not believing

her.

"I'm serious. Most of us don't even have enough credits to take a spaceship trip anywhere. Ann and I got here because the Ataro Empire paid for our passage. Honestly, Tito, there's probably millions of us who would give anything to travel the stars. It's so romantic too."

"Shoot, you could even colonize a new world," added Ann. "With all the money you have, you could buy a new world. There are millions of people who would give anything to colonize a new world. It's like starting life all over. Besides, you ten are the smartest people we have ever known. You would be the guardians, the ones with all the knowledge, making up for your physical disabilities. Don't sell yourselves short. Almost no one can afford to go to the Academy. On my world, maybe one in ten million goes to our Academy, if that many. So you all have what most people don't have: knowledge."

"Say, she has a point," Renato pointed out. "Between us, we have an enormous amount of knowledge. We could be the sages of our new world. That way, we could contribute something of value besides just the initial credits, especially since we need help with damned near everything else."

"A new world. I like that! Think of the flora and fauna we could study," put in Petrona. "Why don't we try to find and colonize a new world? There must be zillions of them out there just waiting for someone to find them."

Vasco decided to speak up. This was an intriguing idea, besides, it offered a way to get away from this dismal existence on Zeta Scorpii-C. "She's got a point. The deep space exploration ships are always finding new habitable planets. Why not us? Come on; this is a great idea. We can leave this hell hole behind forever."

Thus, the idea formed. Within a month, they had finalized their ideas. They would purchase a colonization deep space ship, that is, a modified light cruiser, hire a competent crew, and take applications for colonists to join them, subject to the requirement that they would have to help the ten with their physical needs. When they posted their help wanted ad that stated the colonists wouldn't have to pay for anything as long as they were in total agreement to help the ten with their needs, they were flooded with emails from a dozen other worlds. They had no idea there were so many others who wanted to leave their worlds behind and start a new life on a new world somewhere.

Each of the applicants was given an interview by the ten, who also paid for the applicant's round trip and all expenses just for them to come for the interview. Whenever possible, they chose younger couples who would be, in their views, best suited to help them colonize a new world and who had no qualms in helping them with their many physical needs. As one young woman put it in her interview, "Look, if you are paying for the ship, all the supplies, and getting us all there, I will owe you so much that I would feel horrible if you didn't let me help you guys with whatever you needed. It's criminal what they did to you with that biogenetic agent."

***

Spring of 1506, they were finally ready to set sail on their voyage to their new world. They named their new ship the Zeta Zephyr, a converted light cruiser. The lowest level contained their farm animals, horses, cows, chickens, and sheep, along with vast amounts of seed for crops, such as wheat, corn, and potatoes. The one hundred twenty colonists occupied the middle section of cabins and half of those on the upper level. The ship had a crew of a dozen under the control of young Major Jon James, fresh out of the Academy. His crew looked forward to establishing a profitable commercial travel line between this new world and the inhabited planets.

An important side note: Tito Alvaro did not come from Zeta Scorpii-C. Rather he came from Ashford-5, and yes, he was a telepath, though he had many other mental abilities that so many from that world possessed. He had jumped at the chance to go off-world when Queen Mary Linn finally allowed it. Not getting his arms re-grown was a minuscule price to pay for this extraordinary opportunity. He'd come to Zeta Scorpii-C, ran into Luisa and the others and soon fell madly in love with her. Thus, of the entire group, Tito was the only telepath, just as Renato was the only astronomer among the group. Again, this would prove to be a key detail.

113

As a result, Tito, with his special skills, was elected to be the leader among this group of ten, while the ten were the leaders of the other one hundred twenty colonists, some of whom had some fighter training. Just as Lilly and Ann had predicted, the colonists held these ten Academy members in very high esteem, not only because of their wealth and what they were doing with it, but because they obviously had vast knowledge that they lacked.

Their destination was Forsythe-C, a newly discovered world on the rim of this spiral arm. Many lamented they couldn't name their world New Zeta, a name the colonists desired.

Loaded with all the supplies they could possibly desire, the Zeta Zephyr lifted off from Zeta Scorpii-C on May 12, 1506, amid cheers from the many passengers. The trip was to take three days, primarily because they were heavily loaded. At this relatively slow speed, they minimized their fuel consumption. Yet, even this aspect was taken into account. They had sufficient fuel cells to make the trip twice over, just in case.

Sixty hours into the flight, the unthinkable happened. They were cruising along in the black of hyperspace when the ship hit something! This was not supposed to happen—collisions in hyperspace. However, over the many millennia of hyperspace travel, more than one ship had become stranded in hyperspace, primarily by running out of fuel and thus drifting endlessly through the blackness. The unlucky Zeta Zephyr ran into one of those derelicts. A resounding explosion shook the ship. The sudden lurch tossed many out of their beds or off their feet. Several suffered broken limbs, and many had some nasty bruises. Worse, though, the collision knocked out their hyperdrive. Instantly, the ship dropped out of hyperspace at a wholly unknown position!

Frantically, Major Jon tried to stabilize the ship, which was rolling, pitching, and yawing madly about. Worse, the sub-light engines refused to come online! Only by clever releasing of some of their oxygen from various locations around the hull was Major Jon finally able to stabilize their flight. That done, he sent his men out to assess the damage, while he used the comm to make the awful announcement. He

114

ended with, "Renato, I need you here in the control center now!"

Renato made his slow, careful way to the command center of the ship. He'd taken a bump on his head from the sudden, unexpected lurch. A big red welt was in the process of forming, and he wished he could rub it. "What the hell happened?" he asked when he finally made it there.

One of the hands helped him get seated, gently moving his long hair to his front so he could sit down. "We ran into something in hyperspace. Lord knows what it was; probably a derelict ship would be my best guess. Knocked out the hyperdrive engines, and I can't get the sub-light engines started up. I have men on that, but we've no idea where we are. I need you to look at the viewport monitors of the star fields and figure out where we are. Can you do that?"

"Sure, if someone handles the controls for me," he replied. *No time to panic yet. Surely, I can recognize some of the star patterns,* he thought. He stared at the dots on the screen and the milky streak, which was the main body of the galaxy seen edge on. "Well, we're definitely near the rim of the galaxy, major," he offered his initial assessment. He swallowed. There were too few resolved stars to make any real guess as to their location. He had the assistant sweep around, slowly examining the skies about the ship, covering all three hundred sixty degrees of it. That alone convinced him they were far out on the rim. However, he felt sick at his stomach. He recognized nothing at all!

"We're lost, aren't we?" Major Jon finally broke in on his silence. He was both angry and frightened at the same time.

Renato swallowed hard. "Yes, we're lost. We're definitely on the rim of the galaxy, but lord knows where. I've never seen this star pattern, but that's not saying much. Do the instruments tell us anything? Hyperspace readouts?"

"Dead. The whole unit is gone. We got nothing," Major Jon sighed.

"So we're drifting?"

"Yes. At least, I have us stabilized. You should have seen it up here when we came out of hyperspace. Just looking at

115

that monitor made me dizzy. Used up half our reserve of onboard oxygen just to get us more or less stable. I'll know more when I can get the sub-light engines started. Keep on trying to figure out where we're at."

"Of course," Renato replied, though he didn't hold out much hope. He had never felt so utterly lost in his life. Nothing out there looked familiar except the Milky Way, and even it looked different from the many views he'd seen of it before. He wanted to scream, to cry, to wail, to curse, and to yell out that this couldn't be happening, not after all he and the others had endured—lost in space! Yet, he didn't. He'd already done all that when he awoke from the coma induced by the biogenetic attack on his world, one that left him completely helpless, dependent upon others just to survive. Oh, how he'd screamed then. Now? Well, they were just lost but alive and intact. Mechanically, he continued to stare at the star fields, wishing for a miracle he knew wasn't coming.

"We're screwed, major," one of the damage control men reported. "The whole damned hyperdrive engine is fried. We need a whole new one, boss."

"What about the sub-light engines? Why don't they start?" Major Jon asked, his face red with anger. It was all he could do to suppress the growing terror knot in his stomach. As long as he maintained anger, the knot stayed somewhat at bay.

"Not sure. We're working on that now." He turned and headed back to the rear of the ship.

A couple hours later, Major Jon again addressed the entire ship, outlining what little he knew. Yes, they were lost. Yes, the hyperdrive engine was toast. No, the sub-light engines were not in operation yet. Around the ship, many worried and frightened conversations echoed. At this point, Major Jon had little recourse but to send out a distress call. For an entire hour, he hovered around the comm center, hoping and praying that someone out there heard their calls for help. He tried all known frequencies, but only static hiss replied. At last, he gave that up as well.

During this time, Renato finally calmed down his own raging emotions and put himself wholly into the tasks. It

116

helped that Ann brought him some coffee and spooned it into his mouth for him. "Thanks. That hits the spot about now." After she left, he continued to calculate their trajectory. Well, his assistant did the actual data entry under his direction.

"Shit! That can't be right!" his assistant declared. "I must have goofed up something."

"No, you entered the data correctly. Look at the monitor screen. The red dwarf is definitely a magnitude brighter than it was two hours ago. We are heading straight for that small sun," Renato declared. A sickening feeling began to form in the pit of his stomach. "Major, you've got to see this and get those damned engines online soon!"

Two minutes later, Major Jon cursed a blue streak and smashed his fist into a chair. "Damn, damn, damn. We're heading straight for it, aren't we?"

"Actually, we're being pulled into it, major. We best get those engines going soon," Renato replied nervously.

An hour later, the red sun was significantly larger on the monitor, but still the sub-light engines refused to start! They were close enough to the sun that Renato could begin a search for habitable planets. *Why not?* He asked himself, since that's what everyone on the ship wanted, a new planet. Perhaps, there was one in this unknown system. *At least, it will give me something to do.* Slowly and methodically, he began his search, though his assistant operated the controls, a practice that annoyed Renato, but by now, he was used to being annoyed at nearly everything in life.

Two hours later on, they were close enough to the red dwarf system and its planetary system for Renato to conduct long-range scans. "At least, these instruments are still working," he muttered. It had several outer gas giants, and then he spotted a rocky planet. Focusing his attention on that one, his assistant worked the controls and entered the calculations for him. Its mass was a bit low, but it definitely had a compatible atmosphere for humans. At this point, Renato made the decision that would affect everyone on the ship.

"Major, we've found something—a planet that can support human life. It's just inside the orbits of those two gas giants. I think if we can somehow nudge this ship a bit towards the outer gas giant, its gravity will alter our course to intersect that of this new planet. I'd rather crash on a habitable planet than fall into the red sun."

"Well, finally we get a break. Okay, tell me what thrust vector you need, and I'll see if I can find a way to give it to you," Major Jon replied, grateful for a positive suggestion. Now he had something to occupy his mind besides worrying.

He had sufficient time. He had his crew fire up their single deep space transport and take off. The ship then attached a grappling line to the crippled cruiser and began to pull it in the proper direction under the guidance of Renato and his assistant. In an hour, they felt the gentle tug of the gas giant's gravity pull, and the slingshot effect permanently altered their course and speed. After a few more minutes of observations, Renato pronounced that they were on course for the habitable planet.

At this point, Major Jon again made the broad announcement to the entire ship. "We are heading for a new, habitable planet of this red dwarf star. With luck, we'll manage a safe landing. More when we know more. Out."

Wisely, Major Jon decided to disconnect the transport and send it on ahead to check out the planet and attempt to find a soft landing point. In addition, they would send back all manner of field reports on the planet, which Renato and Major Jon watched intently on their monitor. "Looking good so far. My, what a dense cloud cover," Renato observed.

An hour later, the transport reported that there were two continents beneath the dense cloud cover, but that the larger one was entirely too rough for a landing. Dropping below the clouds and in between two tall mountain ranges whose peaks poked above the cloudbanks, they spotted a zone of relatively flat land close to a large river. Major Jon decided to attempt to land there. When the transport returned and re-grappled the cruiser, it was Renato's job to work out thrust vectors the transport could provide to get the Zeta Zephyr on course to make landfall at that location.

A feverish hour passed, made all the longer because he couldn't just enter the data himself, rather he had to have his assistant calculate it and then enter it for him. Once again, he silently cursed his genetically modified body, for all the good that did him, which was none. Still, he held out a faint hope the major's men would be able to get the sub-light engines online in time to make a controlled landing. If not, well he rather not think about that.

A half hour before the calculations suggested they'd be landing, Major Jon again addressed the entire ship. "We are making for a relatively soft landing spot on this new world. At this time, I want everyone to strap themselves in tightly. If we don't get the engines online soon, it's going to be a hard landing. So make sure you are well padded and strapped in. Someone should make sure the livestock are also secure. I'll give you a five-minute warning. Out."

Twenty minutes out, Major Jon concluded the engines were not going to operate and had the transport grapple the cruiser from its rear and use all its reverse thrust to slow the ship down as much as possible, softening the hard landing as much as possible. In the end, this saved the lives of everyone on the ship. He gave the five-minute warning and then counted down the minutes and finally the seconds, figuring this would give the folks something to listen to instead of fretting.

The landing area was composed of very soft humus soil, further cushioning the landing. Nevertheless, it was a hard crash landing, jarring everyone and everything onboard. Later, his damage assessment men discovered the hull had been ripped apart and the central supporting I-beams had cracked. This ship would never fly again. Still, after the massive jolt, everyone held their breaths, expecting more. Explosions, fireballs, something. Only silence. Finally, Major Jon used the comm system to let everyone know the worst was over, but the comm system was now out.

He unstrapped Renato and headed down the corridors calling out his message, while ordering his crew members outside to survey the damage and the scene. Carefully, Renato made his way back to his cabin, where Lilly and Ann were waiting along with his wife, Isabella. "Well, we're down in one piece. That's something. Come on; he wants everyone outside."

Isabella admitted, "I was terrified. Thank the gods I married an astronomer!"

With Lilly supporting her and Ann supporting Renato, the four headed down the corridors making for the rear exit, trailing along behind all the others, most of whom could walk briskly. The ten and their assistants were the very last ones off the ship and to see their new world firsthand, aptly christened New Zeta.

Chapter 8—Establishment

Vastly different. Weird. Strange. Highly unusual. Spooky. Gloomy. Dismal. These were some of the first impressions the colonists had of the unknown planet on which they found themselves, though *strange* quickly took hold. Most took one look at the remains of the cruiser and realized that it wasn't ever going to fly again. None needed Major Jon's later damage assessment to tell them that. They were marooned here, but while this wasn't the planet they had planned to colonize, still, it was habitable, just very, very strange.

After many days, the group knew several facts. One, the dense cloud cover was a permanent feature of this world. The clouds never broke, though the degree of solid overcast did vary a very small amount. Two, each morning brought a very dense fog. One could only see three feet in front of oneself, though the fog broke by late morning. Three, everything was always red. Actually, the shades varied from dark and somber to a fiery red around noon and returning somber again later near dusk. Four, nearly every day, it rained at some point during the afternoon hours. Five, telling time and days was problematical. Soon, days were estimated to be closer to thirty hours long, but just how to adjust everyone's thinking about time and days never got resolved for quite some time. However, Major Jon began record keeping, based on their normal universal dating system of twenty-four hours per day and three hundred sixty-five days per year, wholly ignoring the actuality of the world around them. For over a score of years, this separate system of reckoning was carefully maintained, though it was finally abandoned. Six, there were no apparent seasons, though this wasn't finally concluded for nearly a year. Seven, the temperature variations were extremely unusual, varying from around the mid-sixties late at night to the low eighties in the mid-afternoon, dropping into the seventies after the rains ended.

Per the original agreements the colonists agreed to before they signed on, certain organizational and procedural matters became the basis for their new colony. The five hermaphrodite couples with their Academy degrees were the top rulers of the colony and were called given the title of *jefe*. Hence, *Jefe* Tito Alvaro and *Jefa* Luisa Alvaro became the rulers of their *tribu*. The colonists were equally divided among the five *tribu*. Each *tribu* began with another twenty-four subordinate colonists.

Four of these two dozen formed the *Querrero Agente* for the *tribu*, that is, the protection-fighters, charged with the total security of the *tribu*. Initially, they were armed with various weapons, including d-guns, though everyone knew eventually more primitive weapons would replace the high tech weapons, since they had no way to purchase more, build them, or even recharge them. One of the four, their leader, was chosen to be their *comandante*. Their wives and/or husbands became the *castillo siervo*, the servants, of the *jefe/jefa*, assisting the mostly helpless hermaphrodites, one of whom became their leader, the *major-domo*.

Another eight who had various trade skills became the *artesano* and would live with their *jefe* and *jefa*. They were charged with manufacturing all the necessities of life. The remaining eight were skilled farmers and were called the *granjero*. Their task was raising crops and animals.

The adopted system was indeed a feudal one, with everyone being a vassal of their *tribu*'s *jefe* and *jefa*. Part of the farmer's produce would be delivered to the others in the *tribu* in exchange for goods that they'd manufactured, the protection given them, or the knowledge and educations provided by the *jefe* and *jefa*.

Jefe Tito, elected to be the top-most ruler of the ten hermaphrodites, took charge at once. The various *agente* were sent out to reconnoiter the land around them, securing their perimeter. Others then began collecting samples of the plants, water, and animals they could find, bringing them back for Petrona and her fancy machine to analyze. The machine performed a chemical breakdown and identified what was safe and nourishing to eat and what was poisonous to the humans. Petrona insisted on putting everything through her analysis machine, since a wrong guess could result in death. They were too few to lose anyone through such carelessness.

Major Jon sent the transport out to survey the area. Within days, the colonists knew that their habitation zone extended some thousand miles across from the West Range to the East Range of mountains. The Zeta River, nearly a half mile wide at the ocean, divided the land in roughly half. The northeastern portion became called the Aspero Hills, rugged foothills from which the river sprang. Here was superb horse country. The northwestern portion was called the Huso Woods. Great stands of trees grew here, tall and spindly. The rest of the land was called East and West Fernland, since these relatively flat areas were filled with vast fields of these beautiful giant ferns, which their livestock quickly favored, even over the grain and hay they were being fed from the ship's stores.

Jefe Tito knew that they would have to learn to depend wholly on what their new planet could produce. Hence, the first week, under the watchful eyes of the many *agente*, everyone began scouring East Fernland for native plants and animals, bringing samples back for Petrona and her assistants to test. Quickly, they discovered no plants or animals, which were known to anyone. Here was a whole world filled with hitherto fore unknown species! While Petrona desired to give each a new, unique name, soon she backed off and began calling them what the colonists called them. "Hey, this one looks sort of like a sweet potato," one young woman said, bringing in the tuber for sampling. While it technically wasn't a sweet potato, it looked and tasted enough like one. The name stuck, as did all the other names the colonists called these new species, based on its similarity to what was familiar to them.

The agente did have work to do. The first day, wild boars were discovered, and a colonist was nearly gored to death before the giant pig-like creature was killed by a d-gun. It was roasted and served up for the evening's meal. It tasted pretty much like pork, and against Petrona's wishes, these animals were subsequently called boars.

A few days later, a cat-like creature now called a tiger was discovered. This was their worst predator, but fortunately, these cats soon gave the human settlements a wide berth. The following day, a herd of llama-like herd animals was found. Their wool was incredibly soft. They were quite docile creatures and easily tamed, feeding upon the ferns. Before too long, many were rounded up and became their primary source for clothing and eventually pack animals as well.

An exploratory trip to the Huso Woods yielded a major factor. All the trees, which grew here, were quite soft and spindly, often reaching towering heights, but they were weak. Their wood quickly rotted in this climate, while mushrooms flourished with wild abandon, many quite good to eat. Thus, permanent shelters could not be made from wood, because they'd rot away in less than a year. With the daily rains, permanent shelters had to be constructed and the only remaining construction material was stone, which was found aplenty in the two mountain ranges.

The rock was soon discovered to be extremely soft in comparison to the hard granites and basalt known to the colonists. Thus, by the second week, *Jefe* Tito realized that their new buildings would have to be made from stone. Hence, he established two quarrying operations, one in each of the two mountain ranges. The Manolo *Tribu* settled in the West Range, eventually building Manolo Castle, while the da Casa *Tribu* settled in the East Range, where *Jefe* Renato oversaw the construction of Casa Castle and even sooner the Escalera a las Estrellas, the stairway to the stars.

After two weeks on this dark, gloomy world, everyone was desperate to see the actual sky and stars, anything to break the horrible red gloom and fog. Besides, visibility was seldom even a mile distant. Hence, couples took a few days off every so often to make the journey to the East Range in order to climb above the cloud layer at Escalera a las Estrellas and finally *see* properly and to look at the spectacular sight with the gigantic galaxy spread out like a stream of milk in the nighttime sky, which was nearly devoid of stars in all other directions.

Laser cutters were used to quarry the stone, though everyone realized eventually stone would have to be cut and fashioned by hand tools, once the lasers could no longer be charged up from what power remained in their ship. Hence, part of *Jefe* Renato and *Jefe* Fidel's tasks was to search for usable ores. A mineralogy study was subsequently conducted, aided by Major Jon's crew.

To their initial dismay, the planet was extraordinarily rich in silicates but lacked most all heavier elements. No iron ores were found, only minute traces of that element. Copper and tin were located in the West Range. *Jefe* Fidel joked that their civilization would be always in the Bronze Age. Hence, since iron was needed for weapons and tools, among other things, *Jefe* Tito decided to use the remains of their ship as their iron ore mine. Over the subsequent years, he oversaw the cutting up of the ship, bit by bit, providing the steel that was needed by the colonists.

The Gonzalo *Tribu* settled in the Huso Woods, building their Gonzalo Castle there. Why? They discovered vast deposits of peat, which would supply everyone's need for cooking, smelting, pottery firing, and heat. In addition, they supplied vast quantities of mushrooms and nuts. They called them *pecans*, but whatever this new species was, it wasn't pecan trees, only that their nuts rather tasted like pecans. In time, other nut-bearing trees were located and given similar names, such as almonds and peanuts, which grew on a tree-like bush.

The Vega *Tribu* settled in the Aspero Hills. After constructing Castle Vega, they raised horses and cattle, which found the strange pale grasses more to their liking than the lower land's ferns. In addition, clay deposits were found here, suitable for pottery construction. Soon, all the pottery needs were met by the Vega Tribu.

Jefe Tito Alvaro built their Castle Alvaro not far from the ship in East Fernland, close to the Zeta River. Here, they eventually raised herds of the llama-like creatures, providing the cloth needs of the colony. In addition, he oversaw the slow cutting up of the ship's steel. However, from day one, he knew none of their seed crops would grow on this world. The red sunlight that made it through the dense clouds was insufficient for their plants. Hence, with assistance from *Jefa* Petrona, he began crop cultivation using native, edible plants, beginning with the *sweet potatoes*.

Three months after their arrival on New Zeta, *Jefe* Tito decided the survival situation was well under control. No new surprises had surfaced for a couple of weeks. Major Jon had given up all hope of salvaging much from the cruiser and had not made any contacts with his Mayday calls on any known frequency. Further, Renato continued to study the star formations from his East Range perch at Escalera a las Estrellas above the dense cloud layer, but was unable to get any better hold on their position within the galaxy.

Hence, *Jefe* Tito reasoned the next step in their long-term survival was procreation. With everyone convinced beyond any doubt this was going to be their new permanent home, the time to establish formal breeding methods was at hand. Women were their most precious and valuable *commodity*, for without new children, their colony would die off with this generation. Complicating the issue was the comparatively small gene pool, only one hundred-twenty men and women, most already married. Thus as previously agreed to, New Zeta became a matriarchal society. That is, the women owned the homes and lands, supervising their operations.

Initially, every couple was allowed two offspring before beginning inner breeding with others. Children from the crossbreeding would belong to the mother and be raised in the mother's home. All parents had to teach their children all that they knew, passing their skills and knowledge on down to their offspring.

The long-range plans called for the hermaphrodite children of the ten *tribu* leaders to move off and establish new villages, following the same pattern as the founders. That is, the newly married hermaphrodite pair, the new *jefe* and *jefa*, would take with them four new *Querrero Agente* for their new *tribu*, while their four wives would become the new *castillo siervo*, the servants, of the *jefe* and *jefa*. Another eight newly trained, young *artesano* would go with them and live with their *jefe* and *jefa*. Finally, another eight young men and women, trained by their parents in farming skills, went with them as their new *granjero*.

Thus, as their children grew into adulthood, *Jefa* Luisa's eldest daughter would marry another hermaphrodite and form up her two dozen subordinates. They would then eventually replace her mother's group when they passed away. All other daughters of *Jefa* Luisa would marry and form up their own sub-*tribu* and establish a new village not far from Castle Alvaro. Her male offspring would marry another *tribu*'s daughters and move to her new location. Initially, *Jefa* Luisa anticipated that when she retired of old age, there would likely be two more villages around her Castle Alvaro. In the following generations, the numbers would continue to grow rapidly, forming a unified, solid base for everyone's long-term survival.

However, not all was ideal in the normal human colonists' minds. This procedure forced all their children to remain in the same positions that their parents' had. Born a farmer, always a farmer. That didn't go over well with the hundred-twenty others. Thus, a compromise was reached.

Beginning with a woman's third child, she could request to be bred by one of the hermaphrodites or any other male of her choice. While no one actually knew what such a union with an hermaphrodite would bring in such children, it was hoped that one of more of these children would also be born as an hermaphrodite. If so, then that child would be raised by one of the other *jefa* women and trained with all the knowledge that the *jefa* possessed, as though the child was her own. This offered a way for a farmer's wife to have a child who could become a ruler.

Further, Jefe Tito agreed that each normal human child should be given a choice in his or her training, subject to their capabilities, intelligence, and the world's needs. In this way, a farmer's child had a route that he or she could follow to become an *agente*, a *castillo siervo,* or an *artesano.* If the child needed to be trained in a discipline that their parents didn't possess, then the child would be fostered by an appropriate alternate family, thus allowing the child to have a different societal position from their parents.

Initially, those in the *castillo siervo* group had a special skill, the ability to understand the garbled speech of the *jefe* and *jefa,* whose giant lip disks prevented them from making certain vocal sounds, such as those produced by the lips. Indeed, most colonists found their rulers very hard to understand and allowed their servants to repeat what their rulers had said, but that aspect changed in a rather dramatic way, but not until long after Major Jon and his crew departed from New Zeta.

That happened eight months from the crash landing. At this point, *Jefe* Tito had made all the uses he could from the deep space transport, the major, and his men, who had helped on castle construction and the ferrying of cut stone from the two mountain ranges. For the last couple of weeks, the major and his twenty men were idle, and Tito reasoned it was time to let them go. They hadn't signed on to become colonists, just ferrying their passengers to their new world.

Thus, loaded with plenty of food stores and double the usual number of fuel cells, Major Jon and his crew departed from New Zeta. *Jefe* Renato gave him his best guess at where they were and what route to try first. All the colonists hoped and prayed that somehow Major Jon would find the civilized worlds and eventually return with far more supplies, establishing solid trade with other worlds, particularly for steel. Unfortunately, Major Jon and his crew vanished from history, their fate unknown to those on New Zeta, though for several years *Jefe* Tito didn't give up hope that they would return one day, loaded with supplies for them.

A year after they arrived on their new world, everyone was eating locally grown food. The stores of grain and supplies they'd brought with them had long been exhausted. At this point in time, it happened. The first to be affected was *Jefa* Luisa. One morning as she was staring off into the dense fog just outside her window, she began hearing voices of her servants in her head! Later when she was dining with the others, the combined *noise* of all the others around the table became annoyingly deafening. Tito noticed something was wrong with his pregnant wife, though he too was also pregnant.

After they finished eating, or rather being fed by their servants, he took her aside, presumably to check on their babies. "Dearest, what's wrong? I sensed you were most troubled as we dined," he whispered gently to her.

"Voices. I keep hearing their voices inside my head!

Deafening. Oh Tito, what's happening to me?" she wailed, releasing her fears and worries.

It didn't take Tito long to discover that Luisa had somehow miraculously developed telepathy! At once, he began training her in how to block the thoughts of others and to keep from broadcasting her thoughts to others. He no more than got her stabilized when several of their servants complained of the same thing! Inside of a month, every colonist developed telepathic ability!

For the next two months until he couldn't travel any longer being in his ninth month, Jefe Tito trained each of the one hundred twenty colonists in how to handle their newly developed telepathy. Of course, no one had the slightest idea how or why they suddenly developed this incredible gift, only that everyone had. Later on, they discovered all their children also possessed basic telepathic abilities. As hopeful as Tito was that they'd also develop other mental gifts similar to those he had, such never materialized. Years later, Jefe Tito discovered the basic soil of New Zeta was flush with silicon and germanium crystals, and he wondered if that had anything to do with their gift of telepathy. Certainly, Ashford-5 had a similar composition.

A year after their landing, a new problem arose. Nearly every couple now had a baby to raise, including the ten hermaphrodites, each of whom had a child, following the guidelines *Jefe* Tito had established. The complaint was a simple one. Since this was now supposed to be a matriarchal society, how could the colonists tell which of the hermaphrodites was to be given the high honor of being the woman, since for all practical purposes, physically there wasn't any difference between Jefe Tito and Jefa Luisa. (There was one, but it hardly counted. Their urine came out from different locations.)

True, both had the same ten-inch lip disks. Each had to wear a tight corset to help their back support the heavy weight of their enormous breasts, made even heavier now that they were both nursing. Since every colonist demanded an answer to this question, Tito took their complaint seriously. While there was obviously an observable physical difference between male and female colonists, such didn't exist between the hermaphrodites.

"Look, Luisa, we have to solve this one somehow," he explained while they lay on their sides nursing their newborns. "With us, it is simply how we ourselves have chosen to view our positions in life."

"I know dearest. I chose to adopt the ways of the human females. It suits my temperament, as you well know. And you, the strong leader. I know. We've chosen our own paths. But they have a point. We look so much alike. It's important, dear, now that we've made this a matriarchal society. I figured this point would be raised one day, but I kind of hoped it wouldn't." She giggled slightly.

"So what do we do? We need a visible way for them to tell the difference between our bodies," he replied.

"Well, women traditionally like to decorate themselves with jewelry and such, though wearing a broach probably isn't going to cut it. Anyone could don one," she suggested. "No, we need something that is truly unique and that can't easily be removed, something that sets me apart from you. Let me think on it a bit."

Gemstones had yet to be found, but the copper-tin alloys that made bronze were just coming into full production. The initial goal was to provide bronze utensils and vessels for cooking and food storage, in case there were actual seasons on New Zeta. While looking at their new, shiny, golden goblets and silverware, Luisa got an idea.

"Dearest, what about us hermaphrodite women wearing bronze neck rings? They would stand out at a glance," she suggested.

"Hum, you have a good idea there. They'd match your lip disks well, and they'd be rather hard to put on and take off. Certainly, we couldn't manage doing that ourselves," Tito replied.

He summoned his new bronze-smith, and Luisa explained her idea to him. Bill responded well, as Tito hoped he would. "Why yes, golden neck rings would let everyone know that you were the matriarch of this *tribu*! But they should be a work of art. Let me see what I can devise, *Jefa*

Luisa."

During the next few days, Bill and Luisa experimented with various designs for neck rings. One ring wasn't sufficient, so he stacked several rings, one on top of the other. While the overall look was pleasing, the loose rings didn't work well as far as Luisa was concerned. They slipped and slid over each other, but Bill explained that he dared not make them smaller in diameter, for they might choke her. After more experimentation, Bill found a way to keep them from slipping and sliding over each other. By careful design, he added to the series of inch-wide rings until the last one fit against the others very tightly. While it made her neck immobile, the rings stayed put and didn't slip and slide around. No longer did her servants have constantly to readjust them for her.

"This is much better, Bill. Only now I can't move my head at all," she explained.

"That was the idea. It holds them securely in place, my *jefa*," Bill countered.

She added, "But look at me. I'm so golden this way. Everyone can tell at a glance that I'm the woman here, can't they?"

"You bet they can," Bill replied, pleased she didn't object strenuously to his latest idea. He had run out of notions to try. If she didn't like this one, he had no idea what to try next.

"Since my servants do everything for me anyway, this shouldn't be much of a problem. Let's see what Tito thinks about it and everyone else here too," she suggested, knowing their opinion mattered a very great deal. She knew the normal humans just had to have a way to tell the difference between those hermaphrodites who chose to play the role of the "female" and those who chose the role of "male." To resolve this potential rift between the colonists, she accepted a little more discomfort and restriction, especially since her new look was praised by all those in her *tribu*.

The final obstacle these new rulers faced was how to train and educate their hermaphrodite offspring. Lacking arms, they couldn't write anything down. They couldn't ask their servants to constantly hold book pages for them, and the computers' batteries would soon lose their charges forever, unless Major Jon somehow returned, something few believed would happen. Everything would have to be done orally, which turned out to be a monumental challenge, one that over time slowly failed.

Still two years after their landing, their population had doubled, most encouraging. Further, all were convinced this world didn't have seasons. The weather was always perpetually warm and humid. However, the constant gloomy, red overcast and fog nearly drove them all mad. At least four times a year, everyone just had to make the journey to the Escalera a las Estrellas to view the real world and the nighttime skies. Thus began a tradition that future generations would follow, though the bodies of their children and children's children began to change and adapt to this new and strange world of New Zeta.

This much of the early history of New Zeta is known because Lilly and Ann continued to make digital recordings of the events that happened during the first two years. After that, the computer's power failed completely. However, Tito ordered the solid-state drive containing the record be preserved in a sealed, weatherproof box, and guarded at his castle for posterity.

***

Present day, 2007. Nearly half a millennium past on New Zeta, whose known population surpassed the five hundred thousand mark. Why so little? Food resources and wars constrained them, though many believed that some of their ancestors had managed to travel across the oceans to another land, while others believed that many had traveled beyond the two edges of the world, namely the two mountain ranges, East Range and West Range, which marked those borders of their world. Still others claimed that ancestors moved north beyond the known forest and hills, that is the Huso Woods and Aspero Hills, but today none who lived here in New Zeta had any actual knowledge of what may lay beyond those borders, for none ever dared travel that far into the dim unknown. The tale of the evolution of these people and their society must have been quite interesting, for today, their world and society are vastly different than that defined by *Jefe* Tito.

132

Chapter 9—First Contact

"Good God! We can't see a blasted thing," Hard Ass declared, as she and her platoon swarmed out of the Hyperion onto New Zeta. It was around noon, local time. Overhead, one had a hint of a red orb up there, giving the dense clouds a rather crimson or bright red color or hue. However, visibility was far less than a mile. Worse, they had landed in the middle of a giant fern patch. Four foot tall, pale green ferns surrounded everything, hiding the soft, spongy ground beneath their feet.

Major Lu Ann barked orders, finally looking at her. "Captain Janine, have your platoon setup a defensive perimeter around the Hyperion. This planet is inhabited, but likely by primitives. Use stun settings and set up the electro field poles about five feet apart. We can't see anyone or anything until they are on top of us. Stay alert. There could be wild animals and snakes here too." She then began issuing other orders to her repair crews while Hard Ass barked her corresponding orders. All this happened before Peter, Kathy, and Dr. Alison finally made it outside of the ship and got their first look at the world they'd crash-landed upon.

Wobbling wildly on the soft ground, she maneuvered around so she could see what had happened to the LD array, knowing that getting it to work was vital if they were ever going to be rescued. The diagnosis was correct. The cannon fire from the attacking CAM ships had definitely disintegrated the entire array. Only mounting bolts remained. Well, their spare one could be mounted, which meant that she really did have to get that motherboard repaired so they could call for help.

The three wobbled about just trying to stand in one position while watching the many activities going on. Crew members and her sister were rushing about. They saw Janine and her group carrying pole-like devices. Peter explained for Kathy, "Those are the electric fences. They'll set them up about five or six feet apart all around the ship. When they are turned on, they will act as an electric fence, which won't allow anyone or any creature past them. They'll get an electric shock if they try. That way, we can be safe here."

Kathy replied, "Cool. Now I feel safer. But daddy, are there wild animals around here? I heard some say that there are primitives on this world. What's a primitive? Are they dangerous?"

"Less civilized people. That's what I think they mean."

Dr. Alison added, "As we approached this world, we didn't detect any signs of a modern, space faring world, Kathy. No power plants, no space ships, no orbiting satellites, no electrical grid, and no TV or radio signals. But they did see signs of human habitations."

"Okay, but what signs?" she asked naively.

"They used infrared scanners, which pick up body heat. Otherwise, you can't see through these dense clouds," she explained. "So they saw lots of human-like bodies down here, but I don't know where they were located from where we landed," Dr. Alison answered as best she could.

"So they could be close or far. I get it. But what are they like? If they don't have TV and electricity, how can they even live?" Kathy asked. "And how soon are these clouds going away so we can see everything? Is it almost night time?"

Dr. Alison smiled. "Kathy, this is high noon. It's as bright as it's going to get. I bet the nights are pitch black here. I think the scouts suggested the clouds never clear up. It's so dismal here."

"I agree, mom. Dismal," Kathy said, inserting a subtle hint to Dr. Alison of what she really wanted. "I sure wouldn't want to live here."

"I don't think anyone of us wants to stay here any longer than needed to get the ship repaired or to get rescued, honey," Dr. Alison replied, giving Peter a nod. He smiled back as well, while wobbling a bit just to keep standing up.

Kathy saw a number of the children dashing about the ferns. "I wish I could go play with them, but I don't think I can, daddy."

"Nope. It's all I can do to keep from falling down just standing here. This ground is really soft and spongy. It must be water logged," Peter suggested. Just then, they heard the sound of thunder in the distance, and a few sprinkles began to fall. However, those outside ignored that, continuing their work.

Janine finally walked up to her sister. "Well, that's done. We should be safe now. Got the electric fence up all around the ship. Best go report that to the major. Dismal world."

Dr. Alison laughed, "That's what we just said here. Dismal." Janine smiled and spotted the major. She began moving towards her to make her report.

Just then from several locations, sparks flew, along with startled cries. Everyone turned to look towards the north. "Put the lights on the fence there," Major Lu Ann barked, drawing her own small d-gun.

"Crap," barked Janine. "First Squad, to me. Second squad, form up down there. Keep alert. Something is trying to get through the fence!" Dr. Alison, Peter, and Kathy continued to stay where they were, merely wobbling to keep afoot, while all around them, men and women rushed to take up defensive positions. Everyone strained their eyes to see what was out there, some hundred feet beyond the ship. The tall ferns and pathetically dim light made spotting anything difficult.

Suddenly, a dozen native men stood up above the tops of the ferns. Each carried a bronze shield, and a sword or a spear. A band of gold metal surrounded their heads, but their heads looked large. In addition, they were quite tall and thin. The shortest, Hard Ass estimated, was at least six feet tall, while the tallest of these men had to be over seven feet tall. Their skin was a ghastly pale white. Their eyes seemed gigantic in size, but perhaps that was due to the poor lighting. They wore a brownish loincloth and leather-like sandals, though the latter wasn't visible initially. They said nothing, but observed the rather large group.

After a minute, several pointed to Dr. Alison and Peter. More undecipherable grunts and gestures directed towards them followed. "Are they the primitives, daddy? Will they hurt us?" Kathy asked.

"Yes, but I don't think they can get close enough to harm us, dear. Aunt Janine and her soldiers will protect us,"

Peter answered, feeling more helpless by the minute. He was a trained security guard, but now all that training was useless. He couldn't do a thing to protect his daughter.

"But why are their heads so tall?" she asked. No one answered.

Meanwhile, everyone else was talking. Major Lu Ann's voice barked above the others. "Okay. This is a first contact situation. Let's not make enemies of them if we don't have to. Jonesey, see if you can establish communication with them. Who are they pointing at?" Someone told her that it was Dr. Alison and Peter. Then, Jonesey walked slowly towards the electric fence.

The armed natives watched his approach, but didn't otherwise react. When he was sufficiently close, Jonesey began speaking, saying "Hello," in one language after the other, looking for a response from the six men. He got none. Then, the six men backed up and disappeared into the ferns. "Well, that didn't work well," Jonesey exclaimed, walking back to the major. "I tried every language I know. They didn't respond to any, and they didn't say a single word, major."

She barked, "Okay Jonesey. Stick around. They might be back. Okay everyone listen up. Natives have found us. So watch yourselves. Captain Janine, keep your platoon on constant patrol around our entire perimeter. I don't think their weapons will give us much trouble. Still, we can't afford to be speared or cut up by those swords. Do we have an archaeologist or anthropologist among us? If anyone has any such training, have them report to me at once. Otherwise, carry on everyone." Everyone headed back to their duties, still chatting about the weird looking men.

A bit later, Major Lu Ann came over to Dr. Alison and Peter. Her alto voice said calmly, "Well, you two certainly got their attention, just as you do the members of my crew. I guess some things are universal."

Dr. Alison chuckled. "Indeed. Did you see their heads? I swear that they were at least twice as large as ours are. What does that mean?"

Now it was the major's turn to chuckle. "Doctor, if I knew that, why, I wouldn't need an anthropologist. Hell if I know. You three stay here close to the ship. I don't want them returning and trying to abduct you two hot babes," she jested. Alison smiled, but Peter flushed.

After a moment, Peter said, "Major, they will be back, probably bringing reinforcements with them. Will the fence be enough to hold them?" He looked down at Kathy, and Major Lu Ann picked up his hint.

"Oh, I'm sure the fence will keep them back. I think you are right. They will be back in force next time. Probably just a scouting party," she answered. "Still, I don't want to antagonize these primitives if we don't have to. Besides, I've no idea how long we're going to be stranded here. If we run low on food, we may have to depend upon them to tell us what is safe to eat. Those heads of theirs—I've never seen anything like it. Tall heads. I think that's what we'll call them for now. Times like these, I sure wish we had an anthropologist onboard. I admit I'm out of my league on this one."

"Well, if no one else comes forward," Peter volunteered, "I've done a little studying in that area. I've always been interested in digging up old fossils on Ragnar-B and took a few courses in it. I know enough to know you're going about this the right way—by not antagonizing them. If they come back, we need to figure out their language. Has Jonesey tried all the languages he knows? We couldn't hear much over here. Did those strange men say anything back to him?"

"No. They didn't make a sound, and Jonesey tried all the languages he knows. I guess I should see if anyone has linguistic skills. Good idea. I'm making you my official anthropologist, Peter, unless someone else shows up who has more training. I'll go see about a linguist now." She turned and ordered one of her aides to go inside to search the personnel records.

She then asked, "So Peter, any idea why their heads are so tall? Why they are so darn pale, almost like ghosts? Why they are so tall? I swear some had to be seven feet or more."

"If this is as bright as the days get on this world, then you can expect their skin pigments to be this pale. That's my guess anyway. I heard someone say this world is lighter than Ragnar-B, so maybe that accounts for their heights. I suspect if this is as bright as it ever gets, then their eyes have adapted to it. My guess, major, is their eyes see well in this infernal gloom, while we can't see beyond a short distance."

"That might account for their giant-sized eyes, if eyes those were," she mused. "Ah, then they probably won't like our bright lights." She ordered another aide to setup another bank of quartz lights, training them onto the perimeter, ready to be turned on with a moment's notice.

Just then, the electric fence fired again, attracting all eyes towards the noise. They saw a herd of strange looking, furry animals gathered near the fence. Those farther away were munching on the ferns, while those who had gotten shocked bolted away into the ferns, out of sight in a few seconds. "Damn this dim light. We can't see much until they are on top of us. What are those creatures?" Major Lu Ann barked.

Someone close to where they were yelled back, "Major. They look rather like llamas, sort of. Docile enough."

"Daddy, can I pet one?" Kathy asked. "Oh!" She shut up, realizing that she no longer had hands to pet them, even if they allowed her to do so. Wisely, Peter didn't answer right away.

"We should observe them from a distance. They are wild animals, I suspect," he finally answered her, and she seemed satisfied with that and didn't start crying, which is what both Peter and Dr. Alison thought would happen.

Meanwhile, Peter began to suspect this herd of llamas was there for some purpose. Perhaps, he thought, the natives were using them to test out the fence defense. Shortly after that, his suspicions were confirmed. Hundreds of natives suddenly appeared, but stood just at the edge of the fence. "Crap!" Major Lu Ann exclaimed. "We're surrounded. Okay, everyone. High alert. Remember, this is a first contact situation. We don't want to make enemies if we don't have to." She moved a little closer to Peter, knowing that if he had any advice for her, he couldn't come to her with it.

At first, they squinted to see these men. All were as tall as the first six. All were very pale skinned and had what appeared to be very tall heads. Their hair was black and short. All were armed with shields, spears, and swords, probably bronze, Peter guessed from their golden color, if it was truly golden colors he was seeing in this very dim red light.

Several men and women who were close to the fence tried calling out various greetings, but got no response. Then, they detected movement in the ferns behind the men. Suddenly, ten women appeared. Once more, everyone stopped and stared at these women, who were even stranger looking than the men. True, while they were equally tall, thin, and ghastly pale with large eyes, they also only wore a loincloth, their breasts, bare. Their hair was long and likely never cut, Dr. Alison guessed, based on its length, falling to below their knees, much like hers and Peter's and even Kathy's now. All had black hair. No variation there.

Rather what got their full attention was the fact that they seemed to have very tall necks, surrounded in golden disks! Further, each woman had her lips slit and wore enormous golden lip disks. Some were ten inches in diameter, while others were more like a foot across. From the first sighting of the women, everyone could tell two details about them. One, their necks were immobile. Two, all stood with perfect posture.

However, none of the natives had yet uttered a single sound, even though all around the ship, men and women were talking among themselves and occasionally talking towards the natives, who simply didn't respond verbally. Very strange, thought Major Lu Ann, wholly uncertain what to do next. *I'm not trained for this kind of mission. What do I do?* She ordered, "Okay, hold your positions. Don't fire unless they attack." Just then, all hell broke out.

One of the privates in Captain Janine's platoon took clumsy steps towards one of the electric poles. "Benson, what are you doing?" Hard Ass yelled at him. The man seemed to be in some sort of trance. He ignored her and everyone else, and slowly his hand reached out for the control switch. "Benson, stop that!" she yelled. His hand jerked forward and backwards several times as though he was fighting against some kind of overriding force. Two others moved over towards him to restrain him, but too late. His fingers turned the switch off.

These primitive warriors seemed prepared for this and

rushed through the five-foot break in the fence barrier, waving their swords and spears. "Fire at will," yelled Hard Ass. The two who had almost reached Benson drew their weapons. Again, one seemed to hesitate but the other fired. He was using the stun setting and one of the pale-skinned natives went down.

More streamed through the breech. Half of the platoon stood frozen in place, unable to move or fire or even defend themselves, but Hard Ass and the rest of her platoon began firing as fast as they could, while dodging the swinging swords. Major Lu Ann thought, *I don't want to kill these primitive people*. However, with some twenty-five of them now attacking her people, she acted. Her alto voice barked, "Flood lights on now!" Instantly, the hastily installed bank of ten quartz floods fired up, casting brilliant daylight on the entire area on this side of the ship.

The reaction was just as she hoped. The attackers cried out, shielding their eyes with their hands, and stumbled back outside the fence as fast as they could go, while the others outside covered their eyes, seemingly in great pain, and backed far away, before ducking down hiding in the heavy ferns.

"What the hell just happened?" the major barked. "Why did you turn off the fence? Why didn't your soldiers fire?" she yelled angrily.

Benson threw his hands up to his temples, rubbing his head. He mumbled, "Inside my head. Something was inside my head, forcing me to turn it off. I didn't want to. I tried to not do it, but it was too powerful."

"Same here, captain. I tried to shoot, but something took over my body. I couldn't move a muscle," another called out. Within a minute, the others who failed to defend the ship called out similar stories.

Hard Ass yelled to the major, "They're right. I felt it too. Like something was trying to overpower my mind. I fought it off."

"Hey, so did I," Fel called out. Many other "me too's" echoed from the others who were able to fight back.

"What the heck is going on? Who? How is this

possible?" yelled Major Lu Ann over the confusion of everyone talking at once. "Medics, front and center. Looks like we have wounded. Captain Janine, get those stunned natives out beyond the fence. We can't have them waking up inside our perimeter. What the hell?" She threw her hands up to her head as though fighting off an attacker.

***

Some hours before this, one of *Jefe* Sancho Alvaro's *agente* reported to him at Castle Alvaro. *Yes, Comandante Sancho, I have confirmed it. Cloud people have descended all over New Zeta. What are your orders?* Rumors suggested that mysterious flying things had appeared in the clouds, and he'd sent his trusted man out to confirm them. No one spoke. No one ever did. They had no spoken language nor any need of one. Telepathy was nearly instantaneous, and concepts seldom were misunderstood.

The imposing seven-foot tall Sancho, now in his mid-forties, ran his hands over his tall head, beginning with his bronze band, something he often did when working out serious problems. The arrival of these mysterious cloud flying birds was just such a one, far worse than the war-like encroachment of the Vega *Tribu* from their hill lands down into the fertile northern fern lands of Alvaro. *Just what are these mysterious birds?*

Sancho sat on his throne in the Great Hall of Castle Alvaro. True, the soft stone steps were worn with age and countless footsteps of his ancestors. Even his throne seat was quite worn down, despite his soft seat of llama wool. Nearby, his wife, *Jefa* Adelina, sat perfectly erect on her Judgment Throne. While she had no say in what he did, it would be her duty to adjudicate the matter, should anything come from this mysterious appearance. She was forty-two with soft black hair that reached just below her knees. Sancho glanced her way. Such a beauty she is, he thought, so perfect. Like all women of New Zeta, her head was held immobile by the many tight-fitting neck rings, which at her age gave her the appearance of having a very long neck, befitting that of the *tribu*'s supreme adjudicator, their *jefa*, her sole real duty. Of course, the immobile neck forced her to have perfect posture at all times, just as it did for all women.

Her lip plates were the largest of any woman of the Alvaro *Tribu*, some eighteen inches in diameter, befitting the *tribu*'s adjudicator. Only the four other *tribu*'s adjudicator's lip plates as large as hers, though all women wore them. Adorning a woman with their neck rings and lip plates marked their rite of passage from that of a girl into the flower of womanhood, and usually occurred after her first bleeding. During her special ceremony attended solely by the women of her *tribu*, she was given her neck rings, her lips were slit, and her first plates installed. Over time, the lip loops stretched, requiring larger plates. However, no one was allowed to have them larger than their tribu's *jefa*.

However, *Jefa* Adelina also had no arms, just like the other four *tribu*'s *jefa*. This tradition extended far back into the dawn of their history, though on one living knew the real reason for this detail. When the *tribu* selected a new *jefa*, due to either the retirement or death of their current *jefa*, this most honored woman would undergo the anointing ceremony during which her arms were removed and burned as an offering to the gods, ensuring that they would guide her in making her future *tribu* adjudications. *Jefa* Adelina had been *Jefe Comandante* Sancho's wife for over twenty years now, having ascended to the throne upon her mother's untimely death.

Using her feet, she pivoted to look at Sancho. *Jefe, what do these flying things mean? Should we be worried? Some new invention from the de Casa Tribu or Menolo Tribu, perhaps?*

No, that cannot be. I'll send out armed patrols to observe these mysterious flying bird things. Then, we will know more, Comandante Sancho replied. He gave the order to his *agente*, who bowed respectfully and departed to carry out his orders.

Jefe Comandante Sancho Alvaro led close to one hundred twenty-five thousand men and women in the Alvaro *Tribu*. Many were artisans and farmers, spread out across East and West Fern Land, on either side of the Zeta River. Here, they raised both crops and llama herds, which provided all their cloth needs. Both men and women only wore a llama wool loincloth. With the constant mild temperatures, nothing more was needed or desired, though at night, everyone slept on and under llama wool blankets. Also, they wore sandals made from the hides of cattle to protect their feet from sharp rocks, particularly in rockier areas.

The *comandante* position meant he was actually the supreme leader of his entire *tribu,* and he had well over ten thousand *agente* or fighters under his command. It was their job to protect the entire *tribu* from attacks from the other four *tribu.* Wars were commonplace on New Zeta, though in all these centuries, none of the five had ever achieved domination over the Alvaro *Tribu,* for whom luck always seemed to be on their side. Many claimed their luck came from their taller heads. *Jefe* Sancho knew better. It came from superior fighting skills and tactics, along with their efficient intelligence gathering methods.

That's just what he needed now, intelligence. Soon, if not already, the other *tribu* would know about the sudden appearance of these flying bird things. Even the lowest *granjero* or farmer tilling their fields could see far up into the clouds and spot these *hot* things, which appeared redder and hotter than their own sun. So yes, *Jefe Comandante* Sancho was under pressure to ascertain the meaning of these flying bird things.

Hours later, he finally received word from six scouts whose report was even more chilling than the sudden appearance of the flying things. Cloud people. They reported one of these giant flying things sat down amid a fern field, and strange human-like people swarmed out of it. Carefully, he had the frightened *agente* describe them, and he listened carefully, as did *Jefa* Adelina, who may well have to perform her adjudication skills.

Sire, they are all short in stature, but they wear strange apparel. Some are men; some are women, at least we think so. They have brought many strange things with them, out of the flying thing. They make many strange noises we cannot understand. What are your orders? he asked.

Do they have swords and spears? he inquired.

Nay sire. They have set up strange poles around their flying thing. Yet, they may be like us, a tribu.

What? How can that be?

Well, maybe two tribu are there. We have seen two jefa-like women, though they don't compare to you, your majesty. They're not adorned properly and hide their bodies beneath strange apparel.

I see. If they don't have swords and spears, perhaps they aren't warlike.

Nay sire. These strange poles cause us great pain when we try to pass them. Much like the stone walls that keep the llama herds in their fields. Many seem to be carrying what may be weapons at their sides, much as we carry our swords, sire.

Then, they must be here to attack us, Jefe Comandante Sancho concluded. *How many of these strange human-like creatures are there?*

We counted nearly two hundred, but some keep going back into the flying thing, and others come out. So we are not sure, sire.

Okay. Sound the alarm. Round up four hundred agente. We must go to this flying ship and see for ourselves what threat they pose to us, he ordered.

Jefa Adelina spoke up, *Jefe, they may not be warlike. We should first see what their intentions are. I so declare. I must see them for myself.*

But this could be dangerous, my jefa, but it shall be as you have decided, he conceded her point. After all, he needed her adjudication if he wanted to declare war on these potential enemies. Besides, perhaps this flying thing was made of the rare metal. If so, capturing this flying thing would be worth more than all the Alvaro *Tribu* combined! The ancient steel swords and spear tips were the most valuable items anywhere on New Zeta.

The flying machine lay on the ground some two miles from Castle Alvaro proper, though only the top of the thing could be seen from the tallest castle tower. As the large group assembled and headed out of the protection of the stone castle, four *castillo siervo* women accompanied *Jefa* Adelina, two keeping a steadying arm around her, preventing any accidental fall she might have.

Two hours later, the large group could see the flying thing and the myriad human-like creatures around it, but wisely, they stayed well back from it. Soon, *Jefe* Sancho realized a key detail. *Jefa, these aliens are mostly blind! Look, they can't even see us, while we can easily see and smell them from here. They can't see my agente until they are near those pole things. That gives us a decided advantage.*

My jefe, what is the meaning of all the noise they make with their mouths? They are all making many strange noises, all the time, Jefa Adelina asked. *I'm confused. I sense minds but they are quiet, not like us.*

Jefe Comandante Sancho declared, *Quiet minds, like llamas and cows. Perhaps, these are mere primitives and not real people, like us, my jefa.*

She replied, *Yes, primitives. That must be what they are. And yet they are able to fly. How? Where did they come from? Beyond the mountains perhaps? If so, why have we never heard of these primitives before?*

I don't know, my jefe. I think we should move in close and see what their true intentions are here. We will have to force them to remove that strange hurting pole thing.

Yes. We must make first contact with these strange foreign primitives. If we do not, soon the other tribu will come and make their own attempts to contact them. They are on our land, so it is our duty and obligation to find out their purposes, friendly or not. Our tribu is depending upon us, my jefe, she adjudicated, giving him the okay to proceed with making the first contact with these strange primitive people, if people they actually were.

They appeared so very strange to her eyes. Meanwhile, she scanned over the hundreds, looking for their *jefa*. Two had been reportedly sighted before. Finally, she found them. How very, very strange they appeared to her large eyes. She'd never seen such monstrous bosoms before, though well hidden from sight beneath the shiny looking apparel they wore. Are they horribly disfigured, she wondered? Why would any sentient being hide their bodies almost totally from view? She concluded they must be horribly disfigured, a ghastly sight for them to wear all that apparel. She watched as the many well-armed *agente* moved in closer to the strange poles and this swarm of primitives, amazed none of the primitives had yet even spotted them. *Are they truly blind?*

In awe, she watched as several got too close to one of the poles. She saw sparks flying, and heard and sensed the cries of pain from the men. *Agente* Rodrigo saw one of the primitives drawing what must be a weapon and moving towards the pole. He focused and attempted to take control of the primitive's mind. *Turn it off,* he ordered. The primitive fought against his will, but Rodrigo's will was stronger. The man did as ordered, the pole went inert, and his *agente* flooded through the opening. Rodrigo reported to *Jefe Comandante* Sancho, *Jefe, their wills are weak like llamas and cows. Ah, they have mysterious weapons!*

The unexpected battle began. Several of his *agente* fell to the ground, presumably dead. In retaliation, he ordered a full-scale attack. He sent, *Force them not to use those strange weapons of theirs!* Battlefield chaos ensued for several minutes.

While this was going on, *Jefa* Adelina tried to make sense of what she was seeing and sensing. *Jefe* Scancho was focused on the battle taking place at their breakthrough, so she put her attention onto who was actually controlling these primitives. Their minds were dead, that much she sensed, and yet they continued yelling and making all manner of sounds with their mouths. Ah, their *jefa* were standing back out of the way of the battle, just as she was. That made sense. Yet, all the primitives seemed to be working together. Could the strange noises they were making be some low-level form of communication among these primitives? The more she looked, the more convinced she became that these noises were somehow a form of primitive communications. Further, this one woman may well be their *jefe comandante*! Although such was totally foreign to her—that a woman could be their *agente* leader, it appeared there were two of these strange primitive women that were in command, one subordinate to the other. But what orders was their *jefa* giving them?

With quite a few of her own *agente* likely dead from these strange weapons of the primitives, she decided to act. She focused and made mental contact with the woman *agente* and one of the *jefa* women. To the *agente*, she placed into her mind, *Why are you attacking our men? We mean you no harm. Are you trying to conquer our world? If so, we can't allow that. You must stop this senseless slaughter now or you primitives will all perish.*

Into the mind of the *jefa*, she placed, *Jefa. Why are you allowing your primitive people to attack and kill our people? We mean you no harm, and yet you are killing our fighters. You must put a stop to this senseless slaughter or we will be forced to kill all you primitives.*

She used considerable mental force to enforce her will upon these two women, but found that both were highly resistant to her will. Then came the overwhelming bright lights, temporarily blinding all those who were close to the battle. Taken by surprise, the fighting ceased, as the many blinded *agente* made a hasty retreat back beyond the range of vision of the primitives and away from the blinding light, if only to regroup.

Jefe Sancho took stock of the combat results. Twenty of his *agente* were gone, but by all reports coming up the line to him, his men had wounded eight of the primitives. Still, his men had made a poor showing, primarily because some of these primitives had very strong wills and were not easily mentally dominated. He'd take that into account in the next battle. He reported their final tallies to *Jefa* Adelina, as he was required to do. Then he set about making counterattack plans, sending word to mobilize another thousand of his fighters.

Meanwhile, *Jefa* Adelina continued to observe, squinting because of the brilliant lights. Then, she saw something hopeful. *Jefe, look. I believe they are returning our dead agente. Send some to retrieve their bodies that we may honor them in death for their valiant defense of our tribu.*

He acknowledged her and issued the orders. Before long, a report came back that these men were not dead, but were waking. He personally went over to one of the reviving men and examined him. *Jefa, they're not dead. They have*

147

been merely stunned. I don't know what to make of this.

She sent back, *Jefe, we have dishonored these primitives. Our agente inflicted actual wounds, perhaps maiming or killing the primitives while the primitives have only temporarily stunned our agente. The dishonor of the battle lies upon us.*

Sancho cursed silently to himself, now knowing his adjudicator was right. He and his *agente* had drawn blood, while these primitives had not. He contented himself to assisting the fallen recover, hoping that little would come from the dishonorable action. *How could I have known that they weren't killing my men with their strange weapons?*

Jefa Adelina took the only option that was available to her. Her *tribu* had dishonored these primitives. As their adjudicator, it was her responsibility to find a way to rectify the affront, even if these were mere primitive peoples. To *Jefe* Sancho, she sent, *I must speak with their jefa and comandante, even though she is a woman.*

As much as he didn't want his wife to do this, he knew honor dictated it. He sent, *Be careful, my jefa. They may try to harm you too.*

Slowly and carefully, she made her way through the fern field towards the brilliantly illuminated battlefield where the strange flying thing sat with the swarm of primitives dashing about. She could barely see so bright was the light, but she was honor-bound to make this attempt to salvage their honor. When she finally drew close to the poles, she stopped. She kept her eye lids nearly shut, allowing only a tiny crack, just enough to spot the two with whom she needed to speak. Even so, the bright light was giving her an enormous headache already. She focused and placed into the major's mind and the jefa's mind, *Please primitives, turn off the brilliant lights that we may see each other and speak. I am unarmed and mean you no harm.*

Holding her hands to her head, Major Lu Ann looked up and out across the field of ferns. She gasped, just as Captain Janine spotted the primitive woman as well. They saw an armless woman with a very long, bronze neck and with two giant lip plates dropping down to her chest standing alone just before one of the poles. Major Lu Ann barked, "Kill the lights now, but be ready to turn them back on if they try to rush us." The lights vanished and everyone blinked. Once more, they could just barely see this very strange looking woman. Hard Ass issued orders left and right, getting her platoon properly repositioned, while Bite Me and the nurse continued to wrap emergency bandages on the eight wounded men, now arranged in a line close to the side of the Hyperion.

Primitives, we are sorry we injured your people when you clearly did not injure ours. We are honor bound to heal your wounded men, if you will allow us to do so. I give you my word as our tribu's jefa they'll be fully healed within a few minutes, if you will allow us to do so.

Major Lu Ann called out in her alto voice, "I'm sorry. But we don't trust you. Are you talking in my head? My medic is seeing to their wounds now."

You are making strange sounds with your mouths. Is this how you primitives communicate with each other? How primitive indeed. Please, just think your thoughts, and I will hear them.

We don't trust you. You're the primitives as far as we're concerned. Is this telepathy or something? Is this what you mean by thinking thoughts? Major Lu Ann thought.

Yes, very much better. Our methods of healing are fast and efficient. If you'll permit us, we'll fully heal your wounded primitive soldiers in just a few minutes. It is the least we can do, since the fault lies with us. We misinterpreted you primitive's response to our attempts to communicate with you. I'm Jefa Adelina Alvaro, the adjudicator of the entire Alvaro Tribu. If you don't believe me, ask your own jefa, who is standing with the other jefa and the young jefa girl.

Major Lu Ann looked confused. *What does she mean?*

That one with the enormous breasts.

Oh, you mean Dr. Alison? The blonde woman who lost her arms?

Yes. She is your jefa, correct? She must be horribly disfigured to so hide her body beneath all those apparel things, as must all of you. I'm so sorry for you primitives that

149

your bodies are so terribly disfigured and too ghastly for eyes to see. Yes, ask her.

I don't understand all this. We're not disfigured. Well, perhaps Dr. Alison and Peter and his daughter are some. They have had a horrible accident that gave them those monster breasts, distorted their feet, and cost them their arms, Major Lu Ann fumbled, trying to get a grasp on what this strange woman was saying or implying.

Bite Me interrupted the major's thoughts. "Major, we have to get these eight into the ship soon. Somehow, someway we're going to have to try to sew up their wounds or they're going to bleed to death."

"Hold on a second, Jascar," she replied. "These primitives are suggesting they can heal them in minutes. I don't believe them or trust them, but this strange woman is claiming it's a matter of honor that I allow them to do so."

"You can't be serious? Allowing these savages to work on them?" Jascar called back, now even more worried about the eight men.

Peter spoke up, "If it's a matter of honor, major, I would suggest you let them try. That would go a long way to establishing better relations, I think."

"Okay Peter. Jascar, you keep a sharp eye on what these primitives are going to do to the men. First sign of trouble, stop them. Got it? We're not risking their lives," Major Lu Ann barked her orders.

Of course, we won't harm them. We're honor bound to heal them, since your people didn't harm our men. I'll send in eight, but they will come unarmed, Jefa Adelina placed in the major's mind and in Dr. Alison's mind. After a brief pause, eight men wearing loin cloths appeared above the ferns. They had left their swords, spears, and shields behind and walked hesitantly past the pole, where their *jefa* bravely stood alone, facing these primitives from the clouds.

Hundreds of eyes watched the eight men who walked up to the eight wounded men and women, lying on the ground and trampled ferns beside the giant Hyperion. Jascar said, "I'm not going to let you hurt them any further. You got that?"

In his mind, he perceived, *We will not harm them. We*

will heal them. His face looked rather shocked. As everyone watched, these eight men merely bent over the bleeding, bandaged victims. They didn't even touch them and apparently were doing absolutely nothing. For over ten minutes, Jascar and the others watched the eight closely, but they seemed to be doing absolutely nothing to the wounded. Finally, Jascar declared, "Major, they aren't doing a damned thing. Permission to take them inside and start sewing up their wounds. This is ridiculous."

As if sensing what he was saying, the eight men rose in unison. *There, it's done. Your wounded are healed. Jefa, we have restored our honor.* The eight turned and departed, leaving Jascar completely confused.

"Well, Jascar?" Major Lu Ann asked.

"They didn't do a thing. Okay, I suppose I can check," Jascar replied, realizing he needed proof, visible proof, for the major. Carefully, he removed one of the wounded's bandage, hoping it wouldn't start bleeding profusely once more. While there was a plasma supply in the medical center, he didn't want to have to use it if he didn't have to. He gasped.

"What's the matter, Jascar?" a worried Major Lu Ann barked.

"It's, well, it's healed!" Jascar pealed the whole bandage off, revealing the pinkish skin of a healed sword cut. "Good God! The whole damn wound is healed! It's healed as much as I would expect it to be a couple weeks from now!" Hastily, he and the nurse began unwrapping their emergency bandages from the others. As promised, all eight were fully healed, though a bit weak from loss of blood. This made a huge impression on the major and everyone else who was watching!

Major Lu Ann swallowed hard and went over to see for herself. *Good God! They healed them! They actually healed them far better than our medical doctor ever could have if he was still living! I don't believe this. And from primitives too!*

In her mind and in Dr. Alison's, she heard, *I'm sorry, but we're not primitives. Rather, we consider you're the primitive ones. You can't do this simple healing, and your minds are dead. You have to make all those strange noises with your mouths to communicate with each other. You can see why we consider you and your people to be the primitives here. But then maybe you're an unknown human species who come from the clouds. However, it was our wish to welcome you to New Zeta and the lands of the Alvaro Tribu. We mean you and your people no harm, though soon the other more distant tribu may come to see you. Some of them are warlike and may well cause you trouble. If we grant you honored guest status and if your jefa are with me in my castle, you would be under our protection, and the other tribu wouldn't dare to harm you or your people.*

Major Lu Ann thought, *Are you saying there are others like you who are warlike and would try to attack us?*

Yes. Particularly the de Casa and Menolo Tribu. They could bring tens of thousands of their agente, their fighters, down upon you. However, if I grant you honored guest status and have your jefa with me, they will be honor bound to treat you and your people as our honored guests. Our Castle Alvaro is only two miles from here. We would be honored if you and your three jefa would come back to the castle and visit with us. We would like to learn more about you cloud people, and I sense you wish to know more about us. Your flying machine is in trouble, is it not?

Er, yes. How did you know that? Well, I guess our crash landing tells all. Okay, but our jefa as you call them are quite helpless. I insist we bring along some to help them and some of my guards as well. Trust must go both ways.

Agreed. However, we'll not harm you unless you harm us. When you're ready, walk to where I'm standing. I too need some assistance. Walking among the ferns is rather difficult for me to do without help. I'll send orders back to the castle to prepare a great feast in your honor. Thank you, cloud people. The strange woman turned and seemed to vanish into the dim light of this strange world.

Major Lu Ann relayed the gist of this, the strangest conversation she'd ever had, to everyone else. "Okay, Captain Janine, pick four others. You will accompany the others and me. We're going to be their guests and try to figure out what the heck is going on around here. Captain Billington, you are in charge until I get back. For God's sake, don't antagonize

152

these primitives further. We've got a tentative truce going."

"Hammerhead," Captain Janine barked, "you got the platoon while I'm gone. Fel, Sam, you're coming with me." Major Lu Ann ordered one of her aides to accompany her, though all four were well armed, especially Fel, who never went anywhere without a supply of her "boom-booms." Within a few minutes, the small group moved to the indicated spot. Janine kept a supporting arm around her sister, while Fel did the same for Peter, and Samantha helped Kathy. "Can't see a damned thing," Janine muttered. "I hope it isn't always this darn dark and dreary here."

"Sis, I think this is as bright as it ever gets," Dr. Alison whispered. "Thanks for holding on to me. This is really hard for us." She wiggled and wobbled about, but Janine held her securely. One of the primitive men silently joined them, motioning for them to follow him. Soon, they caught glimpses of hundreds of these men moving in a long line off to the southwest. They were following a very clear path and spotted what had to be corral fences. Animals that looked much like llamas grazed about them, as they passed along through the land of tall ferns.

Chapter 10—Understandings

An hour later, the red sun turned the dense clouds a dark crimson, but ahead, they spotted what could only be a large city. A stone wall encircled the city, and once inside the metal gates, stone buildings rose all around them, precisely laid out as though a surveyor had been here. In fact, except for the stonework, the layout looked much as any civilized city did such as Brussels, Ragnar-B.

Hundreds of men, women, and children thronged the street, all staring at the *primitives* who followed along behind their guide. They were all dressed similarly, loincloth and sandals. The women all had seemingly long, golden necks and sported lip plates in varying diameters. Fel whispered, "The men will go nuts seeing all these boobs." Janine laughed.

All the buildings were single story, and many had pictographs above their metal doors. All had numerous open windows, far more than anyone might expect. Here and there, they spotted what had to be storefronts. Pottery, bronze household items, and weapons were prominently on display. What so surprised the group as they walked through the packed streets was the silence. Unlike Brussels, not a single person made any sound. No talking, idle chatter, nothing. Slowly, it dawned on the group; this was a telepathic society. Since everyone had the ability to send and receive thoughts, there was no need for a spoken language, though obviously the women wouldn't be able to speak understandably with their lip plates.

Dr. Alison noted everyone had their arms and hands. So far, only *Jefa* Adelina didn't, and she wondered why that was. The many children, both boys and girls, were unadorned. That is, the girls had neither the neck rings nor the lip plates, but the boys definitely had elongated heads and wore tight bronze headbands, just like the men. Already, the boys' heads seemed far taller than they should be.

Ahead, they saw a two story, huge stone building, though it had more windows than they could count. Major Lu

Ann rightly concluded the castle wasn't built for defensive purposes, but as living quarters. Thus far, they hadn't seen a single tree. Yet they had bronze works and steel doors, here and there. Then, in their minds, they all heard, *Castle Alvaro.*

"Hey, at least on this solid ground we can walk again," Dr. Alison commented to her sister.

Peter commented, "You know, some of their metal doors we've seen sure look like cut up parts from a space ship. They weren't originally built to be doors."

"You noticed that too, Peter. So did I, curious," Major Lu Ann added. "I think we've arrived."

They entered another set of doors and found themselves in a Great Hall. All along the four sides, large windows allowed in fresh air and what light was available. Everything was quite dim. There were no electric lights, gas lamps, or even torches. The only illumination came from the meager sunlight, which as the sun began to set, wasn't much. Still, these people could see quite well. Their pupils and eye lenses filled their entire visible eyeballs, nearly double the size of normal humans, which gave the illusion they had enormous eyes. Major Lu Ann now began to understand much. These people likely had vision adapted for this world, which meant they could see just as well as she could back on her own world of Ragnar-B! No wonder the bright lights blinded them. What worried her more was some of these people had managed to force some of her people to obey their orders and not hers. In a crisis, this would be a disaster.

It dawned on her as they walked towards a stone table in the center of the spacious room that the definition of primitive wasn't applicable here. While they lacked all the trappings of a modern civilization such as her own Brussels, they had powerful mental abilities, so much so that they didn't need a spoken language. Their minds could heal wounds in minutes, as well as dominate some of her crew's minds, forcing them to do their will. She began to see these people in an entirely different light.

(Note to the reader. While almost all the following conversations took place telepathically, they will be presented as though they were speaking.)

Ahead, the group saw a long stone table with stone benches covered with brownish mats serving as seats. *Jefa* Adelina sat at the table with another young woman at her side. *Jefe Comandante* Sancho, now less his weapons, sat on her right. Adelina welcomed them. "Welcome to Castle Alvaro, the seat of power of the Alvaro *Tribu*. Please have a seat. Dinner will be served now. After we eat, we can talk. I have much to ask, as do you. My *castillo siervo* will assist me. Let me know if your *jefa* also require someone to assist them in dining."

"I've got my sister here," Janine thought. "Am I thinking this right?"

Adelina smiled. "Yes, we are picking up your thoughts quite easily." Fel and Sam sat beside Peter and Kathy to assist them. The major and her assistant sat directly across from their hosts. Then, six more servants entered carrying bronze trays laden with steaming food. The odors made their mouths water.

"We are having roast boar, sweet potatoes, and beans. There is a lettuce salad sprinkled with a variety of nuts, pecans, almonds, and peanuts. I do hope you enjoy our food. It is very delicious," *Jefa* Adelina explained.

While the items on the menu didn't look quite like their namesakes, the group did find their tastes rather similar. Further, the meal was in fact quite delicious, a hundred times better than shipboard cuisine, a fact that Major Lu Ann pointed out, much to their hosts' pleasure. As they finished, Captain Janine commented, "That was fabulous. Now if we only had a good dark ale to round this off."

"Ah, an *agente* after my own heart!" Sancho exclaimed. Shortly, two servants entered carrying a bronze pitcher with the ale. Fel, Sam, Janine, and Sancho partook, and he was very pleased the three soldiers enjoyed his favorite brew.

"So, are all your *agente* or fighters females on your cloud world? Here, ours are males," he asked.

Janine laughed. "Hardly. No, we pick the best qualified person, male or female. Major Lu Ann there is the best flight commander, and we're the best grunts." She then had to explain what a grunt was. Soon the conversations broke into two groups. Janine, Samantha, and Fel chatted with Sancho, while Peter, Dr. Alison, Major Lu Ann, and her assistant chatted with Adelina.

However, before they got going, *Jefa* Adelina saw Kathy was likely to be very bored, and she sent for her own children. Gaily, Kathy headed off with several to play some games. "So Kathy, you are already in training to be a *jefa* too. That's wonderful," one said, as they watched her taking her tiny steps following them.

Jefa Adelina asked first, "So tell us about yourselves. Where do you come from? What is your purpose here? How long are you staying?"

Major Lu Ann took charge, since she was in command, though Adelina truly believed that Dr. Alison had the final say in significant decisions. She explained they came from Ragnar-B, but quickly found herself explaining about the many civilized worlds of the Federation. Once she got across the vastness of their many worlds and space flight, she then told about the treachery on her own world and how Peter, Dr. Alison, and Kathy had been victims of an attack that had so modified their bodies. She explained that telepaths were extraordinarily rare on all other worlds, though in ancient times, there had been rumors of an entire planet of telepaths who also had strange powers.

She ended up explaining how they had been attacked and their engines put out of commission. They then made an emergency crash landing here, but had done their best to avoid crashing into their city, for which Adelina was grateful. "How long we're going to be here isn't known yet, but certainly for a number of weeks. We have much to repair before we can depart. I must also say that it may well be impossible for us to repair the damage, in which case, we may be stranded on your world indefinitely, but I will do my best to get my people rescued."

Peter then asked about their world and specifically about their unusual metal doors that he'd seen. Adelina told of ancient legends in which a metal ship from the skies landed. "We don't have any metals on our world harder than the bronze our artisans make. Yet, there are many ancient doors and roofs in Castle Alvaro and the other castles that must have come from our distant ancestors. The metal is very hard and nearly impossible for us to work. Steel, it is called. A blade of steel is perhaps the most expensive item on our world, worth a year's crop from a farmer at the very least. We have axes, plow blades, and other steel implements that must have come from our ancestors, though as they wear out, our artisans replace them with the inferior bronze replicas."

This discussion was then followed by a description of New Zeta. The population estimates put their numbers at close to a half million, though they were about evenly divided among the five *tribu* groups. She had one of her servants bring in a metal map that showed the layout of her known world, etched into the metal, showing even the newer settlement expansions as well. They learned each group provided basic survival needs for the others. Here at Alvaro, they produced crops, llamas, wool, and cloth from the llama wool. Stone blocks for construction came from the two *tribu* near the East Range and West Range of mountains, run by the more warlike de Casa and Menolo *tribu*. Bronze works came from the Huso Woods and the Gonzalo *Tribu*, along with all the peat used for fires and pottery. Their meat, cows, and horses came from the Aspero Hills and the Vega *Tribu*.

With a basic understanding of the layout, Major Lu Ann asked about their society, its organization, and just what was a *jefa*. *Jefa* Adelina giggled, one of the rare times these people ever made a vocal sound. Soon, she had a very good understanding of the political situation. As she guessed, *Jefe Comandante* Sancho yielded immense powers here in Alvaro, a dictator's role, though in judicial maters, he had to defer to *Jefa* Adelina's decisions. That he had tens of thousands of soldiers under his command wasn't lost on her. Besides, the other four groups also had similar numbers. Further, she learned wars were commonplace, and she correctly surmised the constant battles kept their population lower than it may have been.

What surprised her group the most was to learn this was a matriarchal society. The women owned their lands and buildings. Men fundamentally worked for them, at least in theory. Women were considered immensely valuable because they gave birth to the future generations. In ancient times, women donned the neck rings to let men know that they were of breeding age. Their lip plates, called *placas del labios*, denoted a woman's rank in society. No one was allowed plates larger than their sole *jefa*, which usually meant no larger than eighteen inches across.

When a girl reached womanhood, she was adorned with her neck rings and her lips were slit. Plates of about four inches were inserted. As her lip loops stretched, her plates were enlarged. Older adult women's plates were around a foot across. When asked why this was done to their lips, Adelina giggled a second time. Her answer took them all by surprise. "Kissing. Our men find our kisses are very erotic."

When they asked about the men's tall heads, they learned that every newborn boy child had their heads bound. By the time that they reached full adulthood, their heads had formed into the accepted tall heads. When asked why this was done, Adelina replied, "With bigger heads, the men believe they have a bigger brain and can think and do more than women can. No one knows if this is true. I think it is men's vanity at play." The women chuckled.

Jefa Adelina then followed up with what she truly needed to know, based on all she'd learned. "As I've told you, this metal called steel in invaluable to us. Do you have any of that metal you could exchange with us for whatever you might desire?"

Major Lu Ann thought for a moment. "We have to use some to repair our ship, Jefa Adelina, but I think we have some that we could trade. Give me time to see just how badly damaged our ship actually is. Before we leave, I will see you and your people get what steel we can spare. However, I do have some smaller ships that can fly. I will send them on a mineralogy exploration trip around your world and see if we can spot any areas that are worth exploring for metals. That much I can do starting tomorrow. However, it would not be fair to the other four *tribu* to give all of this to your *tribu* only. We must donate some to the others as well, but since we are your guests, much should come to you, our kind hosts."

That satisfied Adelina and later Sancho, who was

159

extremely pleased that his *jefa* had worked out such a deal for steel. By now, it was dark out. Major Lu Ann and her group could barely make out their guests at the table, but they apparently were still seeing them quite well. Sensing her guests' discomfort, she suggested they stay the night, an idea readily accepted. Then, she added, "It would be best for all of us if your *jefa* stayed here with us for a time, especially when the other *tribu* arrive and demand access to you and your people. Having your *jefa* here with me will ensure they honor our offer of guest protection."

She added, "And perhaps some others of your people would also like to spend time here with us as well. They would be most welcome. Sancho would also like to position a few guards around the field where your ship is at, for your protection. There are occasionally wild boars around and a few tigers, though those are rare. Plus, they will keep the locals from interfering with your work."

Major Lu Ann agreed to allow the three to remain here. While she needed Dr. Alison's assistance on rebuilding the blown circuitry, right now, the long distance comm array was the very least of her problems. Time enough to get that working once the ship was again flight-worthy. She also thought having a few of their men around would allow her to learn more about their special mental abilities. Thus far, she'd not dared to inquire about them, believing that might not be a wise line of inquiry until stronger ties of trust were established.

The many servants laughed heartily when they discovered their guests were almost completely blind. They had physically to lead them down the halls to the guest bedrooms and help them find the beds! All this, they found most amusing, somewhat reinforcing their notions that their guests were primitives in many ways.

The next morning, everyone could see once more, well sort of. It was dim, dingy, dismal, and red-hued, but they could see. Breakfast was again a very delicious meal, very well balanced with a goodly amount of protein. Major Lu Ann concluded that her people would be fine staying here. *Heck, they are eating better than the rest of us. At least if we end up being marooned here, we won't starve.*

"You be careful, sis," Janine whispered her goodbyes to Dr. Alison. "I'm leaving you a communicator just in case. I think you can use your toes or nose to activate it. If trouble comes, just push it. I'll come charging in here with my platoon's guns blazing, sis."

Dr. Alison felt relieved, even though she actually had no way to carry the device around. "Thanks. I'm sure we'll be safe. *Jefa* are very important women in this society. You keep everyone safe so they can repair the ship. Let me know when the major wants me back to work on the electronics." Janine hugged her sister and left the three still sitting at the stone table in the Great Hall. She joined the major and her assistant, Fel, and Sam, who were just heading out of the doors.

"How about a tour of our city?" *Jefa* Adelina suggested, as her servants carried away the breakfast dishes. *Jefe Comandante* Sancho had already taken off, leaving his wife with her three guests.

"I'd love to, but walking in these heels is hard for us. If we take a fall, it's very hard for us to get back up," Dr. Alison explained.

"Okay. So is Peter really a man? We've never seen a man who looks like a woman and *jefa* before," she asked.

Peter chuckled. "I am, but I'm going to need to use the bathroom soon. So one of your servants will be able to tell you so." Several servants chuckled, and one proudly put a steadying arm around him and led him off to do just that. Kathy and Dr. Alison followed along. From the chuckles she heard as she and Kathy made their slow way back, she guessed they'd verified Peter's sex.

This time, the servants led her into the Throne Room, where they found *Jefa* Adelina sitting on her throne. "Here is where I adjudicate all matters of justice for our *tribu*. I've asked one of our best healers to pay us a visit this morning. With your feet so bent, you can hardly walk. We might be able to heal them."

"That would be wonderful. Too bad you can't do anything about our monster breasts," Peter sent back.

"We can try. If we can do this for you three, I would like

Dr. Alison and Kathy to consider allowing us to ornament them properly. It will help if your people's *jefa* look like ours. Trust me, that will go a very long way when the other *tribu* come and make challenges," *Jefa* Adelina explained. Just then, another man entered. Peter thought he looked a bit silly bowing to *Jefa* Adelina with his long, distorted head bobbing up and down.

Nothing was said, but Dr. Alison suspected *Jefa* Adelina explained about their malformed feet and monster breasts. She didn't hold out much hope he could do anything about them, since her body had been genetically modified to get it this way. "He needs to get you dressed as we dress so that he can see your body," *Jefa* Adelina requested. After getting the okay, her servants came into the room carrying three loincloths made from the incredibly soft llama wool. Even Kathy had a laugh while watching the servants struggle mightily trying to get them out of the unfamiliar apparel. Of course, everyone stared at Peter and Alison's bosoms, but Kathy was proud of hers, which had started filling out, and looked more or less like the other adult women around her.

That done and now dressed in the typical loincloth, the trio was helped to lie down on soft llama mats, and the man began his examination, beginning with Dr. Alison, the alien *jefa* and the more important of the three in everyone's opinion. Alison felt a tingle, a strange sensation of something gently probing here and there on her feet and then her breasts. He then moved on to Peter and finally Kathy.

Jefa Adelina spoke at last. "He believes that he will be able to repair your feet and probably your breasts as well. Shall we give it a try?"

"Yes, by all means. But will it hurt? What do we have to do?" Dr. Alison asked for the other's benefit as well as her own.

Jefa Adelina laughed. "No. It shouldn't hurt. He has sent for other healers. Together, they will join and become even more powerful healers. You will see. Each of us has some ability to heal our bodies, but a few are exceptional at it. Renaldo here is a master. Trust him."

Three other men and a woman arrived and quietly took

up sitting positions around her. Each had brought their own soft llama cushion. After making sure she was comfortable lying on her mat, they began. Dr. Alison watched but the five just sat there, their giant eyes seemingly staring at her feet. Finally, she closed her eyes and relaxed. She dozed some. An hour later, *Jefa* Adelina coaxed her awake.

"*Jefa* Alison, it is done. Look at your feet and breasts." She struggled a bit to sit up and stared at her feet. They looked perfectly normal! She gasped and Peter had tears in his eyes. "They were able to reduce your breasts by half. While they are still larger than any of ours are, they are much smaller. I hope this will do."

"Oh thank you, thank you! This is a miracle. Now I can walk properly once more! Thank you," she exclaimed, joy flooding through her.

While the group began working on Peter, *Jefa* Adelina said, "Now are you ready to be adorned as a proper *jefa* should be? It is also painless." Dr. Alison had already given this considerable thought. She knew the population of this world and thus the number of fighters or the *agente* as they called them. Tens of thousands. She had been cautioned several times that some of these other *tribu* were warlike. While she knew her people's weapons were deadly, she also had witnessed these telepaths taking control over her people's bodies, as witnessed by the man who had unwillingly lowered the electric fence pole and others who had failed to draw their weapons to fight back.

She reasoned if tens of thousands of these fighters really wanted to capture the ship and cut it up for scrap steel, her people would be hard pressed to stop them. Even if they went inside, using their strange mind powers, they could force someone inside to open the doors. Against tens of thousands, her people stood no chance. However, *Jefa* Adelina had said that if she appeared as one of their own *jefa*, that would go a long way to helping keep the peace and accepting them on this world. *What's a little discomfort if by doing that I can prevent a major battle?* She replied, "Yes, I must appear as a proper *jefa* to help keep the peace between our peoples."

"You have the wisdom of a true *jefa*," *Jefa* Adelina

replied. "As soon as they're finished with Peter and Kathy, we'll have them adorn you and Kathy properly, unless Kathy shouldn't be."

"Oh, I want to look like all the other girls here," she broke in. Peter also understood the ramifications and gave his parental agreement. *Jefa* Adelina did check to make sure that Kathy was officially a woman, that she had at least one period.

An hour later, Peter gushed, "I feel like a hundred pounds has been lifted off of me! And I can walk normally now!"

Alison laughed. "Dear, they weren't *that* heavy!" Both laughed.

After that, Peter was led out of the room and given a morning coffee. Okay, it wasn't any type of coffee he knew as coffee, but it was this world's equivalent of caffeine, which he greatly appreciated. Meanwhile, the five began to work on adorning the two women.

Still lying down, the healer pricked her lips with a thorn, numbing them. Soon, she drifted into a light sleep, while they worked their "magic" on her and on Kathy. When she awoke at the gentle mind-touch of *Jefa* Adelina, she felt a solid pressure downward on her shoulders and an opposite one on the bottom of her head. Her lips felt very heavy and stretched, and she could see the giant golden, bronze lip plates resting on her chest. One of the servants helped her sit back up and held a shiny mirror for her to see her new look.

Her lips had been slit but the loops, which should have been enough to surround a pair of four-inch plates, now held a pair of eighteen-inch disks! They rested below her bosom, just as they did with *Jefa* Adelina. Further, her neck was entirely immobilized by the rings, forcing her to have the perfect posture she'd seen the other women have. "Oh my! So strange. I can't move much at all. Oh, I can't understand my own speech!" She spoke aloud and couldn't recognize her own words.

Fortunately, *Jefa* Adelina anticipated this, since these aliens didn't have telepathy and depended upon their strange vocal sounds. "Don't worry. I'm assigning you your own personal servant. This is Rosina. She will assist you when needed. It takes getting used to, just as it does with all our young girls when they first become adorned. You look ravishing, Alison. Peter will certainly love your magnificent appearance. Now, anyone on our world, who sees you, will know you're the alien's *jefa,* and they'll treat you with the highest honor. Between us, we should be able to keep the more warlike men under control. Come, now that you can walk, let me show you our city. There's much to see."

"What about Kathy?" Alison thought.

"Oh, she's up and off playing with the other children. We can visit her and pick up Peter for our walk. He's watching the children play. He'll make a fine *jefe,* well not fine in terms of protection, but as a father. I can sense how loving and caring he is. You'll have many happy children in time, I can feel it." Alison flushed at this suggestion and got to her feet.

Quickly, she discovered like all the other women of New Zeta, she had to turn her body now, instead of her head, which was held immobile by the neck rings. Still, her feet felt wonderful on the ground. Gone was that awful sensation of not being able to keep her balance. Besides, she was now going to help everyone survive when the other *tribu* fighters arrived. She didn't think about what would happen if they ended up being stranded on this world.

"Oh, I can't see anything in this fog. We'll have to wait a while, I suppose," Dr. Alison said, hoping that *Jefa* Adelina would hear her thoughts.

"Oh. You mean you really can't see anything?" *Jefa* Adelina sent back. Dr. Alison sensed a real concern for her handicap. "I see very well through the fog. It is foggy every morning, but it usually is gone by noon."

"You mean you can see through this reddish-grey fog?"

"Of course, we all do. It must be because of our eyes. Everyone is calling your people *small eyes.* Kind of a joke," *Jefa* Adelina explained. "Let's tour the castle until after lunch."

"It is pretty dark in here, but okay."

"Wow. You really can't see well can you?"

"Our worlds are many times brighter than the artificial lights we use around our ship. You know—the ones that rather blinded your people when we first met." They began discussing

165

light, visibility, and even stars. Dr. Alison learned away to the east in the mountains lay Escalera a las Estrellas. Everyone took at least one pilgrimage to see the stars once during their lifetimes, but they only climbed up above the clouds at night. In the daytime, the red sun was just too brilliant for them to see anything. Later, Dr. Alison relayed this data to Major Lu Ann, who sent her astronomers up there to set up a permanent observatory, in hopes they could locate where they were at in the galaxy.

For a time, Dr. Alison continually fought against the immobility of her head, but with the constant assistance of her new servant girl, Rosina, she soon relaxed and accepted it, just as Rosina and all the other women did. After another delicious lunch, mouthwatering in fact, they headed off to walk the streets of Castle Alvaro.

This proved interesting because she and Peter got to see some of the *artesano* at work. Both were fascinated with the foot looms of the weaver women. Sitting with their erect backs against the stone walls of their shops, these women pushed one end of their loom outwards with their feet. The other end was tied around their waists. This part held many long strands of wool tight, though they were close together. The strands were tied in alternating bands. One group was slanted upwards, while the other went downward. These were called the warp threads. The weavers slipped another long thread, the woof, attached to a metal needle-like pointer through the opening between the alternating warp threads. Then, they used a long metal rod to push the woof down tightly. That done, the cleverly raised the lower set of warp threads, while lowering the raised set, firmly fixing that woof in place, before running the small needle back through the warp threads again.

For several minutes, the pair stood and watched the women weaving. They were making cloth from the llama wool. Each finished piece was about three feet wide and four feet long. Adelina explained that these pieces would be sewn together to make large bed covers or folded over and sewn up to make seat cushions, or into bags or loincloths. Dr. Alison was fascinated to see how cloth was actually made.

They visited a pottery shop and a bronze utensil maker.

There was only two smelters in this city. *Jefa* Adelina explained most all bronze came from the da Casa or Menolo *tribu* during monthly trading visits. Thus, when Captain Janine and several others returned to check on her, Dr. Alison had a good deal of information to relay.

Of course, she immediately ran into a communication barrier. No one could understand her speech, but Peter came through and pretty well knew what she wanted relayed. She didn't trust Rosina to translate for her. Starting now, Major Lu Ann began receiving valuable information on the people of New Zeta. That they could see easily through the morning's dense fog alarmed them all. Plus, they now had a good idea when they would be facing the more warlike *trubu*, five days from now, when the next monthly trading delegations would be arriving here.

During the ensuing days, *Jefa* Adelina also took her guests on a tour of neighboring towns. Each town was built of stone, carved from either East Reach or West Reach and painstakingly carried here, some five hundred miles overland. While the roofs of Castle Alvaro were made of steel sections from an ancient spaceship, some of these had domed stone roofs. Obviously, these were constructed long after the steel from that ancient ship was used up. Dr. Alison did learn for the Alvaro *Tribu*, obtaining the stone blocks for building new homes was their most costly item. In fact, lack of inexpensive building materials was also a factor keeping their population from expanding rapidly. Wars were needed to keep their numbers manageable, a sad tale indeed, Dr. Alison thought.

On one of the many "check on how they are doing" trips, Fel came along at Dr. Alison's insistence. Via Rosina, she sent to Fel, "There is a big difference in the cutting of the stone blocks here and in the other towns. Can you have a look and see what the difference is? These people are desperate for stone blocks. They use wars to keep their population from rapidly expanding beyond the available homes."

It didn't take the engineer long to see what was going on. "Look, doctor, the stones here were obviously cut by modern cutting tools, lasers most likely. The others are rough cut, meaning done by crude hand methods. Does this help?"

Via Rosina, Dr. Alison suggested, "Can you see if the major can spare a crew to fly to the mountains and quarry stone for these people? Stone blocks cost these people an enormous amount of their produce. It would make a great exchange between our peoples."

"She's already sent out mining surveys and scouts. I'll see what can be done. You're right. If we could provide some stone, that would certainly endear us to these people for their help," Fcl replied. "Much is going to depend on how the four other groups treat us. We'll know in a couple of days. Major Lu Ann is worried about that. Since they can control our minds and make some of us do their bidding, we can't depend on our people for security. So she has been having me set up some booby traps around our perimeter. Those can't be defused except by me, but the natives don't know that. Scary, when someone can take over your mind and force you to do something against your will, but then you already know that." Dr. Alison shivered. That she certainly did.

Chapter 11—Dealing with Natives

Jefa Adelina sat erect on her throne, while a well-armed *Jefe Comandante* Sancho sat on her right. A special stone chair was brought in and placed on her left. Dr. Alison sat equally erect on it, as her honored guest *jefa*. It was around one in the afternoon, and four high-ranking *jefe comandante* men from the neighboring *tribu* had arrived. Just as *Jefa* Adelina had anticipated, word of the arrival of the aliens had spread to these other *tribu*, who had sent their top men and fighters along with their trade delegations. All four demanded an audience with the leaders of Castle Alvaro. The four well-armed men barged into the Throne Room, accompanied by squads of their *agente* fighters.

As far as Dr. Alison was concerned, the men looked pretty much the same, tall, elongated heads with their bronze headbands, short black hair, thin, pale, and with large black eyes. Their physical demeanor looked antagonistic to her. Plus, several had visible scars on their arms and chests. All were far taller than she was, but by now, Alison was used to having others tower over her shorter frame.

The exchange was telepathic, and unfortunately, Dr. Alison wasn't always included. She felt very ill at ease during the lengthy exchange. *Jefa* Adelina was right; these men were far more warlike than she had hoped they would be. Wisely, *Jefa* Adelina had asked Peter and Kathy to remain in another room out of sight of these men. His situation would cause quite a stir, and she didn't want to throw peat onto the fires.

After several tense minutes, *Jefa* Adelina insisted they include *Jefa* Alison in their discussions, rather forcing the issue. At last, Alison began "hearing" some of the exchange in her mind. She couldn't tell who was talking, but it was obviously one of the four key men. "Look, these alien primitives are here. We demand our fair share in the dismantling of their metal. You know as well as I do that this must be agreed to, Jefa Adelina. It is only by chance these primitive people landed close to your city. Hell, they can't even speak to us."

Jefa Adelina countered, "It is true that these people do not possess our telepathy. Yes, it is true that they communicate by making strange sounds with their mouths. But I caution you, *Jefe* da Casa, that doesn't make them primitives! They possess a vast knowledge beyond our comprehension. They have magical weapons and are determined fighters. Besides, as you can plainly see, they too have their own *tribu jefa*. She's sitting beside me. Does not *Jefa* Alison look like me and the other four *jefa*? Of course, she does. Her *comandante* is back guarding her flying ship as we speak."

"That's all well and good, *Jefa* Adelina," broke in *Jefe* Manolo, "but our reports tell me that this flying ship of theirs can no longer fly, that they are marooned here on our world. I want to make them an offer to settle in our *tribu*."

"You can't do that. We want their weapons too and their steel," protested *Jefe* Vega. "Who gives you the right to all their magical things?"

"So we attack them, defeat them, and divide up the spoils between our *tribu*. Balance must be maintained. That is the law of New Zeta, *Jefa* Adelina. You know that as well as we do. We're not going to let you confiscate all their magic and steel for yourselves. We'll destroy you and your entire *tribu* if necessary," barked *Jefe* da Casa.

Dr. Alison cringed. She had no doubt that these men would do just that, gang up on the Alvaro *tribu* and destroy them all just to gain total control over the Hyperion and its contents. She had no idea if they were listening in on her thoughts, but she tried anyway. "You foolish *jefe*! If you harm one of *Jefa* Adelina's people, my *tribu* will destroy you and all your *tribu* and castles. Our cannons and disintegrator guns will turn your stone castles and men into dust! The Hyperion doesn't have to fly for us to do that. We can wipe out whole planets and everything on it, if we have too. You're foolish men. There are hundreds of other worlds out there in the galaxy. We have spaceships that are larger than this entire Castle Alvaro! Just one of these can totally annihilate your entire New Zeta in just a couple of minutes. We're here as the honored guests of *Jefa* Adelina and *Jefe* Sancho. We of the Ragnar-B *Tribu* are prepared to defend our honored hosts. I so warn you."

"It might be true, what she speaks," *Jefe* Vega sent. "We've seen some of their smaller flying ships over our lands before we departed., and we've seen some others on our trip here. What kind of weapons do these smaller ones carry? We need to know that or she may be right. If we attack them, they could retaliate against our homes and castles."

"We've seen them too," *Jefe* da Casa countered. "But they are small and didn't attack us. Perhaps she is bluffing. How could such a devastating weapon be on such small ships?"

Dr. Alison brought up a mental image of some of the delta wing fighters swooping down on Brussels during the robot battles just as she was evacuating with Peter and Kathy. "I don't know if you can see my mental pictures, but this is only a small part of what they can do." She concentrated on holding those images in her mind.

"She could be imagining such things just to frighten us," countered *Jefe* da Casa. "I know I would try that if I were her."

"She can't call up their home world for help. They are marooned on our world and don't know where they are. We've heard they're lost," added *Jefe* Vasco. "I say it's a bluff."

"Likely. Besides, we heard you attacked them after they landed, *Jefe* Alvaro, and were defeated," broke in *Jefe* Gonzalo. "You Alvaro's are pathetic warriors. You always have been. We would have wiped you all out long ago, if we didn't need farmers to grow crops for us."

"That was a misunderstanding, not a battle," *Jefa* Adelina defended her people.

"Still, it proved these are a weak-willed bunch of aliens, did it not?" countered *Jefe* da Casa.

Dr. Alison answered before *Jefa* Adelina could. "My *Jefe* Major Lu Ann ordered our people to not harm *Jefe* Alvaro's *agente*, but only stun them. We didn't want to harm your people. If you attack us now, my *jefe* will not be so kind. She will give orders to shoot to kill."

"Ah, but we outnumber you primitives a hundred to

one," *Jefe* da Casa countered.

Dr. Alison fumed. "For men with big heads, you're sure foolish and dumb! Just because you have telepathy and other mental powers that we do not. Ha. You stupid men, we consider your people to be the primitives here. You lack nearly everything a civilized, modern world has. Worse, you are so ignorant that you don't even know that you don't have such things! Well, that's not entirely true. The people here at Castle Alvaro are wise, and we are sharing much knowledge with them. They are wiser and smarter than you men are. That's plain enough to this *jefa*, though maybe your own *jefa* are far wiser than you *jefe*."

Jefa Adelina spoke up, "Look. I have granted these aliens honored guest status. By our laws, you have no choice but to honor that or you dishonor me and all the Alvaro *Tribu*."

They made some grunting noises and took their leave, rather stomping out of the Throne Room. "You did well, *Jefa* Alison, but I fear they will not honor our ancient law. I will send word of this meeting to *Jefe* Lu Ann and warn her to be alert for treachery. Unfortunately, my *tribu* isn't strong enough to fight all four of the other *tribu*. I'm sorry about that. It was my hope that they would be honor bound to abide by our ancient law of honored guests. That may not be enough."

"Please warn *Jefe* Lu Ann," Dr. Alison thought.

***

"Okay, I just got word from the castle. The other warlike fighters have arrived and met with Alison. Jefa Adelina doesn't think they will honor their ancient law and might try attacking us. So here's what we're going to do." Major Lu Ann barked her orders.

The electric perimeter fence was still in its original position. They couldn't see much beyond that distance from the ship, so why extend it. All the portable quartz lights were brought out and positioned on both sides of the ship. Further, Fel connected them to six different circuits. While it would take six people to activate them, at least some would be turned on when the natives tried to control the six minds. Surely, some would be able to resist and turn them on. It was better

172

than placing her lights on one circuit, depending upon only one man.

Captain Janine and her platoon donned their personal defense shields and armed themselves with many weapons. She placed Sam and her mortar group on the outward side, the side that the original attack had come from. She put Fel and the RPGs on the other side. Hammerhead took charge of Second Squad, armed mostly with MK40's, while she took First Squad with her, armed with d-guns and grenade launchers.

Inside, Major Lu Ann placed her Hyperion security guards near the main entrance bay, armed to the teeth. Then, she had One Shot, Killer Diller, and her other delta wing fighters ready their ships. If an attack came, they would launch from Bay One and Bay Two, taking up positions from which they could strafe the ground beyond the outer perimeter.

This time, Major Lu Ann decided to issue the orders to shoot to kill. If they were hit with overwhelming numbers, her small force could be wiped out, especially if half of the men and women's minds ended up being controlled by the natives, as they had during that first attack. Plus, she counted on Fel's booby traps as well. No, this time, these primitives had to be taught a lesson. Now she could only wait and see what developed. Had Dr. Alison been able to convince them to respect them or not? She hoped so, for all the torture the doctor was enduring just to establish good relations with these primitives.

By late afternoon, everyone was in place. Major Lu Ann then toured her defenses. "When do you think they will strike?" she asked Captain Janine. She already had her own conclusion but was seeking input.

Hard Ass looked out across the reddish, dim world, and replied, "For my money, I'd hit us in the morning when the fog is thickest. They can see through it and we can't. Besides, in the fog, our bright lights won't do us any good."

Major Lu Ann smiled. "Damn, Hard Ass. I picked the right captain. You and I think alike. Yes, that's what I figured too. I will issue orders to turn on the bright lights only when they've broken through the electric fence. That should inhibit them from close quarters combat. Plus, I think I have a way that I can get us some advance warning of their numbers and when they are going to hit us."

"How?" Hard Ass asked, feeling really privileged to be having such a frank discussion with the major.

"I can send up a deep space transport with an IR scanner onboard."

Captain Janine laughed. "Perfect. It will help to know their disposition when we can't see them. Sam and my mortar squad can be effective if the transport can relay their locations to her."

"I'll see that they have a direct line to Samantha. Good thinking. I firmly think we're going to be forced to have to give these big heads a lesson. I think I can understand why these people are so aggressive. We've been here two weeks, and already I'm so depressed with this world—dismal, glum, fog, rain, and continual dim reddish hues everywhere. My God, it's enough to make me stark raving mad."

Hard Ass laughed. "No kidding. Dismal is being kind about it."

A short while later, One Shot complained, "Killer, this isn't fair. You get to shoot'em up down there, and I get to fly and run the stupid IR scanner."

"Suck it up, big boy," she replied. "Besides, you get to direct Sam's mortar fire. Bet you'll get many more kills than I do." Both laughed.

Back at Castle Alvaro, *Jefe* Sancho entered the Great Hall for supper, an angry look on his face. "What's up?" asked *Jefa* Adelina.

"I just got word from some of our outlying farmers that these *jefe* secretly brought a thousand *agente* along with them. You can bet they're going to attack the aliens."

"Oh no, Sancho, four thousand against their few hundred!" exclaimed *Jefa* Adelina, her face suddenly quite worried and frightened. "Should we send help?"

"No, they'd just get killed," *Jefa* Dr. Alison replied. "Please let Major Lu Ann know for me. I'm afraid four thousand of their fighters are about to die if they attack us. The Hyperion is a war ship, after all."

174

Both locals turned to look at her. "You're kidding us, right? Four thousand against a handful? Surely, your people will be wiped out," *Jefe* Sancho replied. "We took control of some of their minds, forcing them to help us when we attacked you."

"We weren't expecting an attack, that you had telepathy, or that you could control our minds. Now we know better. Besides, we had orders not to harm your people. I doubt Major Lu Ann will give that order this time. She's a war commander, after all, and a damned good one. No, I bet four thousand of these foolish *jefe*'s men are going to get themselves killed."

Very early morning, One Shot reported, "My goodness, here they come. There's so many of them, I can't count them. Most are going to come at us from the north, but several hundred I think are circling around, probably going to hit us from all sides." Thus, they had advance warning of the enemy's positions beforehand.

Early morning came. The dense fog reddened; visibility wasn't more than twenty feet ahead. "Okay, they are about to hit us on all sides," Hard Ass barked her orders to her platoon. "Remember, they want to take over your minds. So think of them as the tin cans! Fight back. Don't let them into your minds or you'll be dead. Spray the area with fire. They're densely packed so we're going to mow them down even if we can't see them. Remember, you're fighting for your lives. Give them hell!"

Hammerhead took his ten men around to the south side and Samantha got to her mortar, nodding to her crew. They had boxes of mortar shells at hand, and she felt confident, ready for action. Hammerhead positioned the others around the mortar crew and near the main entrance to the Hyperion. Six delta wings launched, and the bay doors were then sealed.

Meanwhile, Hard Ass positioned her squad strategically around the northern side, close to the main entrance. They were giving the enemy all the openings they desired up front where there was no access to the ship, preferring to defend the single main entrance. Inside, six men were positioned at the light switches. All she had to do was give them the order to turn them on. That would blind those who broke the perimeter fences. Now she waited, hunkered down. All PDSs were active and would prevent any sword strikes or spear thrusts. She felt confident.

Without warning and believing they had surprise on their side, the four *jefe* led the charge. Battle was joined, only it wasn't as they had anticipated, far from it! Sam's mortar began rapid firing, guided somewhat from One Shot flying the transport above the area. The primitive fighters were bunched together. There were so many of them, that whenever a shell landed, it took out many fighters, far behind the front lines.

Hard Ass barked the fire at will order, and the MK40s and grenade launchers fired away, making a devilish noise. While they couldn't see any enemy fighters yet, they knew they were hitting some. Moans and startled cries told all. The defenders kept up a steady rain of fire, shifting from one zone to the next, spraying deadly fire in outward cones.

Several minutes passed before they finally saw many natives trying to smash their way through the electric fences. This they did by sheer brute force, men falling onto the poles, knocking them down, though those that did this died from the electrical sparks. When others tried to pour through these openings, several triggered Fel's booby traps. Loud explosions sent bodies flying in all directions. Still, the enemy pressed forward and gained a strong foothold at the front of the ship. Some hacked at it with their swords, but only metal clanking sounds resulted.

At this point, Hard Ass called for the quartz lights. Brilliant illumination followed, lighting up the entire front area of the ship. Even in the dense fog, the lights were extremely bright, the fog aiding its effect. Screams from the fighters close in echoed in the defenders' ears. The native fighters had no choice but to throw up their arms to cover their eyes, had to back out, and retreat, all the while taking a rain of deadly fire from First and Second Platoons.

Some fifteen minutes after it began, One Shot reported, "They're all retreating!" Still, Killer Diller and five other delta wing fighters continued making their strafing runs, their cannons mowing a path through the retreating fighters, who now broke into an all-out rout! "Cease firing! Cease firing!" Hard Ass yelled above the din. "Get those fences back up!"

Major Lu Ann poked her head out. "Any casualties?"

Hard Ass looked at her group. "None here, major." From the other side, Hammerhead reported none as well, but that the mortar group could use another box of shells. The major smiled and headed back inside to recall the delta wing fighters.

"What? I have to keep on flying and keep an eye on them?" One Shot complained.

Killer Diller called back, "Serves you right. That mortar fire was more effective than our cannons. So stop complaining." Both laughed.

As usual, by noon the fog had lifted. *Jefe* Sancho and a hundred of his men arrived to see what had happened and thus got to see firsthand the slaughter that had occurred. "My God! *Jefa* Dr. Alison was right. Not one of your people was harmed and there are thousands of dead *agente*!"

"Of course," Major Lu Ann replied. "What did you think would happen? Anyway, I've decided that if your people will handle all the dead men, you may keep their weapons to help arm your own soldiers. Just give me a report on the number of dead *agente*, please." She had a very good idea what this offer meant to Sancho. Suddenly in possession of thousands of swords, spears, and shields gave him a decided advantage over the other *tribu*, who had just lost these. By nightfall, he reported that one thousand seven hundred sixty-three were slain. He had no idea how many wounded men managed to flee the battlefield before his men arrived.

Meanwhile, Major Lu Ann and a security squad paid a visit to *Jefa* Adelina, requesting her to summon representatives of these four other *tribu*. An hour later, four men arrived in her Throne Room, but none of the original four *jefe* was present. *Jefa* Adelina translated for the major.

"We have killed thousands of your *agente* fighters. I'm pleased to report not one of my fighters took a single wound. However, your blatant disregard for *Jefa* Adelina's honored guest status has upset me. Take this warning back to your *jefa*. If we're attacked again, then I shall launch a counterstrike

177

against your entire *tribu*, destroying your cities and all your people, once and for all. After that, your *tribu* will cease to exist. Do I make myself clear?"

After the four shocked men left, a shocked *Jefa* Adelina asked, "You wouldn't really do that? I mean destroy the entire *tribu* would you?"

Major Lu Ann smiled. "No, of course not, I just wanted to put the fear of God in them so they won't dare think of causing you or us any more problems." *Jefa* Adelina made a rare noise, a huge sound of relief.

After that battle, hostilities died down completely. Later on, the four *jefa* sent emissaries to *Jefa* Adelina and *Jefa* Alison, apologizing for the attack and asking for forgiveness, which Alison accepted. Finally, things calmed down for now and Major Lu Ann sent some of her people to the other four castles to establish friendly relations with them. The most important one was with the de Casa *Tribu*, because she wanted to station her astronomers there on the Escalera a las Estrellas, in hopes that in time, they could work out their position within the galaxy.

Chapter 12—Unexpected Development

Three months since their crash landing brought one vital development. After two months of work, her engineers finally got the Hyperion's sub-light engines running. A day later, all the ships power cells had been fully recharged, much to everyone great relief. At this point, everyone knew they could take off and leave this world behind. Work then began on restoring or rebuilding the hyperdrive engines. The astronomers established a small base at Escalera a las Estrellas, but as yet still had no idea where in the galaxy this red dwarf sun was located. Still, they had hope in time they would.

Major Lu Ann's geological survey began paying dividends, especially for the more belligerent *tribu*. They'd discovered several new and large deposits of copper and tin, from which bronze was made. Further, they found a copper load just beneath the soft soils in West Fernland. Suddenly, the Alvaro *Tribu* had their own source of copper! Plus lesser deposits were also found in the Aspero Hills and the Huso Woods, much to the great benefit of those *tribu*. This went a long way to improving the relations with the locals there.

Meanwhile, Jason and the nurse spent long hours cleaning up and repairing Sickbay. While repairing the d-gun damage to the supply shelves, Jason made an unexpected discovery. Not all the genetic bio agent cures had been destroyed. Three of the six vials of cures fell down inside the cabinet when the shelf disintegrated along with three other vials and a number of other antibiotics. A very pleased Major Lu Ann personally reported this find to Dr. Alison and Peter. However, considering her current position as their *jefa*, Dr. Alison wisely decided to put off getting the cure until the major needed her services repairing the electronics. Until they got the hyperdrive working or discovered their location in the galaxy, the LD array was useless. Besides, she was maintaining their societal connections to those on New Zeta.

On the other hand, Dr. Alison encouraged Peter to get

his cure right away, which he did, but he insisted Kathy also get hers along with him. A week later, Peter and Kathy rejoined Dr. Alison at Castle Alvaro, bringing with them two additional discoveries. The genetic cure had definitely worked. Peter and Kathy now had arms and hands, though they were still weak but strengthening each day. However, Kathy's slit lips healed themselves, and she gaily had her lips redone once she was back at the castle so that she would look like all the other girls. There was a down side to the genetic cure. Their feet ended up distorting again, forcing them to have to wear six-inch heels, completely undoing the special healing they'd received here at the castle. Fortunately, *Jefa* Adelina didn't mind having her healers redo both Peter and Kathy's feet a second time.

Thus, Dr. Alison realized that her own split lips would likely also be healed when she underwent the cure, though her feet would end up being slightly malformed as a result. *Perhaps*, she thought, *I can get the healers here to redo my feet too. At least these alterations to my body aren't going to be permanent. I can endure this much better now.* All her unspoken fears for the future evaporated.

Then, it happened. One morning over breakfast, Dr. Alison began hearing many voices in her head. "Oh please, can only one of you talk to me at one time? It is so confusing to be hearing all of you talking at the same time."

"What are you saying, *Jefa* Alison?" asked *Jefa* Adelina.

"Oh, you are louder than normal. I'm hearing all of you at the same time, I think. Please, only one at a time," Alison attempted to respond properly.

Jefa Adelina gave her a strange look and sent for her healers and for *Jefe* Sancho. After a few more minutes, her healer declared, "Isn't this interesting. *Jefa* Alison has developed telepathy, just like one of us. *Jefe* Sancho, it falls upon you to train her. She's broadcasting all her thoughts to everyone here."

"What? This isn't possible. I've never had any telepathic ability before," she exclaimed startled. This shouldn't be happening!

"Well, it certainly is happening. Come with me. I must

train you. Right now, you are sending your thoughts off in all directions to everyone here! Besides, you need to be able to block out other's thoughts so you don't hear everyone talking at once," *Jefe* Sancho pointed out.

Two days later, both Peter and Kathy began hearing other people's thoughts in their heads, all at the same time, confusing them. Minutes later, the healer declared that they too had somehow developed telepathic skills and sent them off with Alison and Sancho to be trained as well.

A week of training later, found all three in control of their newfound telepathic skills. Kathy was truly happy for she fit in perfectly with all the other young girls on this world, except for her vision that is. Peter then made a trip back to the Hyperion to relay this incredible and miraculous news.

"How can this be, Peter? Developing telepathy? All three of you? Medically, it's unheard of," Major Lu Ann declared. "Get a full checkup from Jason right away. We have to find out what the blazes is going on here, Peter. How did this happen? Why you three? We've all been here the same amount of time, and yet none on the Hyperion have come down with it," she protested, as though this was some kind of illness the three now had.

Complaining bitterly that he wasn't a doctor, Jason, with the assistance of the nurse, gave Peter a full checkup but found nothing amiss. He was perfectly healthy. They did attempt to test him to see if he really did have telepathy. Both flushed with embarrassment when Peter told them what they were thinking. Jason reported back, "Major, he's just fine. Nothing wrong with him. So how did those three suddenly develop telepathy? There's no history of it in any of their lineage, as far as Peter knows."

Janine was elated to hear this news. "My sister, a telepath. Wow! Super cool! But how?" she asked. This became the next project for Major Lu Ann. She met with Janine, Jason, and Peter, seeking the answer to that question. For hours, they discussed all manner of wild possibilities. What had the three been exposed to that no one else had?

After a lengthy discussion that got nowhere at all, Peter protested, "The only difference is that we three are eating really delicious meals while you're eating bland ship's provisions. I'll take the local fare any day over the ship's meals."

"Say, could that be what caused the change? Something in the local food?" Major Lu Ann asked. No one had an answer to that one. They knew the local names of the edibles did not imply they were the same as their namesakes. Their sweet potatoes, whatever they were, were not real sweet potatoes, but some local tuber that more or less looked like one, though its taste was somewhat different than a real sweet potato.

Major Lu Ann commented, "Well, the ship's stores are running low. My engineers are not predicting the hyperdrive engines will be operational anytime soon. Perhaps it is time to make some trading deals with the Alvaro *Tribu* to get food from them. If it is their food that caused the change, then maybe after eating local food for three months, some of my crew will also develop telepathy."

Peter chuckled. "It's worth a try. Besides, you're going to have to eat local food soon anyway. This could be a fortuitous side benefit, major."

"Yes, but Peter, are you able to do any of the other magical things the locals can do? Force someone to do what you want them to do? This strange healing?" Major Lu Ann asked.

Peter smiled. "Nope. Don't know if I ever will be able to do any of that stuff. It's just kind of cool that I can now chat directly with Alison." He then headed back to the castle, while Major Lu Ann headed to the ship's galley. There, she ordered her chefs to prepare a list of what food supplies they needed, assuming they ceased using of the ship's stores, which were running low anyway. If nothing else, she wanted some available should they finally depart New Zeta.

A week later, the arrangements were made with *Jefe* Sancho. Major Lu Ann was truly surprised to discover that five pounds of steel was sufficient to feed her entire crew for a week. Hence, she made arrangements for weekly deliveries, pleasing *Jefe* Sancho, who was finally getting his hands on much needed steel!

Around the same time, Dr. Alison discovered that she

was pregnant, pleasing Peter and Kathy too. Kathy was ecstatic that she would have a little brother or sister. Quietly, Peter and Dr. Alison were married by Major Lu Ann. After that, Dr. Alison continued to represent the aliens as their *jefa*, though she was now extremely bored with the whole thing. She longed to get her own cure and to get back to her electronics work.

The geological survey finally ended not long after that. The only additional fact they'd turned up was that this planet was rich in silicon and germanium crystals, which could be refined into the fuel all Federation spaceships needed.

During these weeks, many hands were working on the complex task of rebuilding the hyperdrive engines. It was slow going, but the engineers in charge of the project felt certain it could be done, given enough time. Well, time they had aplenty.

Three months after the entire crew began eating locally grown food, changes began occurring with them as well. Crew members began complaining about hearing many voices in their heads at the same time. They refused to eat in the galley and began cloistering themselves in their cabins, trying to find relief from the voices.

Wisely, Major Lu Ann sent for *Jefe* Sancho. She wasn't surprised to learn that they now possessed telepathy as well. Hence, she made another trading arrangement with him to get those who developed it trained in its use. A month later, everyone on the ship, including herself, now possessed basic telepathic abilities and had been appropriately trained. Sancho gained another twenty-five pounds of steel, though he knew he had the better part of this deal.

Nine months after their landing, her engineers reported the hyperdrive would be ready for initial testing in two weeks. Finally, Major Lu Ann decided it was time to pull Dr. Alison back from her post as their *jefa*, give her the needed cure, and get her working on getting their comm center rebuilt. Long ago, her own staff had given up any hope of rebuilding it without her expert guidance.

Dr. Alison welcomed the call from Major Lu Ann. Though six months pregnant, she desperately wanted the cure and to get back to work. "I've never been so utterly bored in my whole life! Thank you, thank you. We probably don't need a *jefa* any longer." While *Jefa* Adelina was sad to see her new friend depart to get the cure and to begin work on the ship, she knew that it had to be done. Besides, she saw just how bored her friend had become. While she had routine adjudications to deal with every few days, poor Alison had nothing to do but sit around, but she did get Alison to promise to come and visit her as often as she could.

A week later, Dr. Alison once more had her arms and hands. Her lips were healed with no trace of the slits in her lips. Unfortunately, her feet were malformed, just as Peter and Kathy's were. Still, she ignored this and wore her six-inch heels for now, though she hoped on one of her visits to the castle, she could get them fully healed again.

With abandon, she dove into the reconstruction work of the motherboard of the communications system, identifying which components were destroyed or weak, replacing them with comparable components from unused boards. More often than not, she couldn't find an exact replacement and was forced to make alterations in the other components as a work-around solution.

During this time, the rebuilt hyperdrive passed its initial tests, to the cheers of the entire two hundred plus crew. Thus, when they were ready to attempt a liftoff, Dr. Alison had the LD comm center back in operation, though they only heard static, confirming they were a very long way from any known location.

Wisely, Major Lu Ann then began settling promised affairs with the locals. A hundred pounds of steel was given to each of the tribu. Further, she stockpiled the Hyperion with as much local food supplies as could be expected not to spoil before use. And she set the day for their attempted liftoff. Given that, Dr. Alison, Peter, and Kathy made a last trip to visit Adelina and Sancho, saying farewell to their new friends. Cleverly, Adelina arranged for Alison's feet to be healed as a parting present. This time, Alison was able to give *Jefa* Adelina a proper hug, though both women had tears at the parting.

Nine months and three weeks from their crash landing, Major Lu Ann issued the order that everyone was waiting to hear. "Fire up the sub-light engines. Get us into orbit around

New Zeta." She and nearly half the crew held their breaths or crossed their fingers. Would it work or would they crash again or even blow up?

Exhaust gassed swept out from beneath the huge ship, flattening ferns all around the ship, but gently the Hyperion rose into the sky, watched by hundreds of locals, many of whom waved a farewell. Quickly, though, it disappeared into the dense clouds, vanishing from their sight. Major Lu Ann breathed a huge sigh of relief when the black sky appeared, along with the dim red sun and the bright milk stream that was the galaxy on edge.

While the astronomers had been unable to pinpoint their location, based on their observations, they had zeroed in on it somewhat. Either they were on the opposite side of the galaxy and at the rim of the other spiral arm or they were in one of two distant locations on either side of the Federation's rim sectors. No one said much about the first possibility. They didn't have enough fuel to get home from there. Rather, they presumed it was one or the other side of their known space sectors.

One major problem remained—that of initializing the hyperdrive unit. Rebuild nearly from scratch, the precise coordinates of their location needed to be entered to initialize it. Once that was done, they could then enter their destination and see if they had enough fuel to reach it. Now the engineers face this problem.

Arbitrarily, Major Lu Ann headed the Hyperion towards the center of the galaxy, away from the rim. Of course, if they could only use the sub-light engines, they'd die of starvation long before they reached any destination. However, it felt good to be going towards the galaxy and away from the rim.

She, her astronomers, and staff met to discuss how to solve the initialization problem. Everything depended upon entering the hyperspace coordinates of their current location, but that was unknown. An aide finally made a workable suggestion. "Why don't we pick one of the two corners of known Federation space and enter that as our location to initialize it. Then, we enter the coordinates of say Scorpi-C and if we have enough fuel to get there, give it a shot. If we are right, we should be able to identify our location when we drop out of hyperspace, make appropriate changes, and reinitialize. If we are at one or the other edge of Federation rim sectors, then it isn't going to matter too much where we end up, as long as we are able to identify our location from matching known star patterns."

"Yes, but Scorpi-C is on the rim. We should pick a destination closer to the mid-arm region. We'll stand a better chance of identifying our location," another advised.

Major Lu Ann brought up the 3-d galactic model and zoomed in on the Federation rim sectors, studying the layout for a moment. "Okay, say we are here or here," she pointed to either side of these sectors. "If we head here, sort of midway between them, we should end up in recognizable space. Minas-C. Okay, enter the coordinates for Minas-C, and let's see what the drive says."

An aide looked them up and entered them. All watched the readout. It suggested that they would need a quarter of their fuel to reach it. Major Lu Ann suggested lowering the proposed speed of travel. When that was done, even less fuel was required, but travel time would be twenty-four hours. She liked that choice and made the announcement ship-wide. "Execute," she ordered and held her breath. Would the rebuilt engines actually work? Would they blow up? The Hyperion lurched slightly, and the blackness of hyperspace appeared. Finally, Major Lu Ann breathed a sigh of relief and announced to everyone they would be in hyperspace for twenty-four hours, and that when they dropped out, they would begin to analyze just where they were. She didn't suggest that they pray to their deities though. She wasn't religious.

This was the longest twenty-four hours that the major ever experienced. If they dropped out in wholly unknown, unidentifiable space, everything would have been for nothing. Their chances of survival would be slim to none. Right on time, the Hyperion dropped out of hyperspace, and the astronomers began doing their vital work. Just where were they? As much as Major Lu Ann wanted an immediate answer, as did everyone else, she knew better than to rush the astronomers.

Ah hour later and after testing several theories, they finally were able to match up star patterns. "We are in Federation mid-arm regions!" one cheerily announced. Hastily, new calculations were made and entered into the hyperdrive unit, re-initializing it. Then, the major issued orders to enter Scorpi-C's coordinates. The results suggested one-half of their fuel in twenty-four hours. Once more, Major Lu Ann relayed the news to everyone on the ship and then gave the order to execute the jump.

She had taken the astronomers' estimates of the error in their position into account and purposely adjusted the arrival coordinates to be four light-years from Scorpi-C. If they were off, they could well materialize inside Scorpi or inside the planet. She couldn't trust the hyperdrive until it had been precisely initialized. This time, the time passed more rapidly and with less worry.

When they dropped out of hyperspace, Scorpi was quite visible, being the brightest star in their field. Finally, Major Lu Ann made contact with Scorpi-C, identifying her ship and its situation. A day later, they docked beside the Battleship Arc Royal, undergoing massive repairs while in orbit above the planet.

Commander Kelly Kay Knight's voice came over the comm channel, "My God, Major Lu Ann, is this really you? We gave you and the Hyperion up for lost months ago. Where have you been? Over."

"Good to hear your voice again, commander. I've quite a story to tell. We must meet in private and under top security, preferably on the Hyperion. Over."

"You got it. Be there in thirty. Welcome back! Over and out."

Chapter 13—Salvage Operations

"You're kidding me, right?" a flabbergasted Commander Kelly Kay asked. Major Lu Ann had just told her the critical news that everyone on her ship now possessed telepathic abilities.

"Yes, all of us. We don't have any way to test the degree, but I'd say probably Class V at least. Let me explain what happened to us and the critical role Dr. Alison Wage has played in this. And yes, we have your complete Shadow Maker systems and the doctor knows quite a lot about how they work," Major Lu Ann explained.

She talked for nearly an hour, outlining in detail what had happened, most, she guessed, would be marked top-secret, something the commander insisted upon when the major finished. "I suppose my crew could now make a fabulous living marketing their new-found skills, but I'd like to keep as many with me as possible. We have bonded, and they're all first rate members of the Hyperion," the major finished.

"Incredible, major. Just incredible. I don't suppose you have coordinates for this New Zeta world?" the commander asked.

"Actually, no we don't. We had to initialize the hyperdrive system three times to find our way back, so their precise location isn't known. It's on the rim and isolated, most likely just beyond Federation rim sectors, but we don't know which side of the rim sectors. Couldn't be helped if we were to get back to civilization," Major Lu Ann reported, knowing quite well this wasn't what the commander wanted to hear. A world of telepaths would be the find of a century, to say nothing of newcomers obtaining telepathic skills merely by living there and eating their food for months. She also knew they couldn't *hire* some of those natives to come to Federation worlds and use their telepathic gifts. Their eyes were adapted for the incredibly dim illumination of their world and its dense cloud cover and daily fog.

"Just the same, I want your navigators to discuss what

they do know with my staff. Considering the magnitude of your situation—two hundred Class V telepaths—my God, major—I must speak to everyone and offer them alternative and drastically higher paying positions in our new alliance with Scorpi-C. I should bring you up to date now, major," the commander declared.

She sighed and continued, "Brussels—well there is no easy way to say this. Every person in Brussels was murdered by those Shadow Makers. After that, the robots and that new battleship vanished, along with all plans and a great deal of machinery and equipment from manufacturing plants. Every computer was gone as well. However, the good news is that the rest of Ragnar-B was left untouched."

"At this time, the civilians have totally overthrown what few lower level corporation executives were left in outlying cities and have declared independence from corporation rule. We've a president now and a legislature as well. President Able Bottomsworth has joined with Scropi-C's Freedom Alliance. Once my battleship has been repaired, we will be returning to Ragnar-B and assisting in its permanent defense."

She became more animated, "The fight against the corporations in our sector escalated dramatically after the corporations attack on our world. Major revolutions are underway on Zelmar-C, Bella-B, and Jarok-C. That means every subordinate world of our Twillis Sector is revolting against corporation rule from our sector's controlling corporations on Willis-C. Those three neighboring worlds have also joined the Freedom Alliance and have just about thrown off the stifling yoke of corporate suppression. The next step is to go after the sector corporation headquarters on Willis-C. If we can drive the corporations off Willis-C, then the whole of Twillis Sector will be free and part of the expanding Freedom Alliance, stationed here in the Abelard Sector. Major, the fight for freedom from the corporations has really been making huge strides out here in the rim sectors!"

Commander Kelly Kay ended with, "So Major Lu Ann, once your people recover and full repairs are finished, your next assignment will be to go to Willis-C and help the rebels there throw off the corporate yoke."

189

Major Lu Ann smiled. She was never one to back down from an honest fight. "Excellent news. One thing, commander, I want to reorganize the Hyperion and its crew. During this last long mission, having a cadre of delta wing pilots and a platoon of ground grunts has actually kept us alive and safe. So I want to reorganize and make these part of the Hyperion's normal crew compliment. I know, space is at a premium with so many onboard, but it has worked out well."

"Permission granted, major. Put what your desired staffing is in writing and I'll authorize it. Mind you, I anticipate some of your new telepaths may jump at my offer of drastically more profitable employment," Commander Kelly Kay advised.

"Of course. I best see to the repairs and get you my ideal staffing. I would like the opportunity to brief my staff on the latest news from home and what my intentions for new staffing will be," Major Lu Ann bargained. The commander agreed, and they discussed lighter events before the commander left. Commander Kelly Kay had some very significant new arrangements and job proposals to work out. Two hundred telepaths was better than a platinum or gold mine.

After the commander departed, Major Lu Ann briefed everyone, smiling when the entire crew cheered loudly over the news of their hard won independence, that their world was now free, and part of this new Freedom Alliance. Then, she explained her reorganization plans. "So from now on, we'll have a fully equipped platoon of soldiers with us, along with two dozen delta wing fighters and their pilots, plus six deep space transports. I know that quarters will continue to be a bit crowded, but we've already seen the survival benefits of having Captain Janine and her ground platoon with us, as well as the invaluable fighter pilots. With these three branches working together as we have done, the Hyperion will lead the way in effective offensive actions to help free others from corporation domination and keep our own Ragnar-B safe in the future."

After the cheering died down, she explained Commander Kelly Kay would soon return and offer high paying employment opportunities for the many new telepaths.

"I know the pay will likely be beyond your wildest dreams, but realize such work could be deadly and is really mostly just spying operations. While I can't remotely offer that kind of pay, I would treasure having each of you as part of my crew. We've learned to depend upon each other. Together, we're one powerful cruiser. That is all. Shore leave will begin after the commander pays us her recruitment visit."

A day later, Major Lu Ann was pleased to discover that only twenty of her original crew accepted the new high paying spying offers from the commander. She set about drafting her reorganization plans that called for filling out Captain Janine's platoon of crack ground troops and adding more pilots. One Shot and Killer Diller were put in charge of finding the needed seven more key delta wing pilots.

"Now I finally feel right!" Peter declared. He stood tall before Dr. Alison and Kathy in their cabin on the Hyperion. He wore a woman security guard's uniform, complete with PDS and an assortment of weapons. "At long last, I'm back doing what I'm trained to do, providing protection for you two and our Hyperion. You are looking at one of Hyperion's new security guards," he declared proudly. While he still looked like a very well-endowed woman, complete with knee-length black hair, he looked the part of a strong security guard and felt it, for the first time since he was subjected to the awful genetic bio agent attack back in Brussels.

"Honey, you look stunning. Now Kathy and I feel truly safe with you watching over us. Just don't go getting yourself shot," she teased him. She recalled the terrible mental state he was in when she first found him and Kathy. The incredible surge of self-respect that shone on his face brought tears to her eyes. Kathy just hugged him tightly. Alison knew she'd married the right man.

Dr. Alison met with a dozen GD research scientists who were assigned to unravel the mysteries around the Shadow Maker systems and to recommend defenses against this diabolical invention. She shared all she knew and her own subjective reality of having undergone its ultra-high frequency, aesthetic energy waves several times. "Honestly, there's nothing I could do to prevent the energy flow from doing what

191

it wanted me to do," she explained. "It was as though I and my mind were just sucked into whatever it wanted me sucked into. I couldn't help myself. Once in that awful robot shell, if I didn't obey orders, I was again blasted with that white energy, which generates unimaginable pain. You'll do anything just to get it to stop. For God's sake, don't experiment with it on other people!"

While they spent long weeks studying it, they were unable to come up with any defense against the Shadow Maker's use. However, since all such units were long gone and completely out of the hands of the corporate executives, except those that had been captured by Dr. Alison's group, the Freedom Alliance believed that this diabolical invention was no longer either in use or a threat. However, several other researchers were quite fascinated with this revolutionary technology, though they were willing to bide their time, patiently waiting to get their hands on it.

The Hyperion was docked for repairs and refitting for three months, during which time, Dr. Alison gave birth to their son, James. There wasn't any doubt that he would look much like his father when he grew up, for he was born with very long black hair, far longer and thicker than normal babies. Still, the three were elated over little James, especially Kathy, who now had a mother and a little brother. From her viewpoint, life had become wonderful once more.

Major Lu Ann was true to her word, pleasing Hard Ass and Fel, but for very different reasons. Captain Janine now had a full platoon, and they were extremely well armed, including their own PDS, MK40 Model 2, grenade launchers, and two complete mortar units, one being added to the Third Squad. Engineer Fel was delighted to discover that she now had her own private demolitions locker, packed with every explosive her heart desired! She would never be without her boom-booms.

With the Hyperion loaded and once more ready for action, Major Lu Ann gave the nav controller the orders many were waiting for: Execute. They were heading towards Willis-C to join their freedom fighters, battling the Twillis Sector main corporate headquarters and their forces. The rebels were fighting around the capital city of Johnsville and desperately needed assistance throwing off the yoke of corporate oppression.

Chapter 14—The Battle of Johnsville

Johnsville, Willis-C, a city of some ten million inhabitants, sprawled across the semi-arid and utterly flat landscape. As the Hyperion circled the city, everyone watched the live video being streamed to large monitors throughout the packed cruiser. "I've never seen any place flatter than this!" exclaimed Fel to Hard Ass. "There isn't a tree anywhere."

"Bushes maybe. Look," Captain Janine pointed out, that must be the rebel's base of operations. The major did say they'd taken the spaceport."

"Hell, you can't tell where the spaceport ends and the open lands begin. Bet it is hotter than hell down there," Hammerhead added his opinion to the mix. Flat and greyish brown. As far as they could see in the distance, which was many miles from this altitude, the terrain varied not at all from the incredible flatness and its ugly shade of grey-brown, which they presumed was the ground itself, since apparently little actually grew here. However, as the Hyperion began its descent towards the spaceport, they realized what they were seeing was some kind of foreign grass that grew on this world.

"Makes good sense to have a major spaceport here. Everything is perfectly flat already," Captain Janine suggested. "Nothing to have to do but pave it. Now the city—that's an entirely different matter. Duh. Corporation standard skyscrapers. They stick up like a cushion of needles."

"So where's all the fighting?" Fel inquired, rhetorically of course. "Seems pretty quiet down there." Many attempted to spot where the current battle was occurring, but nothing was visible, even as they landed at one far edge of the spaceport. However, as they drew closer to the grey-brown ground, they could see a number of nearby buildings that had sustained considerable damage in the battle for the spaceport.

Upon landing, Major Lu Ann asked Captain One Shot, Captain Janine, and Lieutenant Fel to join her in the CCC. When they arrived, they saw that two others from Willis-C had already arrived. "This is the resistance movement's General

194

Victor Stevens and his top aide, Helen Trace," Major Lu Ann began the introductions. "He's here to brief us on their current situation and how we might help."

The general was a young man, probably not even thirty, Hard Ass thought. Lightly sensing his mind, she got the impression he knew what he was doing, that he had led his forces well so far, but he knew he couldn't win. That much was radiating from his demeanor. She looked at his aide, one of those women whose age is difficult to ascertain. She looked fit and trim in her professional woman's outfit. Her hair was light brown and wavy, barely touching her shoulders, easily kept, Janine thought. Yet something about her mind felt different, cold sort of. She focused on her a bit longer while the introductions wrapped up. Cold yes, but she means business was her conclusion. The general began speaking, and she put her full attention on him.

"We are now at a stalemate here in Johnsville. We lost all our delta wing fighters during the battle for the spaceport, which we've obviously taken. Then, our forces began marching towards the skyscrapers, where the corporations have their stranglehold on our city. However, they called in the armed forces of Willis-C. Thankfully, they were up north and I've sent the bulk of my resistance fighters there to delay them. We've no hope of defeating them, obviously. However, I do have their generals' agreement that if we take out the corporation leaders, they will cease-fire and allow us to take control of our world. Meantime, they can't seem to be disobeying orders and are slowly heading here to the capital city."

"Now then, the rest of our forces have been completely stopped on the ground. We don't dare get within ten blocks of that part of the city where the skyscrapers are located. You see, they have six delta wing fighters remaining, parked on the roofs downtown. As soon as our forces make a move towards them, the fighters take off and strafe my soldiers. We don't stand a chance against them. That's why I've asked your major if she can somehow take out those remaining fighter ships. If so, we can again make slow progress towards the skyscrapers. Once there, it will be a ghastly battle to take them from the corporation forces hold up there. Door to door urban combat is deadly. Yet we must proceed and take them before the army generals finally arrive here. If we don't, then all this has been for nothing."

Major Lu Ann replied, "I'm sure we can eliminate those six fighters for you. I've two dozen crack delta wing pilots with me."

"That's more than twice a cruiser's compliment, isn't it?" Helen spoke up, rather curious that the Hyperion had so many delta wings.

"Indeed. We are a special, mixed fighter group, seasoned as well," Major Lu Ann answered. "I don't relish the door to door part, general. You can expect substantial losses. The odds are in favor of the corporations."

"Indeed, but we have no choice but to make the attempt, which we can do once the six fighters are eliminated," he replied.

Fel spoke up. "What about all the civies? Especially those in the skyscrapers?"

Helen replied. "We know they evacuated their UFB women and children already. As far as we know, there are no civies in them. Many others have fled the surrounding area and for good reason. We shouldn't have much collateral damage."

Fel continued probing, "What about avoiding all that bloodshed? There's another way. Implode the buildings."

"What? Well, yes, that would be ideal, but we don't have anyone who knows how to do that," the general responded.

"Well, from the little I could see from the air as we circled, these are corporation standard skyscrapers, right?" Fel inquired.

Helen laughed. "Of course. Isn't everything the corporations build made from the same standard mold?" Everyone chuckled.

"Well, with Captain Janine's help, I can set the charges that'll implode a skyscraper. It's damned easy. Four outer Grade 10 I beams bear the main load, while a dozen inner Grade 8 beams support the flooring."

Captain Janine broke in, "Fel, how can you get in there to set the charges?"

196

"Through the sewer system. Of course, I'll need your platoon to assist in laying them under my direction and to keep their security guards off of us while we do that."

"Incredible! If you could implode GD headquarters, the others may surrender," General Victor said, growing enthused. *Perhaps there is a way to win this war of freedom.*

Janine picked up his thought. She said, "Fel's right. If we implode GD, the general will have a good chance at convincing the others to surrender, major. We can do this, especially if at the same time the general's forces move in close on the street, as though they were making a direct assault. That should force them to commit many of their guards to face them, leaving fewer to charge into the basement and into us."

Since everyone liked the plan, General Victor sent Helen off to retrieve the city sewer plans and those of GD headquarters. The others discussed a timetable for the operation. I-day, or implosion day, was set three days hence. Fel needed time to prepare the needed charges, getting each into an easily attached package, since she wouldn't have time to set each one individually.

"Okay grunts, listen up," Hard Ass briefed her platoon, as they were making their final preparations for the assault. "Third Platoon, you're the mules. Follow behind Fel and carry in the bombs. First Platoon, you're on me in the lead. We're to take out any guards that might be in the basement when we enter. Second Platoon, your job is to weld those crossbars onto the central elevator doors and on the two stairwell doors to the basement. It's vital you weld them shut ASAP. Otherwise, we're going to get swamped with security guards and likely grenades. You're supposed to survive this assault, so get those bars welded fast! Question? Okay, we go into the sewers now. I don't want to hear any talking and no complaints about the smells. I'm trying to get you in and out in one piece. It beats going door to door and room to room, which we will have to do if this fails."

They headed into the sewers. When they were about two blocks from the GD skyscraper, Hard Ass sent word to Major Lu Ann who ordered the air strike. "Game's on, One Shot," yelled Killer Diller over their comm. "Hundred says I

197

get more down than you."

"You're on, Killer," One Shot joked back, as his delta wing shot out of the Hyperion's Bay One, while Killer Diller's came out of Bay Two, swooping high into the air. The others twenty-two followed behind them. In a minute, they were onto the six defending fighters. Aerial combat began at once, with an enemy ship firing a rocket at One Shot, who veered out of the way, aided by releasing decoy flitter that confused the sensors on the rocket.

Another fired one at Killer Diller. She banked hard, executing a one-eighty degree turn with the rocket following behind her. She flew straight into the enemy ship, but veered off at the very last minute to avoid a collision. The rocket trailing her latched onto the enemy ship and detonated, sending flying fragments descending onto the streets and buildings below. Killer Diller called out, "Okay grunts, that's how you take them out without firing a shot. One up, One Shot."

One Shot groaned but got a lock on one and fired his cannons, spraying the back of the enemy delta wing, hitting its engines. In seconds, that one went down trailing thick black smoke. Three minutes later, One Shot reported in, "Skies are clear. I repeat skies are clear, and I owe Killer a hundred, damn it." She had gotten two to his single enemy fighter. Four others each had a kill as well, which only made One Shot feel even worse about it. "We need more enemy ships, Killer." She laughed into the comm, heading back for the Hyperion. Now it was up to the ground grunts.

Major Lu Ann relayed the news to the general, and in turn, his ground forces, some hundred rather poorly armed men and women headed towards the GD skyscraper. As they approached, they began firing at the ground floor. Though the corporation executives had placed shields around the lower floors, that didn't matter. The idea was to convince those inside they were being assaulted from the street.

That was the signal for Hard Ass to cut through the steel grate and climb into the basement of GD. Quietly, she climbed out, her MK40 at the ready. Silently, she signaled the other ten in First Squad, as they climbed up and out of the

198

sewers. All were soaked and stinking from the filth. No one was down here, and they took up protective stances before the central elevators and each of the two side stairwells, as Hammerhead brought his Second Squad up, along with their welding torches and metal bars. In three man teams, the men headed to each of the three entrances and began welding the bars across the doors. While this would not prevent the security guards from entering for very long, it would delay and confuse them, long enough Hard Ass counted upon.

Meanwhile, Fel and Third Platoon climbed up and began planting their charges. Each had a timer, which was set to thirty minutes, but Fel also had a remote detonator inserted deep inside the charges, just in case. Even before Fel reached the first major I-beam, the alarms went off, probably triggered by motion sensors in the basement. Soon, Hard Ass yelled, get that welding done fast. Company is coming!"

The three teams no more than turned off their torches, the job done, when GD men arrived, banging and pounding on the doors, which wouldn't open. Hammerhead then placed his men in covering positions along with First Platoon. Now all waited on Fel and Third Platoon to do their work. It was a race against time. If they figured out a way to blast through the doors, a deadly firefight could well disrupt the laying of the charges.

"Two more to go," Fel yelled encouragement. Boom! An explosion ripped off the northeast stairwell's doors, sending fumes and smoke into the basement area. After a short pause, two security guards stomped loudly down the stairs and ran through the doors, guns firing at no one, though it looked impressive. They were met with fire from four MK40's. At this point, Hard Ass said a silent thank you for these new weapons. These guards were wearing personal defense shields, making them immune to normal weapons, but not these new ones. She saw the double hit of each shot. The first hit drilled a tiny hole in the shield, while a microsecond behind it, the second shot entered the hole, killing the guard outright.

The battle was on. Amid heavy gunfire, Fel and Third Platoon finished and raced back into the sewers. Once they were down and moving back through the sewers, Second

Platoon, led by Hammerhead, followed them, with Hard Ass and First Platoon retreating and giving them covering fire. By now dozens of security guards lay dead just beyond the two stairwells. One by one, First Platoon members jumped down into the sewers. Hard Ass tossed six grenades rolling them towards the doors and then jumped herself.

When they were a block away and still running, Fel called out, "Boom boom time. I'm not waiting on the timers. They could be detaching the charges now. Run like hell!"

"Do we cover our ears?" Hard Ass yelled from the rear.

"If you want too," Fel yelled back.

Boom! One combined blast shook the concrete of the sewer's tiles. They kept running and then a giant shock wave shoved into them, tossing them forward like rag dolls. Their PDS units kept them from suffering any real harm, though they all ended up piled on top of one another. Fel scrambled up, "Come on. Run. It's not over yet, only beginning!" Hard Ass didn't need any more encouragement. Neither did her platoon. All ran as fast as they could, though the dim lights from their headlamps barely illuminated the way. Fel cleverly took them around several bends before heading up to the streets. That was a wise move, for the imploding building came down, thrusting a mountain of concrete dust down into the sewer lines.

Fel got to the street level just in time to see the top of GD slowly sinking down. It was a perfect drop. The hundred-story skyscraper simply collapsed downward, floor by floor, pulverizing everything below it as it went down. "Damned amazing, Fel," Hard Ass commented, as she finally climbed out only to see the top floor vanish from sight, blocked by intervening buildings. "I hope someone captured that on video. I'd like to see it come down." Several others laughed, especially First Platoon members who had seen only the last of it.

"Now that was what I call fun!" Fel called out to the entire platoon. Everyone roared with laughter. Filthy as they were, covered in slime and concrete dust from head to toe, they still were able to laugh with Fel's pronouncement.

When they finally made it back to the Hyperion, Major

Lu Ann congratulated them and told them, "You can't see the video until you've had a long, hot shower. My God, you all stink!"

An hour later as Fel watched the video of GD going down for the twentieth time, General Victor and Helen joined her. "Amazingly well done, Engineer Felicity. Amazing, well done," the general effused, shaking her hand vigorously.

"Thanks. I do hope that I get to blow up some more skyscrapers. I've always wanted to do that. Boom, boom," Fel replied.

Helen laughed, "Remind me never to get on your wrong side, lieutenant."

Fel smiled. "I do so like to make boom booms. Always have. Thanks for letting me blow up a skyscraper. Next time, I can do a better job of it. We were slightly off. It wobbled a bit too much, you see. Should have come straight down. Instead, I rather wiped out one street with it. Sorry about that."

Both just shook her hand and left her to watch the video once more. The two then joined Major Lu Ann in her CCC. "Well, I've sent surrender messages to the heads of GE and GR corporations. Time will tell. I do hope this was enough to convince them to surrender peacefully," he explained.

The plan worked to perfection. By evening, General Victor received the call that he'd been hoping for. Both CEOs of Galactic Electronics and General Robotics surrendered, ending corporation control over Willis-C and thus the entire Twillis Sector on the rim. Since it abutted the Abelard Sector, the two immediately formed the anticipated alliance. The Hyperion spent another two weeks on guard duty, though everyone was bored out of their minds.

What had started as a minor resistance movement on Ragnar-B had ended up removing their entire sector from the vice grip control of the major corporations. Nevertheless, the damage was done. On the average, half of these world's space fleets were gone. Ragnar-B had lost half of theirs, while Willis-B had lost all theirs. Still, billions of people began a new life, free from the tyrannical control of the unethical major corporations. For now, that was cause for great celebrations. The End.

A Favor to Other Readers

How about helping other readers? Many readers rely on reviews to make the decision whether to buy a book. You can help them make their decision by leaving your opinions and viewpoint in a short review of the positive things of this book. Writing the review and expressing your opinion only takes a few minutes, and other readers will appreciate your efforts.

Click this link: Slow Comes the Dark Volume 3 Darkness Descends
                      http://www.amazon.com/dp/B00NVSHV3W scroll down to Customer Reviews; click on Write a Review, and enter your review. Thank you.

Author Information

Visit My Amazon.com Author Page
Vic Broquard Author Page
http://amazon.com/author/vic-broquard

Follow My Blog:
http://www.broquard-ebooks.com/blog/

Follow Me on Social Media

Facebook
http://www.facebook.com/vic.broquard/

Google+
http://plus.google.com/102242823668960002176/

LinkedIn
http://www.linkedin.com/profile/view?id=297732151

YouTube
http://www.youtube.com/channel/UCQWcs-WAX2YqViIiafUqJuw

Other Books by Vic Broquard

Without Warning (fantasy)

The Trident Series: (fantasy)
Volume 1 The Trident and the Book
Volume 2 The Trident and the Scepter
Volume 3 The Trident and the Resurrection

The Adventures of Elizabeth Stanton Series: (science fiction)
Volume 1 The Evolution of the Path
Volume 2 The Great Messiah
Volume 3 Of Kings and Queens and Troubadours
Volume 4 Chaos in the Aftermath
Volume 5 Power Plays
Volume 6 Age of Exploration
Volume 7 Abducted
Volume 8 The Emperor and Empress
Volume 9 A Job Worth Doing
Volume 10 Degradation
Volume 11 The Second Crusade
Volume 12 When Worlds Collide
Volume 13 Dark Ages

The Lindsey Barron Series: (fantasy)
Volume 1 The Rod of the Apocalypse
Volume 2 The Board of Governors
Volume 3 The Crown of Moses
Volume 4 Dominus for President
Volume 5 The National Health Care Program
Volume 6 States Justice
Volume 7 Cross and Double-cross

Zoran Chronicles Series: (fantasy)
Volume 1 A Dragon in Our Town
Volume 2 Dragons, Power, Courts, and War

Planet of the Orange-red Sun Series: (science fiction)
Volume 1 When Kingdoms Fall

Volume 2 Dark Ages
Volume 3 Age of the Towers
Volume 4 Difficillis Exitus
Volume 5 Age of the Lords
Volume 6 The Renegade Tower
Volume 7 Rebellions
Volume 8 The Aliens Return
Volume 9 Power Struggles
Volume 10 Guilds, Genetics, and Gods
Volume 11 Magi, Witches, Swords, and Superstitions
Volume 12 The Voyage of the Eagle's Seed
Volume 13 Eagle's Seed and Origins
Volume 14 Justifications
Volume 15 Responsibilities

The Return of the Wizards: Twelve Companions – The Making of Wizards (fantasy)

Slow Comes the Dark Series: (science fiction)
Volume 1 Creeping Darkness
Volume 2 Serendipity
Volume 3 Darkness Descends